2SS

Who would have though.   .e drama of a
goddess could be so much fun. .RIBUTE FOR
THE GODDESS has many moments of action,
suspense and, of course, a wonderful love between
a great hero and a goddess. It's a recommended
read, and Brynn Paulin is an author to enjoy.
~ *RRT Erotic*

Brynn Paulin has penned a sweltering story. The
characters are hot for each other and the sex
scenes could set the pages on fire. She knows how
to capture the reader's attention, and keep it glued
to the pages. This story was fascinating and had a
few unexpected events. I was enamored with the
characters, and I hope there will be future tales
with some of the secondary characters. TRIBUTE
FOR THE GODDESS is an extraordinary tale that
shows there are no limits to love.
~ *NovelTalk*

TRIBUTE FOR THE GODDESS

Brynn Paulin

A Total-E-Bound Publication
www.total-e-bound.com

Tribute for the Goddess
ISBN # 978-1-906590-41-3
©Copyright Brynn Paulin 2008
Cover Art by Lyn Taylor ©Copyright 2007
Interior text design by Claire Siemaszkiewicz
Total-E-Bound Publishing

Published in 2008 by Total-E-Bound Publishing
1 Faldingworth Road, Spridlington, Market Rasen, Lincolnshire, LN8 2DE, UK.
Total-E-Bound Publishing is an imprint of Total-e-Ntwined Limited.

Manufactured in the United Kingdom by BookForce, Roslin Road, London W3 8DH.

Dedication

For Chris who understands goddesses and their
quirks better than anyone else.

Chapter One

Someday after we have mastered the air, the winds, the tides and gravity, we will harness for God the energies of love. And then for the second time in the history of the world, man will have discovered fire.
Teilhard de Chardin

"I see you failed to sustain the curse."

Thad's eyes narrowed at the woman's superior tone. Gods! Sometimes he hated her. He struggled to keep his head bowed and remove the disdain from his voice. His teeth gritted. "Yes, my goddess."

Reddjedet, Goddess of the Zodiac Quadrant, shifted on her 'throne,' a plush chair on a raised dais. One dainty, sandaled foot tapped on the marble beneath her and signalled her annoyance.

"Why is your hair drawn back like that?" she asked impatiently.

A cascade of white blond hair fell about his shoulders, raising his irritation another notch. How dare she? Although he hadn't seen the flick of her wrist that precipitated the disappearance of the clasp that had held his hair, he knew she'd taken it, and it now rested in her palm.

It pissed him off.

Goddess or not, she had no right to treat his body like this, fashioning it to her pleasure. Yet, she did. How many times had she released his hair, removed articles of his clothing, touched him with invisible hands? More than he could count.

"Thaddeus..." she sighed.

Through his lashes he saw her shake her head.

She set the clasp on the arm of her chair. "Why do you hate me so?"

He shifted. *Trap question.* "I don't."

"Liar."

He heard the smile in her voice. Felt it in his pelvis. Damn it!

It was the same cat-and-mouse game they'd played for the last two hundred years. She always acted the gleeful cat. The predator.

That pissed him off, too. It went against his grain, against everything that comprised his code of behaviour.

Still, today, he sensed something was wrong. There was a change in her demeanour that she tried to hide from him. She might appear smug—happy—but it was a façade. Something troubled his goddess.

Reddjedet was worried.

He took a few casual steps, moving closer but not close enough to touch her. Never to touch her. It wasn't allowed.

He lifted his head and looked directly at her. That she didn't notice his action or the challenge in his eyes told him more than words.

"What's wrong?"

Her light blue eyes clouded, and she swiped her reddish-blonde hair from her face. "Nothing is wrong. Why would you ever ask something like that?"

He tilted his head.

Whatever... if that's your story.

"You seem tense," he commented.

"Tense?" She gave a stilted laugh. "I am not subject to human emotions. What are you suggesting? That I'm—what is that word you've used—*stressed*?"

"Are you?"

She wasn't subject to emotion? Who was she kidding?

She scowled at him.

He crossed his arms and silently challenged her. He'd waited for the opportunity to bait her for years. "C'mon, Jett, what's the problem?"

"What did you call me?" she demanded.

"Jett. Who the hell can say your name anyway?"

"Everyone." She glanced around, and it struck him that she was nervous. She wasn't just nervous. Something was very wrong. What kind of catastrophe was she about to bring down on the earth that she was obviously afraid to get caught in? That would be just like her. Destruction and doom and then poof! off she went.

She wasn't heartless. Apparently, she followed "directives for the greater order." He'd seen the look of grief in her eyes when she'd given the commands.

"So what's it going to be today?" he asked. "Forest fire? Typhoon? Earthquake? It's been awhile since California's been hit."

"We were discussing your inability to maintain a curse?"

Thad sighed. Talking to her was like arguing with a wall. "It wasn't a permanent curse. The man had to find his true love and he did."

"And you did not help him at all?"

He made a show of examining his fingernails. It wouldn't do any good to lie to her, but he bought time to think up something. He wasn't up for a punishment today. Sure, he'd helped the poor guy. Being cursed for two hundred years was no picnic.

He should know...

It really sucked being pledged to a goddess. What had he been thinking? Why on earth had he wanted this? Back when he was stupid and twenty and drunk, it had sounded like a good idea. Especially, since the woman who'd enticed him into it had been the most gorgeous creature he'd ever beheld, with reddish-blonde locks rioting down past a slim waist that sloped gently into the finest ass he'd seen in his life. He'd dreamed of rhapsodising about her sonnet-worthy breasts— of course, rhapsodising *after* he'd tasted them, moulded them with his tongue, taken her up on the promises in her cerulean blue eyes.

Promises she'd immediately reneged on once she had him. He knew her well enough now to know that was how she operated.

Reddjedet, Goddess Bitch of the Milky Way.

She'd claim that she'd given him exactly what she'd promised. Phenomenal supernatural abilities. Wealth. Power. It was the unspoken, unfulfilled promises that irked him.

And the side-effects she hadn't mentioned.

After he'd pledged to her, he'd aged normally for ten years. Until the day he'd placed a curse on his best friend to save the man's life. Technically speaking, it hadn't done that. It had cursed him to a ghostly existence for two hundred years until his true love had come along. Because Thad would inevitably benefit and he'd acted outside the greater order, he'd been cursed, too. Only he'd lived, never aging. Thirty forever. A dream to some. A nightmare to him.

Especially since it meant servitude to a woman who haunted his dreams. He turned a glare on her. He didn't completely hate her. He wanted her beyond reason, but he'd never have her. It was forbidden. Another reason he walked around perpetually pissed off.

She squirmed in a most un-goddess-like way. He'd never seen her edgy or disconcerted. He'd like to keep her this way...except without the worry. He'd like to replace that with desire.

Her worry...that, well, *worried* him. To see the unflappable Reddjedet like this. What was she about to do? Announce that his curse hadn't ended? He'd remain in this stasis of age for an eternity, bound to her?

He discarded that thought immediately. That wouldn't make her uncomfortable. That would just fill her with unmitigated glee. She wouldn't bother to control or shield it from him. She'd flaunt it.

A thunderous crack echoed through the room. Jett twisted on the throne and peered towards the passage that led from the chamber. Thad had no idea where it went. He'd never seen the outside of this portion of Jett's holdings. He merely visualised himself here when his goddess summoned and was immediately transported to her presence.

Her lip caught between her teeth as her hands clenched around the chair arms. The clasp she'd taken from his hair caught under one of them. It gouged into her flesh, a trickle of blood appearing on her fingers, but she didn't seem to notice.

Another boom drove her to her feet.

"We must leave," she whispered, urgency making her voice harsh.

"What's happening?"

"They are coming for me. They plan to seize me during the regeneration. I did not think it would be so soon."

A third, even louder, explosion of sound rocked the chamber and tumbled her chair to the side. Jett jumped from the dais and into his arms, wrapping herself around him. His hands caught in the voluminous, pale peach cloth that wrapped her divine waist. He was actually touching her!

Spirals of heaven, energy Thad hadn't experienced even with his great power, flowed through him. His head grew light, and his breathing stalled.

"Breathe!" she demanded. "Get me out of here!"

"What?" He'd never been dazed by a woman's touch. The goddess's contact sucker-punched him, before raking along his cock. No wonder a mere human wasn't allowed to touch her. He could die from the pleasure. *Oh yeah.*

"Mortals," she groaned in disgust. "I forgot they cannot handle my energy waves."

Her eyes closed for a moment, and he felt his mental abilities returning. *My goddess, she's like a drug.*

She snapped her fingers in front of his face. "Now, quick before they get here. We have wasted too much time already."

"Here? Who?" He winced though a fog filled his thoughts. Enter the human moron.

Jett apparently felt the same about his questioning. "Do you *want* to die? Get us out of here. I can not or they will track me."

"They'll track my energy trail."

"I will mask it. Divert it. I can do that without them finding us." She jumped as a bellow echoed across the chamber.

Three hulking men filled the doorway of the passage she'd watched earlier. Thad quickly assessed them. They were equal to his size, and if they weren't gods, he might be able to take them in a fight. But they were divine in nature. He could sense that.

A lesser man would have cringed at their glares. A smarter man would have shoved Jett away from him and claimed he'd had nothing to do with her jumping into his arms.

Thad clasped her tighter to him. They wouldn't hurt her. And they wouldn't take her from him.

"Go!" she urged.

Closing his eyes, Thad visualised them to the safest place he could think of. His favourite hide-out. A place teaming with magical energy. Somewhere a person could get lost for days.

The cool tingle of magic swirled around him, contrasting her heat burning his front. A rush of air drowned the sound of furious shouts as he and Jett dissolved from the room.

Her arms tightened about him as the wind threatened to rip her from his embrace. He hugged her closer.

Jett! He'd waited so long to hold her. He couldn't imagine letting her go.

Deafening silence rang in his ears, signalling their arrival at his penthouse. They both breathed heavily from the exertion of the journey. Tendrils of magical energy spiralled away from them and dissipated through the walls. As Thad watched the last silvery-clear strand disappear, he found himself alone with Jett, the woman, for the first time.

He could feel the change in her vibrations as she maintained the lower frequency for his comfort. Probably for her protection and hiding, as well. She masqueraded as human now, but it did nothing to dull her radiance. How could anyone look at her and not know she was a goddess?

Jett extricated herself from his arms.

"This is nice," she said, looking around the spacious room that cost him a fortune in this city. She skirted the sunken living room and headed towards the wall of windows. He knew the view was breathtaking, but tension rolled off her as she stared down at Central Park. He admitted to himself that, in her lifetime, she'd probably seen beauty that surpassed his imagination, so the view might be run-of-the-mill to her.

She gave a subtle roll of her shoulders before wrapping her arms over her middle. It tempted him to ask again what bothered her. She probably wouldn't explain. Far be it for a goddess to answer to a mortal. Hey, if she didn't want to admit she was stressed, fine, but he wanted to know what had just happened. The three mountains of doom who'd menaced them in the throne room gave him a pretty good clue.

"Where have you taken me?" she asked before he could question her.

"New York City."

Her shoulder pressed to the window as she watched the constant motion below them. "It is so...busy."

He glanced at Fifth Avenue with its endless flow of traffic, littered with taxicabs. Even at this height, he knew if they went out on the balcony, they'd hear the continuous bleat of horns. People, like streams of ants, hurried to home for the evening.

He loved Manhattan.

"They'll have a hell of a time finding you here.

Of all my territories, this is the place most rife with magic."

She nodded sagely, as if she'd known it all along. "This will be good."

Her never-show-weakness attitude warred with the new vulnerability he saw. She didn't seem to be trying to hide it from him, either. He didn't want her to hide anything from him. Ever. That surprised him as did the sudden proprietary and protective feelings coursing through him. He needed answers, because no one was going to hurt her. He wouldn't allow it.

"What was that about back there?" he demanded. "Who's after you?"

She arched a delicate eyebrow but didn't call him on his tone. In the past, she might have given him a mild smiting, after all she was his goddess and dictated respect. Now she shrugged and turned back to the view. "That was Airyon and his brothers. He thinks to make me join with him."

Hell no, she won't join with him! Everything inside Thad protested. He might despise her with every fibre of his being, but she was his goddess. He wasn't sharing her with anyone. Or letting anyone take her.

The lights in the room dimmed as if hit by a brown-out then flicked back to normal. Jett's spine went stiff, and she wheeled from the window. "Where is the bedroom?"

"You want to sleep?"

She nodded gravely. "With you…"

Thad backed away, alarm bells and victory cannons warring in his head. He hadn't been allowed to touch her until a few minutes ago and now…

"They are searching for me," she told him. "Power fluctuations like that will occur across your territories as they search. They have not found me yet, or they would be here already. Airyon does not expect my resonance to be as low as it is right now. Idiot. Does he think I am as stupid as he is?"

She hadn't reduced her vibrations just for him. That irritated a little.

She sidled up to him, and he forgot his resentment. The goddess wanted him.

Reaching for the hand that hung death-like at his side, she raised it to rest between her breasts. Her luscious, gravity-defying breasts. Her heart thundered beneath his palm.

"I am just a woman," she murmured, closing in on him until her lips were inches from his. The spirals of heaven surrounded him again.

He shook his head against her claim.

"Not just a woman. A goddess." His fingers sank into her wild curls. Her tresses fell around his arm past his elbow. "My goddess," he murmured.

Jett shivered, and he closed the scant space between their lips for a wholly passionate kiss. Hot, deep, full of the need he'd harboured for her. Sinking his tongue into her mouth, he hugged her tighter and splayed his hand on the bare flesh of her back.

She groaned, her hands moving restlessly at his shoulders as if she couldn't decide where to touch him. Finally, she looped her arms around him, threading her fingers into the hair at the base of his neck. Power seemed to radiate from her palm, seeping into his limbs. Nothing mattered more than kissing Jett. Nothing mattered more than fully claiming her mouth.

She settled into the kiss, duelling with his tongue for dominance. He lifted her slightly and aligned her hips with his. Jett gasped at his hard length pressed to her mound. The pleasure warmed him as she forgot her battle for supremacy and softened for him, sucking gently on his tongue as it darted along the velvet of her mouth.

Oh yes, this felt completely right. The more he tasted her, the hungrier he became. He had to sample her skin and discover if it tasted as good as her mouth.

"Bedroom?" she gasped, when he trailed open-mouth kisses down her neck.

My goddess, she tastes like orange cream. He suckled at the throbbing pulse at the base of her neck.

"Thad, take me to bed," she begged.

He trailed a slow path back to her ear. "There's no hurry."

"There is. You must take my virginity."

Virgin?

Ice water splashed over him. He thrust her to arm's length and took a few hasty steps backward. He jammed his hands into his pockets before he tossed caution to the wind. He wanted nothing more than to throw her over his shoulder, run for the bedroom and drill her to the bed.

His primitive urge shocked him. He wanted her. Now. And now, like a cruel cosmic joke, she was cut off from him as surely as that invisible barrier had separated them all these years. She was a virgin goddess. He couldn't defile her. He wanted to howl his frustration.

The lights flickered around them again, but this time he couldn't be sure if it was the electricity or his head.

Jett glanced around, desperation in her eyes. "They are getting closer," she murmured.

"You can't be a virgin. You've got to be a million years old."

She grimaced. "A million years? You tread a

dangerous path."

He continued to stare at her, unamused.

"I am," she insisted. "It is the root of my power. It is the vibration they search for."

"I don't believe you."

Her eyes flashed with fury. "You dare insult me thus!"

"Just calling it as I see it."

"You are mistaken, Warlock Pennington."

Now, *she* was pissed. She never called him that—unless he'd thoroughly gone against her will and fouled her plans. Not that the 'fouling' was always bad. Often the results were perfect. Just not what she wanted.

Jett glared at him, then spun on her heel and headed towards the penthouse's double front doors.

"Where are you going?"

"If you will not do it, then I will have to find someone who will. Surely, there is some man in this city who is capable if you are not."

Hell no! She had to be joking if she thought he'd let another man touch her.

There wasn't a trace of teasing or duplicity in her. Dread settled in his stomach and churned together with his inexcusable pleasure. The mixture nauseated him. Maybe she really was a virgin. A million-year-old virgin? Well, go figure. As good as she'd felt in his arms, he sure as hell wasn't initiating her. He wouldn't be responsible for defiling such a treasure. She was a goddess, for the gods' sakes!

But he couldn't let anyone else do it. It was him or no one. Fuelled by possessiveness, he stormed after her and trapped her against the door before she could open it. His face pressed to the silken hair at the back of her head.

"You're not leaving."

She turned towards him. "You will lay with me?"

"No way. I can't do this. You can't do this. I mean, won't it make a rift in the fabric of life?"

Her eyebrows raised, her foot tapping in irritation. "And you really care about that? You are forever doing whatever you want to do."

He shook his head and refused to buckle under her challenge. "No, I won't do this." Oh goddess, he wanted to, though. His groin throbbed with his need to take her.

She straightened imperiously. "I command you."

A flash of anger stabbed through him. *Now wait a minute!*

"Now wait a minute," he repeated aloud. "We are in my home where *I'm* giving *you* protection. You are not the imperious deity here. I won't allow you to order me."

She opened her mouth to protest, but he interrupted her. "This is on my terms. What I say goes. Until this is over, I am *your* god."

Was that excitement that flashed in her eyes? It was gone before he could be sure and immediately replaced with a scowl. How was it possible even that turned him on? It didn't matter. All he knew was that the goddess was on his time and terms now. If she didn't agree, he'd transport her pretty ass right back to the portal room.

It didn't matter how much he'd fantasised about touching her. It didn't matter how often he'd visualised her cupping him when he'd touched himself. It didn't matter how many times he'd thought of her hands all over him, her soft skin pressed to him. If she didn't agree, he'd take her back.

Sure he would. Taking her back to that god was on the same level as letting another man take her virginity. Wasn't happening.

"Are you clear on that?" he rasped before he called his own bluff.

"Clear."

"Good."

Before his triumph took grip, the power downgraded again, this time for much longer than it had before. Panic filled her eyes. "We must... couple."

As ever, trying to be in charge...

Thad groaned. "Jett— "

"They can trace me through the vibration of it," she offered quickly, then clarified, "Of my virginity."

"Contrary to cultural reports, you're not the only virgin on earth."

"No, but I am the only virgin *goddess* on earth. Do you think they cannot find that pure energy? They can."

Inevitability dropped over him. The picture became like crystal in his mind. Him sinking into her, allowed to fulfil a dream. All because it suited her. She didn't want him. He met her criteria, and he'd pledged to serve her after all. "If it's that strong, won't you lose your powers?"

"I have strengths they have not begun to fathom. The virgin strand is but an inkling of what I am capable of doing.

"Please," she continued. "If they find us—*you*— they will kill you."

"Is he more powerful than you? Is that why you ran?" Thad asked, unmoved by the assertion that this unknown god might murder him.

"No. That is why he wants to join with me. We have equal power. Different, though. Mine are more potent in some ways, and in some ways, his outweigh mine."

"Could you defeat him? Enlist the help of other deities and smite him? That's what you would have done to me or any other irritation. Smiting."

"Airyon is cunning. He does not act justly. I would fight him straight on, but he would fight unfairly. He would attack my people in an attempt to obtain leverage against me. He could crush his thumb over a large city like this one. Everyone would die before they had any idea what was happening. But he will not do it if he cannot watch its effect on me. The longer I evade him, the safer my people are."

She looked away, her sadness flowing from her, the vibrations growing stronger. He wanted, no needed to yank her back into his arms, if only to comfort her. But he wanted so much more.

Her eyes reflected a myriad of the emotions she'd claimed not to have. "Do not dwell on Airyon or his threat. Do not dwell on what I have asked of you. It is not important to this moment." She held out her hands. "In the end, I am just a woman. No one special."

Chapter Two

No one special? Who was Jett kidding?

Another long electric lull propelled Thad into action. The trio searching for her was getting closer, and there was no way he'd let them take her. He wasn't keen on dying, either. Not that it really mattered to him after two centuries. Jett mattered. He didn't have time to mull over the situation and determine another course of action. If Jett said her virginity was leading the gods to her then he needed to get rid of it. It wasn't as if his body wasn't all for it.

His cock fairly wept for need of her. He wondered briefly if she hadn't placed some sort of spell over him to induce such a reaction. He cast aside that thought immediately. He didn't need a spell to want her and she couldn't risk using her magic.

Clearing his mind of everything except the picture of her body in his arms, writhing against him in pleasure as he took her, he crushed her to his chest. Without pausing for her reaction or compliance, he plundered her mouth.

A small whimper of pleasure rewarded him a moment later as she pressed into him. The points of her firm breasts pebbled against his chest.

Reaching between them, he traced patterns on his palm with the nipples while he swept his tongue along her lips. She widened them immediately, giving him access to the ambrosia within. He could quickly become addicted to it, especially the tentative way she darted her tongue against his.

She held nothing back from him, yet he felt the hesitation in her movements. He now recognised them for what they were...her innocence. He still couldn't believe she was so unschooled, and that she wanted him to make her his. Well, she wanted him to claim her virginity. That was all she'd offered. But to him, with her, it equated to the same thing.

He couldn't help his smile as he kissed her. After years of towing her goddess forsaken line, she would be his. She'd obey him—she'd agreed. He'd be the man he really was. How he wanted to command her and bend her to his will, just as she'd commanded him and tried to bend him to her will. To her chagrin, it had never worked. She'd never demeaned him, and he would respect her as well, though as far as he was concerned just about anything was fair game between two consenting adults.

The prospect of what they'd do, what he'd do to her, made him even more painfully hard than he already was. One thing was sure. Starting now, he'd get his way. And he would never follow her orders again.

Slowly, he shuffled them towards his bedroom as he continued to worship at her mouth. He pushed her tight toga-styled dress from her shoulder. The material fell to her waist, leaving her torso naked in his arms.

The bed met the back of Jett's knees, and they tumbled backward onto it, a tangle of limbs that didn't pause in their intent of pleasuring. She clutched his head and pushed him harder to her breast. Complying with her silent plea, he sucked the nipple into his mouth while his fingers glided down her hip.

Quickly, he pushed her dress the rest of the way off, pleased to discover her lack of undergarments.

"Goddesses don't wear panties?" he murmured against her turgid nipple.

"Thad," she cried as he reared up on his knees and spread her legs. His fingertips scored up her thighs to reach her core. Her feminine folds glistened with her arousal. He slipped his thumbs along her cleft, rasping first one then the other over her swollen clit.

"Thad...Thad...Thad," she chanted. Her head tossed as she clenched the sheets. Her hips arched off the bed, seeking more.

"Thad," she begged. "Hurry."

"I'm hurrying as much as I intend to."

He rubbed small circles on the hard pearl, watching her body tighten as her orgasm approached. She'd never been with a man, but had she ever climaxed?

"I am dying," she moaned, and he knew she hadn't. Unmitigated satisfaction lit an out-of-control grin on his face as he called forth her release.

Leaning forward, he licked the cream from her cunt in long lapping strokes, swirling his tongue along her puffy folds while his fingers continued their exploration. Carefully, he slipped one finger into her molten channel. Her inner muscles clenched him, and he could only imagine how tightly she'd squeeze his cock.

He wanted in her now. Forcing control over

himself, another finger joined the first. Slowly, he worked in and out of her as he continued to feast on her arousal. He flattened his tongue on her distended pleasure point.

Jett screamed, writhing as her orgasm crashed over her. Her fingernails dug into his shoulders while violent tremors in her canal clamped down where he stroked.

Then shock nearly paralyzed Thad. Power leapt from her limbs and pulsed into his body like an unbroken circuit of electricity.

His loud cry joined her continued cry.

Jett stroked Thad's head where he'd collapsed against her belly, excruciating pleasure still warming her body. Tremors still racked through him, and she wondered what had happened. It must have been the pleasure so many mortals sought. No wonder sex ran rampant amongst the people.

Before she pondered it further, Thad's fingers started stroking again, his tongue again lapping her over-sensitive nerve endings. "Please, no more," she begged.

He nipped her hip. "We've barely begun."

"But…" her protest was lost on a gasp as his fingers became more aggressive and a third joined the first two, stretching her more than she'd imagined.

The lights flickered again, dimming the room. "Hell!" Thad growled.

"No!" she cried as he leapt from the bed, but she smiled as she realised his intent. He ripped off his shirt and reached for the fastening of his black pants. An unfamiliar rasping sound broke the silence of the room.

"The power surges are getting closer together,"

he said as he shoved his pants down his muscled legs. Gods! The sight of him! With his wide shoulders and slim hips, he was the perfect specimen of what every man should be.

She swallowed hard at the sight of his erect penis. "Is that...normal?" she squeaked. It was *huge*. Long. Wide, the head easily the size of a succulent plum. How on earth would she accommodate that?

He glanced down, his hand stroking over it. "Problem?" he asked.

Her mouth dry, she shook her head. She'd chosen him. She'd begged him. She'd have to take it even if it would be intensely painful. There was no way she could imagine it being otherwise. But she was a goddess. She'd endure.

She'd wanted him for so long. She'd never imagined that he was...deformed.

"Don't look so frightened," he told her as he knelt on the bed. "I won't hurt you."

"I do not see how that is possible."

"Do you have to be so difficult? I'm trying to save your life here, and you're not helping."

"I am sorry," she said. "I just do not see how it will fit."

"It'll fit."

"I do not know..."

"Will you shut up?" He didn't give her a choice as his mouth sealed over hers. Jett moaned as the heavenly sensations from earlier began to vibrate through her again. Her mound throbbed, and she felt herself growing more damp. Thad stroked his fingers over her breast, squeezing slightly, pinching the nipple, while his over-large member prodded at her channel. Hoping to help his entrance and lessen her discomfort, if that were possible, she pulled her knees further up and widened them.

"Oh gods," she cried as the head entered her, stretching her vaginal walls. Instead of pain, ecstasy streamed through her, centring on the place where he joined with her.

"Breathe," he commanded in a strained voice. "It's so tight. Jett, you're so tight. Oh my goddess!"

Blindly, she rubbed her hands over his taut muscles. For some unknown reason, she wanted him to move faster. She wanted him all the way inside her. Deep. She squirmed trying for more of him. Perhaps he wasn't over-huge. She felt full, oh so full. Oh so good!

Good? It was rapture!

"Stay still," he gasped.

"I can not," she whimpered as she continued to rock. "Oh please, Thad..."

He caught her hips and held her still as he inched forward marginally before pulling backward. Before she could protest, he'd pushed forward again.

"This is going to hurt for a moment," he grunted, with obvious strain.

Hurt? He'd told her it wouldn't. How could it hurt when it felt so good right now? "I do not care," she moaned.

Propelled by her assurance, he thrust forward and buried himself deep within her. A skyrocket of pain jolted her. "Bastard!" she cursed. Her voice resonated with the strength of thunder, its fury directed at Thad. She'd smite him! This was the end. She'd kill him!

He leaned on an elbow and looked down at her with a smile. "Now don't bring my parents into this. You know they were married." The dog kissed her neck, gently biting the sensitive flesh behind her ear. "By the way, that virginity problem? Gone."

"Good! Get off me."

"Oh, I don't think so." He remained still, watching her. "All better now?"

"How can I be better? You have impaled me!"

"Are you sure?" He moved slightly. There was a twinge of discomfort in her untried flesh but not pain. Oh sweet heaven what was this?

"I do not understand," she whispered. Pleasant tension and relaxation wove through her as her inner muscles adjusted to the tight fit around Thad.

He glided forward and back in short, smooth strokes.

"Oh, yes," she choked, rocking with him. She'd discuss that conceited smile with him later.

"Now comes the good part," he told her. "Promise."

He'd promised not to hurt her earlier, too, so she didn't put much faith in his statement. While what he did felt exquisite, how could anything be better than before when his mouth had claimed her?

He nipped at her ear. "Stop thinking. Just feel, my beautiful goddess. Just feel."

"It is too much," she cried as the overwhelming sensations gathered inside her. They built larger and larger, threatening to explode.

"Let it happen. Come for me again. Come, Jett. Fly to pieces for me." He reached between them and pressed her clit, tapping it as he picked up speed.

The tremors erupted, starting as small quakes growing ever stronger in intensity. Her head thrashed on the pillow as the unfamiliar sensations, similar to earlier, but far stronger, burned in her belly. They built and expanded, growing farther reaching and stronger until she exploded.

"Oh yes, my goddess," he moaned. "Yes, come for me."

"Thad," she wailed, clutching his shoulders.

Then it happened. And she screamed. Colours flew before her eyes, and she sailed over the precipice to the sound of shattering glass.

* * * *

"Are you back with me?"

Jett slowly became aware of a soft feathering over her ear as she came awake. She sighed rubbing her cheek into it. "I am awake," she said.

"Gods you scared me. I've never had a woman pass out before. Of course, I've never had a woman do the other thing, either."

Her eyes snapped open. "What other thing?"

"Don't move," Thad warned.

"What is it?"

He picked up a handful of shiny, silver gravel from the sheet beside her. "You screamed...then the world seemed to explode."

She smiled, lazily. "Yes, it did."

He kissed her quickly. "No, sweetness, I mean explode in the non-sex way."

"What?"

"The vases, the mirrors, the light bulbs...pretty much everything glass-based in this room except for the windows. It all exploded."

"I am sorry."

"Don't worry about it. We'll just have to make sure to be glass-free in the future."

"In the future? You want to do that again?"

"Gods, yes! Often."

A warm feeling shot through her.

"Don't move!" he cautioned when she attempted to roll towards him. Gingerly, he left the bed then he slid an arm beneath her shoulders and legs. With a sigh, Jett snuggled into his chest as he carried her to the living room.

It was nice to feel protected instead of feeling the need to take care of everyone else.

Her stomach growled loudly as he set her on the white couch.

He pointed towards an area filled with strange white boxes and little doors. A long L-shaped counter separated it from the open living area. "There's food in the kitchen. Help yourself. Or make us something while I take care of the glass. I'm pretty hungry, too."

She stared at him. "I am a goddess. I do not eat."

Her stomach chose that moment to rumble.

"Well, you should."

Jett's brow furrowed. She'd never been hungry before, but there was no denying the gnawing in her middle that had nothing to do with her continued need for Thad. She hadn't spent much time in the mortal realm in the past, only coming here when she needed to speak with one of her pledges. Even then, she hadn't really come to earth. They'd come to the audience chamber—a portal between earth and the heavens.

If she was experiencing hunger, what other human functions would she be subject to? Her nose wrinkled, bathing she supposed, and relieving herself like...a mortal. Well, this was not the vacation she'd envisioned when she'd chosen to run rather than submit to Airyon's demands that she join with him.

He belonged to an unsanctioned faction that believed the feminine deities must be joined with the male deities to harness their power. Misogynistic fool. He'd never get away with this if it wasn't the Festival of Regeneration, the time when the upper servants of the Higher Power convened to regenerate their powers. As a lower servant, she needed no regeneration. Her responsibilities were small in comparison to overseeing *everything*. Horrible events took place whenever the festival occurred. Last time, the Black Death had been unleashed. The perpetrator was in Torment, eternal punishment, but that wasn't until he'd wrecked havoc on her holdings. Of course, the people always blamed her. It wasn't as if she could send them a scroll saying, "It was not my fault, you ungrateful urchins."

She'd known this festival, a long eight days, she'd receive more of the same. To her shame, turbulent weather on earth had been in direct correlation to her unrest. Hurricane after hurricane, tornadoes, earthquakes. Her warlock overlords had worked overtime to keep the effects to a minimum when they could.

Word of Airyon's plans had come to her late yesterday. She'd had little time to work out her own plan, but she'd known immediately that Thad would be the one to help her. Airyon had already seen her mentor, the only other who could assist her, into Torment.

Thad was most unlike her other pledges. He never blindly followed her edicts. As a matter of fact, he often took his own route. Sometimes he eventually followed her wishes, sometimes he did whatever the hell he wanted. Though she complained loudly about it and reprimanded him, she secretly approved of his tactics. He had a brain and he used it. And while he bowed to her power in the audience chamber, she knew it was against his nature. He was a man in command of himself and his environment. It angered him to be placed in any situation where that was removed. Even when in her chamber, he constantly pushed her limits. Looking directly at her, speaking to her without bidding, calling her Jett.

She liked the name. She liked his nature. Liked? Actually, his raw, untamed power aroused her, and it had nothing to do with his magic. When she was placed in the position that she'd have to choose a protector and possibly give away her virginity, she'd had no other choice. He was the only one she'd abide.

Thad looked around the corner from the bedroom. "Go eat something!" he growled. Not unkindly. Still it made her sigh. He was damned pushy. She worried a bit about all that "I am your god" stuff. Exactly how far would he go? He had another think coming if he intended to start ordering her around as if she was *his* pledge.

Some things were not to be tolerated. It didn't matter how hot he made her.

Wandering to the room Thad called 'kitchen', Jett wondered what food it would contain. She stood in the centre of the room, looking around at the multitude of white doors. Everything was white here. Thad would be quite comfortable in her home realm where nearly everything was colourless, save for the clothing of its inhabitants and the wild greenery.

He'd told her there was food here, but she saw nothing save for a bowl on the counter. Was that fruit in it? It didn't look like any of the fruit she'd created. She lifted a piece, examining what she assumed was an apple. What abomination had the mortals performed on her creation?

"Uh, Jett?"

She looked up from her contemplation of the apple. Thad leaned on the entryway, his arms crossed loosely as he watched her. He'd slipped on a pair of loose linen pants that fastened with a button and a drawstring at his waist but left his hard torso bare. She wanted to explore the ridges of his muscles with her tongue and fingers. She'd been far too busy earlier to realise how devastating his body was. He could have any woman, any goddess, he wanted. And he wanted her.

She bit her lip. He wanted more of what they'd done. That didn't really mean he wanted her. He liked the sex. That was different.

She returned the apple, and crossed her arms over her breasts, suddenly aware of her nakedness.

He nodded towards the bowl, his long white-blond hair falling over his shoulder. "That's not edible. It's wax."

"I knew it was not natural."

He opened both long doors on the tall metal box that was recessed into the wall. A chill skated across her skin, prickling goosebumps.

"Cold and frozen foods are in here," he told her. He opened a door next to it to reveal six wide shelves with an array of boxes, metal-looking cylinders and bags. "The rest of the food is in here."

It all confused her. She'd investigate it later when he wasn't around to see her ignorance. She refused to reveal she knew next to nothing about his world. Nature, the workings of the earth and the solar system? Yes. Workings as trivial as technology? No.

Her lack of knowledge spurred a sudden sense of vulnerability and reminded her she stood completely nude in her pledge's presence. Her body was perfection, she was a goddess after all, but her nakedness made her uncomfortable.

"I want to get dressed," she said. "Bring me my clothing."

His cobalt eyes scanned over her, hungry and predatory. She fought to keep from pushing her thighs together. It was impossible to ignore the way her body reacted to the assessment.

"I like you this way."

"Well, I do not like being this way. I would like some clothing."

"My rules..." he rumbled, a nearly inaudible reminder of what she'd agreed to earlier. Her jaw tensed. She'd been desperate for help then. Now she wanted to cover up.

"I want clothes."

"There aren't any here that fit you."

"Then give me back my dress."

He shook his head. "Covered in glass."

Amusement danced in his eyes along with the knowledge he had her exactly where he wanted her. She sucked in an irate breath between her teeth. When she could safely use her powers again, he would pay. She would turn him into a squid. An earthworm. A tumbleweed!

"I'll tell you what," he said, unaware of his impending doom. "I'll feed you this time, then next time, you can feed me." He grasped her around the waist and lifted her to sit on the counter. His words said 'food' but his look said something entirely different.

Jett's growling stomach was pushed aside by her growling lust.

Chapter Three

Jett gasped at the shock of the cold porcelain tiles beneath her buttocks. She squirmed to get down, but Thad held her in place.

"Don't move," he ordered.

Her eyes widened at his tone, but she said nothing, merely adding it to the list of things he'd pay for later. The list was getting lengthy. At this rate, he'd be paying for a long time. That thought made her smile until she noticed the smouldering heat in his eyes. Immediate reaction quivered in her belly. No. She couldn't possibly want him again. Could she?

From his darkened expression, she expected him to touch her. Instead, he turned away to the cool food receptacle.

Her teeth sank into her lower lip at the gut-wrenching rejection that shook her. She felt bereft at his desertion. What a fool she was to misread his intentions. She had to depart here before he realised her hurt and what an idiot his goddess was.

Inching closer to the counter edge, she prepared to jump down and dash from the room. With his back turned, she could get out of the kitchen before he reacted.

As if somehow sensing her intention, he turned from where he gathered implements from another portion of the counter. "Stay," he growled, pointing a knife at her.

She froze. Did he threaten her? Her fingers flexed as she prepared to retaliate magically, if needs be. She'd never imagined such measures necessary against him.

Thad thumped the knife onto the counter, and relief filled her. He hadn't meant any harm when he'd pointed it at her. He pulled a rectangular board from the doors beneath her, and it joined the blade. Two cylindrical red cans, real apples, strawberries and cheese—she recognised all these—followed.

His arm brushed her leg as he began slicing the cheese and apples.

She watched him work, his smooth, sure movement hypnotic.

"Hungry?" he asked and dropped the knife.

Her stomach rumbled in answer, impudent thing, and she had no choice but to nod. Her breath caught in her throat as he parted her knees and stepped between her thighs.

"Let's eat," he said. "Lean back on your elbows and I'll feed you."

She regarded him warily.

He tilted his head, a dare clear in his eyes.

Her fingers tightened on the counter's edge.

Smiting, she thought. *Complete smiting.* No, that would be too good. She'd make him suffer first. Formulating her plan for retribution, she complied with his directive before he spouted his I'm-your-god nonsense again.

He lifted one of the red cylinders. "Thirsty? Would you like a can?

Her brow wrinkled.

"Would you like a drink?" he clarified.

She licked her dry lips. "Yes."

"Me too." He fiddled with the top of the object and it made a loud hissing sound. He held it up to her lips for her to sip. A cold, burning fizz streamed down her throat. She gasped and choked.

"It gets better. I bet before long it's your favourite drink," he promised, dragging the container in a lazy trail along her shoulder to her breast. He nudged it over her nipple, before pulling it away and dribbling a few drops on the crinkled skin. His mouth immediately followed to flick away the liquid with his tongue.

"Mmmmm," he rumbled against her flesh.

The icy trail continued down her stomach until he pressed the can to the inside of her thigh. Slowly, he rolled it towards her heated flesh as she trembled.

Jett let out a yelp as it pushed against her parted folds.

"Oh gods! Thad!" she groaned, the cold nearly unbearable yet so arousing.

He pulled it away and licked the outside where it had touched her. "You taste so good."

Lifting a piece of cheese, he held it to her lips to eat, then shocked her by pouring some of the beverage into her naval until it overflowed and trailed down her sides. Leaning forward, he lapped away the light brown drink.

Jett drove her fingers into his hair. Long after the drink was gone, he dipped his tongue into the indentation, swirling, nipping, sucking. Absently, he fed her a tart apple slice, then straightened.

"Can I have a strawberry?" she asked.

"No. Those are for me."

No? No one had ever denied her a wish.

No one except Thad. She'd given him a little

leeway, and now, it seemed he was ready to run with it. She wondered exactly how far she'd let him go before she yanked him back.

If she knew him, he'd just find a way to cut the binding. Thad only pretended to take her orders. She'd yank, and he'd ignore. That was the way it had always been. He didn't comply with her wishes. He did whatever he wanted.

He wants you *now.*

As if to remind her of that very thing, he moulded her breast in his palm, pinching the nipple before he fed her another apple slice.

With a determined look, he picked up one of the berries. It rasped over her skin, leaving a faint red trail, as he teased her with it. To her shock, he dipped the strawberry into her cleft. A moment later, he lifted it to his lips and took a bite.

Fiery response blazed through her. She fought to keep it under control as she felt her divine power stir. It shimmered along her skin. Any moment, she'd explode into a ball of smiting energy that would destroy all the glass surrounding them. She had no doubt that was what had happened before. Thad was lucky he'd been unscathed.

Unaware of the danger swirling within her, he licked his fingers. "You taste so good. Best creamy dip ever."

Her eyebrows shot upward along with her frenzied heartbeat. A knot clogged her throat. Oh gods, what he did to her!

Thad repeated the process with another strawberry, while Jett's breathing accelerated out of control. Her belly quivered. The rough texture and the cool sensation against her eager flesh sending her nerve endings into panic. No way could she avoid the cataclysmic destruction about to overcome her. She could only hope to shield

Thad...

She should stop him. She couldn't stop him. Arousal flooded her vagina, making her slick.

Thad had plenty of 'dip'. He slipped the final strawberry along her folds, and his eyes danced with fire as he lifted it to her lips.

Her heady scent mingled with the sweet fruit.

"Taste," he murmured, his eyes so full of arousal that she could drown in their bottomless depths.

She sucked it into her mouth, groaning as the flavour exploded onto her tongue and heat soared through her. It crept up her chest to fill her cheeks. To do such a thing...to take her own essence into her mouth...the wantonness of it shocked her. So much related to her interaction with Thad shocked her. She'd never have believed she'd do such things. With him, nothing outside the moment mattered, it all felt right. Embarrassment fled, and she realised her actions didn't just feel right, they were right.

For now. She'd deal with the consequences and loneliness later.

He licked the juice from the corner of her lips. "See how good you taste?"

She didn't answer, instead reaching out and threading her fingers through his hair. She drew him down and kissed him. The kiss sizzled against her lips as he slanted in to deepen their contact.

Her head tipped back, and he left a fiery trail of open-mouthed caresses to her belly that fluttered with her eagerness for him. She nearly cried out when he pulled away and reached for the can again. He took a swallow of his drink as he knelt before her.

His mouth still full of the bubbly beverage, he sucked her clit into his mouth. The same fizz that had burned down her throat, now tormented her sensitive flesh. Mindlessly, she lifted on her elbows, arching into it. As he sucked, he ran a finger along her cleft, sinking it into her. A second quickly followed.

"I could live on the taste of you alone," he muttered, just before his tongue flicked out. He flattened it over her before swiping upward, then back and into the burning passage now filled with three fingers. She already felt so full, but she knew it was nothing compared to his thick cock surging into her. She wanted that unbelievable pleasure again soon.

Not that she didn't love the feel of his mouth on her. The hot, damp warmth and suction coupled with the rasp of his tongue and teeth drove her mad with want. She pressed into him.

He raised her legs so they draped over his shoulders, holding her open for him, his willing captive. As he cupped her ass in his hands, lifting her rhythmically to his thrusts, everything ceased to exist, the flickering lights, the low hum of the electricity, the sunlight, the counter, the rest of their bodies. Her entire focus was on his amazing mouth and her cunt as it clenched in demand. She writhed against him, terrified by the intensity of the sensations clawing from the tormented nub to her womb.

In and out he darted, flicking, pressing, sucking, biting. Unbearable tension coiled in her belly, almost painful in her need. Panting, she clasped his head to her cleft, begging him incoherently for release.

"Come in my mouth," he coaxed. "Feed me, my goddess. Give me sustenance."

Lightning seemed to fly from his words down her limbs, electrifying her nerve endings. With a loud cry, she tumbled over the edge. She fell backward, saved from injury only by Thad's quick reflexes, but he never took his mouth from her.

When she collapsed, boneless, on his arms, he stood. His lips glistened with her syrupy juice. He licked them slowly, his gaze locked with hers.

The tension that had only just released returned with a vengeance.

"More," she commanded him.

"Still hungry?" he asked.

She sat up, wrapping her legs around his waist. "I want to taste you."

He shook his head. "Too soon. I'd never hold out." He stepped back slightly and released the button and tie on his pants. They slithered over his hips, caressing his curves as she'd like to. A moment later, he returned. The wide head of his arousal prodded against her channel, and she swallowed, remembering the last time they'd coupled. The fullness, the intense sensations, the shattering glass. Somehow, she'd have to harness her energy to prevent that from reoccurring. She couldn't destroy Thad's home.

The tapered tip breached her small opening and she forgot everything. She pulled her feet to the edge of the counter and lifted onto him as he slid a fraction further inside.

Jett panted with the anticipation.

"So tight," he moaned.

Her fingers clenched on the countertop. She needed him to move. Gods! She needed him to move! "Is that a complaint?"

"My goddess, no! You're perfect." He pushed further, parting her taut walls. Jett gritted her teeth against the keening sound that gathered in her chest.

Her world spun, and he climbed onto the tile

with her. He positioned her flat on the improvised bed and rose over her. The board, knife and remaining food flew to the floor.

She barely noticed. His thick erection plunged forcefully into her newly initiated pussy. She arched against the welcome intruder and the pleasure-pain that accompanied his deep penetration. She couldn't get enough of the thick, full feeling as he skated through her creamy channel, of the abrasion of his chest hair scraping along her sensitised nipples.

She sobbed into his mouth as he took her lips, darting his tongue in unison with the heavy claiming. Fierce contractions clenched her vagina, hugging his cock, creating a friction that drove her wild. She clawed at his shoulders while her hips met his, thrust for thrust.

"Mine!" he cried, rising to his knees and sinking forward to the hilt. Her womb tightened, her body starting to tremble out of control.

"Thad!" she screamed, her vision blurred as the ecstasy flew over her. Thad's arms convulsed around her middle, squeezing her to him. Hot blasts of semen poured into her.

They landed from their flight over the edge, a jumble of slippery limbs on even more slippery-and-no-longer-cool porcelain. Jett couldn't move. Her muscles refused to cooperate, choosing only to tremor in continued reaction. She fought the weariness that claimed her, but her lids drooped irrevocably. She, the Goddess of the Zodiac Quadrant, couldn't fight slumber.

* * * *

Thad rose on an elbow and smiled at the sight of Jett sound asleep beneath him. *So powerful and so precious.* A wave of tenderness wove round him. Careful not to disturb her, he slid from the counter—how on earth had they ended up there?—and slipped back into his pants.

Tenderly, he lifted her into his arms and carried her towards the bedroom, much like he'd done earlier when he'd brought her to the couch. He liked carrying her. He liked her naked.

She breathed deeply, each hot exhalation tormenting his nipple, an inch from her mouth. Blood surged back to his cock. Gods! She'd kept him constantly hard for two hundred years. Now that he'd had her, he'd expected the torture to ease. Instead, it was worse. So much worse. If not for the few ethics he clung to, he'd follow her down to the mattress and take her again, sleep or not.

Trying to gain control, he surveyed the living room. He hadn't been thinking of anything but getting inside her burning pussy. This room was filled with glass. Aside from one broken light bulb, though, everything remained intact.

He must have done something wrong.

Frowning, he stalked to the bed and slipped her beneath the covers. He'd examine his performance later. Part of him wanted to shake her awake and examine it now.

Jett snuggled into the covers and made a quiet snuffling sound into the pillow. She needed her rest. She wasn't accustomed to the workout he'd given her or the pull of earth's atmosphere.

He stroked a hand over her fiery hair. If he had his way, he'd keep her exhausted and compliant for days. He wasn't fooled into believing Jett would go along with his 'god-plan' for long. Already, she was fighting the boundaries. He only had a few days to convince her he was good for her.

But, he also wasn't fooled into believing their

affair would last forever. He was mortal. She was a goddess. A minute and an eternity. She'd go on long after he ceased to exist.

He wanted as much time as she'd grant him. He scowled. He didn't like that she'd have to 'grant' him anything.

He lifted Jett's dress from the floor. Much as he was loath to admit it, she needed clothes. He couldn't keep her naked and confined to the penthouse even though he'd like to. He wanted to show her New York. He wanted to share the advances of the twenty-first century, teach her everything she didn't know.

He'd realised just how unschooled she was in technology when he'd seen her standing forlornly in his kitchen, staring aghast at the wax apple. He'd known immediately. His sweet goddess was an alien in a foreign land. She'd tried to act knowledgeable, goddesses showed no weakness, or at least, tried not to.

He'd show it all to her, instructing without being obvious.

He glanced at the wadded silk in his hand. She did need more clothes. Something less I've-just-left-my-throne-of-godly-power. Something more Thad-Pennington's-lover.

He balled up her dress and shoved it into the back of his closet behind a box of records. He might let her wear his robe when she woke, then he'd see to garments. The two of them would never stay vigilant with her pert breasts distracting him.

His mouth watered at the thought of tasting her again. He'd like to indulge now. He sighed. He needed to get control of himself.

Time to get some work done. The territories Jett granted him required daily oversight. Much as he'd like to lose himself in other pleasures, he had duties. He headed for his office, though he worried about leaving Jett alone. Would he know if Airyon came into the bedroom while she slept and stole her? He paused in the doorway. Could he leave her? As her pledged warlock he was sworn to uphold her and, by that, protect her.

The power surges were growing much further between. If the god seeking her was still scanning for her virgin energies, the lack in this territory was diverting him. By Thad's estimation, it had been nearly fifteen minutes between power fluxes, where as before it had been more like five minutes. Hopefully, Airyon and his brothers were focusing their search elsewhere, and they'd eventually spread their probe beyond the States. He grinned. They could get caught for days in the magic prevalent in the African cultures.

By then perhaps, he and Jett could form a feasible plan. They had to come up with something. There was no way, he'd let anyone, deity or not, take her from him. He might be mortal, but Jett was his.

* * * *

Jett bit her lip, fisting her fingers in the voluminous folds of the robe Thad had lent her when she'd risen. She smiled at the memory. She'd woken with a start, knocking over a pile of books on the table beside the bed and he'd fairly flown into the room ready for battle.

When he'd seen she was safe and stared for an unduly long time at her breasts, he'd muttered something about distractions and thrust the garment at her. Then he'd stormed from the room, still muttering.

Now, she was alone. And bored. Well, not so

much bored as agitated. She needed to know what was happening elsewhere in her realm, as well as at home in the heavens.

She glanced around. Thad had sequestered himself in one of the other rooms. She wasn't sure which one, though she could feel his strong life force to the north side of his home. He wasn't moving around.

Quickly, she stabbed her empty hand into the air and brought it back with a scroll in her fist— *The Daily Deity Report.* Glancing about again, she unrolled it.

The headline article reported that the upper deities were still convening with the Higher Power and would be for six more moon risings. Below it was a stunningly bad likeness of herself and a small write-up stating she was missing, possibly kidnapped, but that the inner circle had not been disturbed with the news.

"What the hell is that?"

Jett jumped, shoving the scroll behind her before she looked up at Thad.

"What is that?" he thundered, just as the power fluxed. "As if I don't know. As if I'm blind. As if I don't know what the hell a scroll is. I sure as hell know I don't have any around here!"

"There is no need to yell."

"No need to—" he spluttered. "Do you *want* him to find you? Is this just some big game to you?"

"No! Of course, I do not want him to find me."

"Then why would you do something so asinine? You don't think he felt your magic the second you used it?"

She bit the side of her mouth. "Perhaps, he did not notice."

"And perhaps, I just happen to have fucking

horns!"

"I could arrange that."

"*Jett—* "

"I needed to know what is going on," she protested.

"Well, you're going to get firsthand information when he comes to collect you. Just try not to get me killed in your stupidity."

Did he *dare* call her stupid? She flung down the scroll, taking comfort in the way it bounced on the fine wood table. She hoped it left a chink or two. Defiantly, she crossed her arms over her chest. "Airyon did not notice or he would be here already."

"Just because he's not here, doesn't mean he didn't feel it. For goddess sake, *I* felt it. The only reason Airyon hasn't swooped down to drag you away is that he can't pinpoint you. But if he felt it—and I know he did—he'll know where to look."

"Mine is not the only magic on earth."

"It's the only divine magic."

"Hardly. Others visit here."

"Right now?"

She looked away. Visitations were limited during the Regeneration Festival. "No."

Thad's jaw worked. He glared at her then spun away. "How am I going to protect you if you throw out beacons for Airyon to follow?"

She sighed. "It was a minute action."

His lips turned white around the edges as he restrained his anger, very poorly, if his tension was any indication. "Is this whole thing just a charade, a game for you and a punishment for me?" he thundered. "What have I done this time to attract your ire?"

Hurt punched a hole in the new side of her relationship with him, leaving it in tatters. "Do not make me list your transgressions. And do not be ridiculous," she said, her voice devoid of emotion. "If I wanted to punish you, I would see to it myself. Have I ever called upon another to take on a task I find distasteful? I may order the overlords, but I am always there. Always overseeing."

"You are," he conceded, but it was too little too late. He'd crushed the new bud between them beneath his distrust. Not that it mattered. As she replayed his words, she was sure the emotions had been fully on her part. He'd done his duty, no more. Physical hunger was not all she'd fallen prey to. Emotional hunger wracked her, more insidious and insatiable. It shamed her to realise she'd succumbed to human sentiment.

"Small or not, Airyon will track your energy. You can't go pulling rabbits out of hats. He'll find you."

She shook her head. "Every time you or one of the three other overlords use your abilities, it skews his perception. Every time the earth quakes, a volcano rumbles, a storm brews, a child is born...it vibrates with my energy. Right now he is feeling me in every corner of the world. Pulling a scroll is not going to cause a big enough ripple."

He stared at her as if she were crazed, his face taut with unspoken words. "Don't. Do. It. Again," he finally growled.

A bubble of triumph sprung up in her chest, combined with something else. She liked him all growly like this. The realisation humiliated her in light of his obvious distrust.

She nodded before deliberately stepping over the scroll and heading towards the small room he'd shown her.

Thad followed her. She wondered if he didn't trust her to leave his sight. She ignored the 'toilet' and stared into the tiled bathing area. It was large enough to accommodate several people, though she had no clue as to why that would be necessary. Did the people of this time period often partake in group cleaning? The basin, she recognised as a tub, was also huge. She wasn't interested in bathing within the tub. She wanted to try this new thing—without the 'group.'

Turning, she levelled an imperious glare at him. "Demonstrate the workings of this new aqueduct apparatus."

"The shower."

"Whatever it is called."

Moving around her, he pointed to the dials. "This controls hot water and this cold. Adjust them to the desired temperature." He turned on the faucet then flipped a lever and spray shot from several spouts around the enclosure.

She smiled in anticipation. "You may leave now."

He crossed his arms and leaned against the counter. "I don't think so."

Her hands went to the belt of the robe. "Suit yourself."

She let the thick, white fabric fall to her waist and was rewarded by his nostrils flaring as a familiar light flickered in his eyes. She turned and let the robe drop to the floor. "But you may not touch me."

Chapter Four

Jett could order him away all she wanted, but if she thought he'd comply, she was sadly mistaken. Thad scrubbed a hand over his scalp as she stepped into the shower enclosure and shut the glass door, effectively shutting him out, as well.

She thought that, anyway.

He could still easily see her though the clear glass, treated to prevent fogging, though wafts of steam filled the enclosure. The water jets sluiced over her supple body to caress her as he'd like to.

He'd pissed her off. He'd realised that immediately when her light blue eyes had turned to glazed ice. Then she'd stormed away. He couldn't help but follow her.

She had no idea the fear that had surged through his veins, making his blood rush, when he'd felt the current of divine energy. He'd thought that Airyon had found her. That he'd snatch Jett away before Thad could do anything to stop him. She might have laughed had she seen the way he tore into the room...to find her intent on her scroll.

His teeth ground together. She'd risked discovery for something so trivial as a *scroll*. He wanted to shake her. Another part of him wanted to reassure himself she was safe. Mentally, he knew she was. The energy was nothing dangerous. A deeper ingrained primal part of her needed more, needed to touch her despite her order not to.

Jett arched under the water, turning slightly so he could see the curve of her hip bone into her slightly concave belly. Her hands trailed over her skin before disappearing between her thighs.

He drew his brows together as his cock tented his pants. He couldn't take her again. Not yet. She had to be sore. Gods, he'd already taken her more than he should have in her untried state. She needed to recover.

He wanted to bury himself in her again.

Jett's head dropped backward as she stroked her cleft and Thad stifled a groan. She might claim not to be punishing him, but she'd kill him yet.

Turning on his heel, he stormed from the room. Fine. She didn't want him to touch her. He wouldn't. Yet.

* * * *

Jett dropped her head against the wall when Thad left, proving exactly what she'd surmised. She was his duty and he was merely doing what was expected, ordering her about was just a side benefit.

Using the bar of fragrant soap, she lathered it over her body. It smelled like Thad. Her body aching for him, she let the water cascade over her face as she surrendered to yet another mortal foible and cried.

She showered until the water started to cool and when she couldn't get more heat, shut it off. Having indulged her fit, her mind swooped into motion. As long as they were successful in hiding from Airyon, she had six more days with Thad.

A lot could happen in six days.

He wanted her, of that she was sure. The erection that had strained in his trousers before he'd left her alone was silent testimony to that fact. He might not stay with her after the threat passed, but they could enjoy each other until then. Well, as much enjoyment as was possible when one was constantly vigilant for a threat to an entire quadrant. Besides earth, she had life on nineteen other planets with which to concern herself. It often amused her that many earth dwellers believed themselves to be the only humanoids in existence. They'd never discover differently though, since she'd placed the livable planets in far-flung directions. . . and never the twain should meet.

She couldn't help but think that Thad would enjoy some of the other planets. He could survive on all of them. The oxygen to carbon dioxide mix, as well as the temperature, was similar on all. Everything else was different.

She liked variety. But she needed constants.

Thoughtfully, she stepped from the enclosure and dried herself with a fluffy white towel.

White! The man needed some colour in his life and as soon as she could, she'd remedy the lackluster situation. She could see the beautiful home filled with hues throughout the spectrum but especially jewel tones.

She smiled as she slipped back into the robe and left the room. Perhaps she'd add a brilliant-cast article for every time they made love. If she had her way, by the time the sixth night rolled around, the place would be filled with reminders of the passion she'd brought into his life.

The way she saw it, she owed him at least two

bits of colour now.

"What are you smiling about? More magic that you shouldn't be performing."

She jumped with a small shriek. "Will you stop sneaking up on me?"

"Who's sneaking? I was here when you walked in."

Okay, she'd give him that. But she wasn't going to tell him what she'd been thinking. "And goddesses don't do magic. I use my abilities."

"Right. So were you?"

"You told me not to."

"Like you ever listen to me."

"Isn't that my complaint about you? And yes, I listened. I told you I would when you agreed to help me."

He gave her a completely disbelieving look. She didn't blame him. Who was she really fooling? Obviously, deciding to pretend to take her at her word, he began with the orders again. "I laid out some clothes for you on the bed. Go get dressed. We're going out.

"Hurry," he added. "We slept through most of the business hours. . ."

Slept. Okay if that was how he wanted to say it.

"...and the shops I want to visit will close in a few hours. Knowing you, I bet we'll need plenty of time."

"What exactly do you mean by that?" she bristled.

He sighed. "I mean that you are the most pig-headed woman I know. Go get dressed!"

She put her hands on her hips, glaring at him. "I would not say *I* am the pig-headed one in this situation."

He towered over her. She didn't back down,

even when his head bent so that his face was inches from hers. "Do you want new clothes or not."

Oh sweet heavens, clothes. "I'll get dressed."

"I thought you might."

She shot him a nasty look and went into the bedroom where a white—of course, white. The man had some weird hang-up—dress with thin, braided straps to hold it up was laid out on the bed. Her sandals were pillowed in the blanket beside it.

"You told me you did not have clothes here to fit me," she called.

"I found something," he said without elaborating. She wondered if, given the time, he could find more. The dress looked downright perfect in size. As did the filmy garment beside it—she assumed the abbreviated pants were the panties of which he'd spoken. She'd never needed them before. She'd forego them now.

She sat on the end of the bed and dragged a comb from the dresser through her hair until it hung in long golden-red strands to her waist. She dried it as she worked, using such a small amount of natural energy that even the most attuned person wouldn't notice the vibrations of it. Or so she thought until she heard Thad swear from the living room, but by then, her hair was mostly dry anyway.

She stood and slipped on the dress, working the toothed closure in the back the way she'd seen the closure on Thad's pants operate. The bodice hugged her torso, cupping her breasts, while the bottom flared to mid-calf. She spun. The skirt floated around her as she moved. She spun again just to feel it teased around her skin. She liked the way it slid over her bottom as she shifted.

"Hurry up!" Thad called.

"Yes, Master," she grumbled under her breath. He could be the biggest beast. She added his new pushiness to her list of indiscretions.

Sitting, she strapped on her sandals, regrettably white, twining them up her legs until she tied them. She glanced in the full-length mirror, satisfied with her appearance and hoped Thad found it pleasing.

She frowned, irked that such a thought would cross her mind. Who cared what he thought?

* * * *

Jett was the most beautiful woman he'd ever seen. Thad knew immediately that he'd be scowling off plenty of men today. He also realised that buying the dress hadn't been as foolish as he'd thought.

When he'd seen it a year ago, he'd had to buy it. He couldn't see anyone in the one of a kind creation other than Jett. He'd walked into the shop, paid an outlandish amount for the dress and made the woman remove it from the window.

The style was timeless. He'd seen women wear similar in the nineteen twenties, the fifties, the eighties and now. And the colour kept it in style. White. Perfect and pure, just like his goddess.

If she didn't need clothes so damned much, they wouldn't be leaving the penthouse. He could think of some pretty impure things he'd really like to do with her right then.

"What do think?" she asked.

"You'll do," he replied.

Her face fell and he mentally kicked himself for being a jerk. Her rejection earlier still stung, but he reminded himself that he didn't have to hurt her feelings. Especially with a lie. Besides, she'd been pissed about something then. She seemed to be over it now.

Crossing the room, he took her stiff body into his arms, cupping her face so she'd look at him. "You're the most gorgeous creature that's ever breathed," he told her. "I'll be driving off all the men wanting you today."

She pulled from his arms. "You do not have to lie. 'You look good' would have been enough."

He threw up his arms in disgust. "Okay! Fine! You're not pretty! You're as ugly as a toad!"

She looked affronted, then smiled. "You think I'm pretty?"

"No, I think you're ugly as a toad." He pulled her tight against him again. His fingers buried in her silken hair. "C'mere, toad-face."

"Oh, that's just delightful," she laughed. "The best endearment I have ever heard."

His kiss cut off her laugh as he took her mouth with the desperation of a man who would never be able to kiss his woman again. There was nothing gentle about the way he devoured her, his tongue dipping in and out with a tormenting rhythm that made her moan in frustration. He wanted her in his system, in his blood so that he could always feel her, even when he grew old.

Jett was not to be consumed without contributing her hand to the mix. She pulled away slightly, just enough to be able to nip at his bottom lip. She sucked it gently into her own mouth, before letting go to nip some more. Then she angled her head and pressed into him, sucking his tongue into her mouth.

His body responded with the vigour of a standing ovation. Somewhere in the space of a day she'd become a world-class kisser. It both unsettled him and made him a little smug, because he knew where all of her experience had come from. And the rest was experimentation. All for him. And he revelled in it.

"We have to go," he told her, holding her head still while he went in for another foray into her mouth.

He could only imagine the feel of her mouth wrapped around his cock, like a wet vice, sucking on it like she had his tongue moments ago.

At this rate, they'd never leave here. She'd never have clothes. His hands fisted in the material at her waist.

Fine with him.

Breathlessly, she pulled away. "I thought I told you not to touch me," she said, her eyes full of mischief.

"Yeah, well, that was earlier and you know how well I listen," he replied. He deliberately put his hand on her waist as he steered her for the door. "Besides," he said near her ear. His tongue shot out to trace the shell. "I'm your god and what I say goes."

"We will see about that." She scooted away from him, but he pulled her back to the crook of his arm. He wasn't going to be separated from her on the streets of New York City. That might be worse than having Airyon find her. At least, she'd know how to cope with him.

They went into the hall and he pressed the button for the elevator. Jett flinched when the doors whooshed open, but he managed to get her to the street with only a small scream when they began to descend. He tried not to imagine her reaction to the subway and opted for a cab instead.

That would be better. Less men.

* * * *

Jett stared at the buildings that seemed to touch the sky. She couldn't see the tops they were so tall. Amazing. Mortals had done *this*? She wouldn't have believed it if she hadn't seen it. The ones she'd met, aside from Thad and the other overlords, seemed too caught up in themselves to have had the mental resources free to have completed such awesome structures.

But somehow, they had. And there were so many mortals here. They streamed around her, holding objects to their ears, talking to themselves and walking as if the world would stop if they didn't hurry to their next destination. A few looked annoyed as she stopped to gawk at the buildings, then side-stepped around her, and went on their way.

Thad grabbed her hand and pulled her with him. He walked just as quickly as the others. He waved his free hand at large yellow boxes with people in them. She assumed they were vehicles of some sort. The signs on the top said T-A-X-I. One of them swerved, towards them. Jett jumped back while Thad reached for it.

"Get in," he told her.

"We'll get killed."

"A cab's perfectly safe." He leaned towards her. "Besides, you're a goddess. The death clause doesn't apply."

She rolled her eyes, but climbed into the cab. "I think this might override that."

Thad said something that sounded like another language to the man and they sped off into the sea of yellow, occasionally lurching and dodging other cabs. The man in the front seemed very fond of a button that blared at the vehicles.

As they nearly hit another one, she buried her face in Thad's shoulder. "Just tell me when we get there."

He lifted her chin and angled his mouth over hers. She gasped in surprise as he thrust his tongue past her slightly parted lips. His hand squeezed her hip before travelling up to cup her breast. She whimpered as his thumb smoothed inward to make slow circles against her taut nipple.

The man on the other side of the clear divider yelled out the window in another language. They ignored him. Thad pulled her onto his lap, never releasing her mouth or her breast. His arousal, pressed hard and heavy into her leg. She imagined what it might be like to turn slightly and straddle him. Release him from the confines of his clothing. Take him inside her, a long hot rush of man.

She'd decided to do just that when Thad set her back to his side. He handed the man green paper then pulled her out and back to the stream of people.

"You lived," he told her as he dragged her along and then into a shop.

"What is this place?" Jett asked.

"It's a boutique. A fancy place for buying clothes."

"Hmmm," she murmured as she looked around, mostly noticing the haughty women hovering about and looking down their noses at the two of them. Okay, not the *two* of them. Just her. She flexed her hands into fists to keep from smiting the snotty sales people. She imagined their faces with char marks in the centre of their foreheads. "I do not see anything here that I would wear."

Thad took her elbow and led her further into the shop. "It doesn't matter. I'll be choosing."

"I do not want you to choose my clothes."

"I'm your god," he muttered half-under his breath but loud enough for her to hear.

Oh! She'd heard *that* one too many times. Before she could come up with a suitable fate for him, a stunning dark-haired woman emerged from a back room.

"Thad!" she exclaimed, grabbing his shoulders and kissing him.

Smiting! Rage burned through Jett as the woman smiled warmly at him.

Thad deftly pushed Jett's hand back to her side before she blasted. When she moved to lift her other hand, he slipped his arm behind her trapping one hand against his body and holding the other one down.

He smiled tightly. "Anya, we need clothes."

Anya turned her gaze on Jett. Her eyes widened and she bowed her head. "My goddess," she breathed. "Pardon me for not greeting you properly, Goddess of the Zodiac."

Jett's eyes went wide with shock. As the other woman lifted her head, she felt the current she'd been too distracted to notice earlier. Anya was a handmaiden of the gods, specifically to the Archpower, the upper servant, through whom Jett answered to the Higher Power. Her eyebrows drew together. She hadn't been aware of any handmaidens in her territories.

"May I speak, my goddess," Anya asked.

"Speak."

"The Higher Power placed us here to assist you should the need arise. I thought that surely that would never occur."

The Higher Power. Who could argue with that? The Being, after all, only had her best welfare in mind. Still, remembering the woman's familiarity with Thad, she wasn't so sure she trusted the handmaiden.

"At the moment, I require clothing," she said.

"As you wish. You'll be more comfortable in the private dressing area."

Jett wiggled to shake Thad's grip, but he followed her closely. "Oh, I'm staying with you. Remember, I'm choosing the garments."

She pursed her lips, irritated that he'd continue with the charade in front of her servant. Who was she kidding? *He* was her servant.

"Don't worry," he told her, giving her ass a squeeze. "I'll be discrete."

"As what? The plague?"

"Anya," she addressed the handmaiden as soon as the three of them were alone in the room.

"Yes, goddess?"

"You are not to tell a soul that you have seen me. Do you understand?"

"Yes, goddess. I have heard that the God of the Wrath seeks you. Your presence will be kept secret."

Jett smiled at her. "Until later. You may speak of it after the Festival."

She knew it would be hard for the handmaiden to keep the secret with no chance of ever bragging to her fellow servants that she'd personally assisted the goddess.

"God of Wrath?" Thad repeated.

"A nickname," Jett supplied.

"Hell of a nickname," he muttered. He turned to Anya. "Please bring us selections suitable for the goddess. Think of her as a wealthy client—one who must fit into normal society."

She nodded. "I'll be back momentarily."

Jett spun on him as soon as the woman left them. "How do you know the handmaiden?"

"I make it a point to know all of those with

strong magic in my territories. Besides, her name was on my scroll. You know. . . the one with all the rules. You shoved it at me *after* you tricked me into eternal servitude."

"Tricked you? I never—"

"I know you *never.* You offered your body like a high-paid whore then never followed through with your promise."

"I did not. I gave you everything I promised."

"Gods, I never took you for having such a short memory."

"You are an ass."

"Language, language."

She jabbed him in the chest, and she wondered if he realised how lucky he was that she wasn't sending bolts of lightning from that digit. There were too many things in his statement that she'd yet to address. "And it is not *eternal* servitude, though with your attitude, it damned well might be!"

"Oh, it isn't?" he shot back. "It feels like it."

"If it is so bad, I could kill you here and now and find a new pledged overlord!" Too bad. She'd miss the feel of him in her. And the trembles from his touch. Damn the man!

"Um, excuse me." Anya stood in the doorway. She looked ashen and Jett feared the woman might faint from the discussion she'd overheard. Weak. That was why she was a handmaiden. "I have the first selection of clothing."

Jett nodded. "Please bring it in," she said sweetly.

The woman rolled in a two racks of garments. She moved to remove the first article when Thad stopped her. "That's all right. I can assist, J—the goddess. Find her a good selection of shoes and undergarments, but don't return until summoned.

I'll call you when we need further assistance."

Anya looked to Jett for her permission, obviously knowing who the deity in the room was—good woman. Though Jett would have very much liked to send Thad soaring from the dressing area, she knew he wouldn't go. He'd strong arm her into making Anya leave too, with his 'I'm your god' declaration. She didn't need a scene. Not here. Not now.

Reluctantly, she nodded for the woman to leave.

"Good choice. I'd hate to have to summon Airyon to bring on his wrath."

She ignored his asinine statement and railed at him. "You think I'm a whore!"

"Be quiet. You want the whole store to hear? I'm warning you, you won't be happy if the handmaiden returns. She may find you in a compromising position."

"You're threatening me?"

"Gods, Jett! Shut the hell up!"

"You called me a *whore*!"

He sighed. "We all know that you're not." He grabbed her pulling her flush to his rock hard body. "You just play one to get what you want."

"I want you to get out of this room."

"What are you willing to do to make me?"

She thought of all the wonderful things she would do if she could use her powers. Unfortunately, there was little she could do without them.

Little without his cooperation.

She licked her bottom lip, knowing she'd repay him for this. "What do you want?"

He leaned forward until his lips brushed her ear. His hand slid over her ass and pressed her hard to his bulging arousal. "I want for you to take off your clothes," he whispered.

Visions of all the provocative things he could request sped through her mind. Anticipation made her belly quiver as she felt herself become moist.

"And," he continued. "Try on these fine selections so that I can take you home and do all the damned things I've wanted to do since I saw you in the shower earlier."

Letting her go, he went to the clothes and quickly sorted them. Jett stared at him in shock while he pushed one rack to the wall, muttering, "No damned way."

He'd rather have her try on garments than do all the things haunting her thoughts. What was wrong with here? They were alone. Didn't he want her the way she wanted him? The doubts from earlier resurfaced to taunt her. Duty. He was doing his duty.

The hungry way his eyes devoured her when he pulled the remaining clothes towards her, didn't look like duty. It looked like hot sex.

She turned her back on him. "Lower this."

"It's called a zipper," he told her as he slowly lowered it. His mouth trailed the revealed skin, a red hot path of desire.

Stepping away from him, she turned to face him and let one strap fall down her shoulder, then the other. She pulled her arms free and let the dress fall to her feet.

His breath caught when she stood naked before him. And she knew. His desire, whether he acknowledged it or not, ran as deep and as hot as hers. They might only have six days, but it would be filled with a multitude of carnal moments, even if for some reason he was pushing her away now.

To Torment with that.

She stepped from the pool of the dress and moved towards him. She shoved him none too gently onto the wide bench.

Chapter Five

"Jett," Thad warned.

She worked at the closure of his pants. "Sit back and relax," she said and sent him a brilliant smile. "After all, if you are my god, you should let me worship you."

His erection sprang forth into her waiting hands, and she stroked him to the base, squeezing him. "Sweet heaven," he gasped.

Continuing to work her fingers along his great length, she leaned forward and took the wide tip into her mouth. Her tongue swirled over the droplet there, loving the taste of it and hoping for more.

He groaned when she released him. She dragged her tongue up the burning rod, pressing the throbbing vein that ran along it. She flicked at the edge of the head, nipping before stretching her lips over it again. He felt so smooth over the granite that surely formed beneath the velvet skin.

His chest rose and fell as he took ragged breaths, perspiration sprouting on his bronzed skin. She wished she'd taken off his shirt so she could see it coating his wide chest.

Gently, she sucked, increasing suction until he

writhed beneath her and begged in ragged, broken words for her to take more. She would have smiled if it wouldn't have eased his torment. Deftly, she flicked at the crease where another droplet formed and hummed as she lapped it away.

Without warning, she sank lower, taking more. Thad's fingers drove into her hair as he guided her. She clasped his thighs, feeling brazen—wanton—as she knelt before him naked and spread. She knew if anyone entered, they'd see her bared feminine flesh. They'd see how she ached for him, how great her arousal. The area seemed to vibrate with her movements as she stretched over him and worked her mouth up and down his straining shaft.

She wanted to please him. She wanted him to find release in her mouth like she had in his. Determined, she took him until he hit the back of her throat. Her eyes watered but she didn't let it deter her.

Tilting her head, she found she could take more of him. With effort, she remained relaxed and let him slide forward slightly.

"My goddess!" he cried. "My goddess. Yes, baby, like that!"

Her cleft wept with the achievement. She nearly cried out when Thad pulled back suddenly. He stroked her cheek. "Not like that."

"But I want to taste you."

"I have a better idea."

As he stood, he kept her from rising, holding her to her knees. He pushed her to lean over the bench, a far sight more gently than she had pushed him.

She clenched the cushion. Now Thad was behind her, seeing her need-spread flesh. She didn't care. Not with him. Only with him.

He slid his hands over her ass, parting her with

his thumbs. They slid through the thick cream that collected between her thighs. Suddenly, his tongue flicked over her lapping at the juices. She buried her face in the seat to keep from screaming. Pleasure sparked along her veins, arrowing home to her already swollen folds and the stressed nerve endings. Her muscles tightened as she was hurled towards climax, in a dizzying spiral.

He ate, licking and softly biting while she shuddered.

"I like how you feed me, my goddess."

She clawed at the bench, pushing against his mouth. She felt him rise over her. His body draped hers, big and dominating, overshadowing her as his cock probed her folds. It slid up and down the over-slick area. "You can't scream," he told her. "Anya would be in here in a minute."

She nodded mutely. Her ears already buzzed with the need to shout. As he tormented her, it built in her chest.

"Try not to break anything," he said.

"I need you inside me," she pleaded hoarsely, barely able to get out the words.

"You want me to fuck you?" he asked.

It felt so indecent, to have him there at the entrance of her channel, while he whispered such things into her ear. It turned her to molten liquid. As it trickled to her thigh, she thought she might melt there below him.

"Yes. Yes, Thad. Please."

Despite her pleas, he didn't enter her. He skated his hands down her bare back. He scooped them around to worry her breasts. Ignoring her curse, he moulded the soft flesh, drawing them to points. He pulled and pinched her pearled nipples. Gods, she wanted him to flip her over and bite them. She almost told him as much when he moved to knead his fingers over her back again.

His wide hands splayed on her hips. He pulled her towards him. "Do you know what it does to me to see you like this for me?"

"Obviously not enough. You are still outside me."

He chuckled. His cock, thrummed on her clit, driving her nearly wild. Reaching between them, he slipped a finger into her slippery honey. She groaned and worked against it.

"Oh no, baby. Not like that," he whispered, his voice nearly as choked as hers.

Slowly, he worked the slick finger into that part of her that had never been entered. Her eyes went wide, her head coming up so she could stare over her shoulder at him. Her jaw dropped at the unfamiliar sensation. She panted, her mouth forming an 'oh'.

In and out, he moved the finger, while his cock pushed inside her pussy. The width seemed to rend apart the pawing walls. She immediately clenched tighter. He'd waited too long. She needed him too much.

She bit her lip to keep from screaming at the overwhelming sensations. Her nipples scraped along the brocade of the bench, urging the crazed feeling inside to go even more wild.

His lips pressed to the back oh her neck, sending a shudder down her spine. "Just stay still," he told her when she tried to move against him. "Just feel."

"I cannot," she cried. She clawed at the wall and tried to anchor herself. To separate from the overwhelming bolts of sensation shooting between her nipples and inner flesh. Thad played her like a fine instrument, dragging up the keening sound that wailed from her throat as she tried to contain her scream.

His penis and his finger thrust in and out in alternating rhythm so that one or the other filled her.

"Goddess, you feel so good. Perfect. So hot," he rasped. "I could take you forever!"

Her climax came over her fast, the ripping sensation that pulled her soul free of its flesh prison. Suddenly, she was twisting free, a loose sail in the wind convulsing wildly as the tremors tore over her body.

The clothing racks shuddered as her reaction swept over her, wild pulsing raked down her limbs, over her skin.

"Careful, Jett," Thad groaned as one of the decorative lamps fell over. "Baby, breathe. Go with it. Don't fight it. Ah, gods! You're so tight! So tight!"

Hot streams released within her, scalding her womb, branding her his. Forever. Not just today or this week. Forever. She dropped her head to the cushion as her perspiration ran between her shoulders. She'd be his forever. She'd be his long after he was gone.

They lay there panting for several minutes until sounds from the shop drew them back to reason. He climbed to his feet, albeit slowly, and she wondered where the hell he got his stamina. He pulled her up. "There's a bathroom over here. You can freshen up before we look at the clothes."

"I cannot try on anything while I am sweaty and sticky like this."

He dropped a kiss on her frowning lips. "That's okay. I picked the ones we'll take. I know Anya didn't bring anything that doesn't fit you."

"Why?"

"She wouldn't want to insult you. You're her

goddess." He stroked her ass, giving it a little pinch. "Now go check out the bathroom."

"You are so pushy."

"Just discovering that?"

"How do you know about the bathroom…in a woman's boutique?" Her eyes narrowed. "Have you lain with my handmaiden?" She didn't wait for his answer, the answer in his face. "And those other women, too! You did!"

"It wasn't that good…" he ventured.

She scowled at him. Without a word, she scooped up her dress from the floor and stormed into the bathroom, with which he was far too familiar, obviously. Fuming, she cleaned up as well as she could without actually bathing and slipped back into the white dress.

She didn't say a word to Thad when she exited. Anya had re-entered the room. Several boxes were stacked on the bench passion had so recently occupied. Thad instructed her to box the dresses on the 'approved' rack. As the woman smiled and nodded, Jett was again struck with the sudden need to smite her. Instead, she struck a serene pose, her hands folded in front of her, her head at a slight tilt, eyes a bit vacant.

She added item five hundred and twelve to Thad's list of things that pissed off Reddjedet Goddess of the Zodiac Quadrant—all of which he would repay.

"Has Thad compensated you?" she asked the handmaiden.

"Oh no, goddess. I can not charge you for these."

Jett was not beyond understanding livelihood. "You must. I command you to give him an accurate bill and include a sizable tip for your expert assistance. I will know if you skimp on it."

"Yes, my goddess. I'll prepare it immediately while I have the other clothing packaged."

"Very good." She struggled to keep the benevolent smile on her face. It begged to drop to her feet. She wanted to follow the woman and ask her what she'd thought of Thad's cock. How she'd found his lovemaking skills. If she missed him. If he still visited.

She turned on him as the woman left. She didn't say a word, only glaring.

He sighed. "It's been over between Anya and me for over a century. We're merely friends."

She snorted, her arms looping over her chest.

"Fine," he grated. "I come here and screw her every day. I barely get enough of her." He stalked into the bathroom. "I'm not going to beg you to believe me. If you choose to, you can sense if I'm lying to you or not."

She turned away, still angry. A moment later, Thad returned and came up behind her, his white blond hair falling over her arm as he kissed shoulder. "She was the closest I could get to you."

"She looks nothing like me."

"If I closed my eyes, the vibrations were similar." His exhale skimmed along her skin. "Not similar enough. I couldn't quite convince myself that she was you."

She reached up and pressed his head to the side of her face, so he wouldn't see the tears that pooled on her bottom lids and blurred her vision.

What would they do? This was an impossible situation. She should leave him to find a life without her. She'd survive Airyon. Since he didn't know where to search for her and couldn't trace her vibration, she could hide nearly anywhere from him. The chances of him finding her were slim. She had only to hide for a few more days.

She should leave Thad now. She could wipe his brain so he never remembered her.

She swiped at her tears before more came. It ached to release him and turn away. She hardened herself. This was nothing compared to what she'd experience later. "Make sure to pay Anya."

She slipped from the room, and for the first time, Thad didn't follow her.

She waited outside the shop for him to complete the transaction and follow. He came out empty handed. The packages were being delivered. She didn't tell him that she wouldn't need them. She'd be gone before they arrived.

They rode in silence back to the penthouse. Jett took in the sights around them and barely noticed that this driver was worse than the previous. Using the same sense that Airyon used to track her and that Thad used to sense magic, she scanned the areas they passed. Wherever she hid, she should choose a place filled with energy. When she left Thad, she'd have two searching for her. One she dreaded, one she dreaded leaving.

Her lips pressed together as her tears burned again.

"What is it?" Thad asked. His fingers traced down her back.

She turned sitting properly in her seat so that he couldn't repeat the tender caress. "Nothing."

"Hmmm. . . I've known you for what, two hundred years?" he asked.

"About."

"Don't you think I'd know if you were lying? Particularly after what we've shared? What's eating at you? Are you still pissed about Anya?"

She shook her head. "No. Believe it or not, I understand about that. It is not like you were committed to me as more than a pledge anyway."

"Oh gods!" he groaned. He pulled her into his arms and cradled her head against his chest. His heart thumped its comforting rhythm beneath her ear. "I couldn't even touch you. It didn't matter how much I wanted you."

"I know that. I comprehend that."

"But you're still hurt."

She shrugged. "I will get over it." *In about two thousand years.* "You have done nothing wrong in this."

"Jett, look at me. There's nothing to get over. I wanted you. I've always wanted you. The one who should be mad is Anya. I used her."

She nodded, still pained. She struggled to summon a smile. Not too faint, not too bright. Something to make him believe everything was all right. Something to hide her pain, just as she always hid her pain. The world could never know her inner torment.

She didn't want to argue with Thad now. Not when she would leave him soon. Sorrow weighed her down as she contemplated the most hateful thing she'd ever have to do. Not hateful to him. It would be merciful. It would give him back his freedom.

No. It would be hateful to her. And she wasn't sure she'd bear it. She'd have to tamp down her emotions far deeper than usual—the earth wouldn't survive the storm brewing inside her.

* * * *

Jett's pain rolled off her in waves. Thad couldn't fathom it. They made love slowly after they'd returned, each savouring every curve of the other's body. He couldn't help the feeling that she was memorising him and preparing to say goodbye.

His arms tightened around her while she slept. He wouldn't willingly let her go. Did she feel Airyon closing in on them? His senses remained on alert while he wondered why she wouldn't reveal such a thing.

He brushed a mass of red-gold curls from her face, looping it in his fingers and letting the silken strands fall away. She slept deeply, not at all troubled or near waking as he suspected she'd be if the god of wrath were closing in on them.

The doorbell buzzed, and he rose, pulling on a pair of loose pants. Jett's clothes. He couldn't wait to see her in them. He'd have her model all of it—especially the panties and bras.

The messenger stacked the boxes in the foyer and left with a generous tip in hand. Thad whistled on his way back to the bedroom.

Today was a good day.

Bone-crushing pain took him by surprise inside the doorway. It drove him to his knees blinding him with twisting agony within his head. Confused, he struggled unsuccessfully to rise under the pulverising weight. A net of energy snapped around him, its lines lashing at him and searing into his skin.

Airyon! his senses screamed. *No! I won't let him take Jett.* The god couldn't touch her. He couldn't steal her from him.

"Jett!" Thad yelled, the sound barely making it past the net as it wrapped his throat. He wanted to warn her, tell her to run.

He clawed at the shimmering strands holding him.

Jett belonged to him. They belonged together. He had to get to her.

Desperately, he flailed trying to free himself

from the magical binding as his thoughts sapped from his brain. His memories, cherished recollections of Jett, pulled from his brain.

He'd kill the god.

No one was taking Jett from him. No one was stealing his memory. He fought back to his feet and nearly collapsed again. It wasn't a hulking god looming over him.

Jett.

Jett? Why would she do this to him?

Tears streamed down her face as she held out her hand, the magic encompassing him flowing from her palm.

"Stop!" he commanded, his words weak, barely audible. He fell back to his knees. His muscles failed him as his cheek pressed into rough carpet. Black shrouded his vision as the last of his fuzzy thoughts were sapped and the beautiful red-haired stranger disappeared from his sight.

Chapter Six

Jett stumbled down the street, her heart rending.

She had to find a place to hide. The deed she'd done had left a huge energy signature. If Airyon couldn't trace that, he was a bigger fool than she'd thought. She'd swept Thad's home free of the magical residue. Her power wouldn't be pinpointed there, but it would direct Wrath to the city.

Since she was already in for so much, and she figured she'd already sent a beacon to the God of Wrath, she'd used her power to materialise clothing on her body. She'd copied the clothing worn by many of the women on the street, and now, she wore heavy pants of a stiff, light blue material and a black stretchy shirt. She'd also materialised money, a purse and a small pack containing similar clothing.

She couldn't bring herself to use any of the clothes purchased by Thad. He'd be confused by the boxes when he woke with no memory, but she was confident he'd figure out what to do with them.

Once she was out of the sight of Thad's building, she waved at a cab the way she'd seen Thad do.

To her surprise one of the yellow boxes screeched over to her. Tentatively, she opened the door and got inside.

In the front, a swarthy skinned man looked expectantly at her. "Are you going to close the door?" he asked.

Oh! Yes, yes. She needed to do that. A spike of frustration speared her middle. She'd depended on Thad for so much since they'd come here. How would she function?

Just fine, she told herself. *You are a goddess. You can withstand this.* She reached for the door handle, swinging it shut. She wasn't sure she could bear what she'd done to Thad.

"I apologise," she said, the words meant for more than the driver.

He shrugged. "Where to?"

She gave him the names of the street signs she'd seen earlier, a place she'd sensed strong magic power earlier. Hopefully, he'd know where she meant. There was no way she could give him directions.

"Okay. Chinatown." He pulled into traffic and like the driver earlier, narrowly missed another vehicle which blared long and loud at them.

"Yeah, yeah, yeah," he muttered. "So what's in Chinatown?" he asked her. "I hear the food is really good, but the place is a little too mystical for me. I'd rather stick with Allah, you know."

"I understand," she answered, not telling him her plans as she stared distractedly out the window. Hopefully, she could lose herself in the area for five or six days.

The buildings flew past so quickly, they blurred together, one shop looking much like the next. She supposed that wouldn't be the case if she was walking. There were so many, too. Perhaps she could ask Thad to show some of his city to her—

She took a shuddering breath. But she couldn't ask him. He wouldn't know her from the next woman. She'd robbed him of huge chunks of his past. If he knew, he'd never forgive her, probably be unable to understand why she'd done it too. She wanted only to protect him.

No one ever appreciated that. Throughout time, whenever she'd taken measures to protect her people, they'd complained long and loud. They never liked restrictions. They liked the way things *were*... The only time they were truly thankful was when she swooped in to save their skin literally, and then they promptly forgot she existed—again.

A surge of magic hit her as they approached her destination, snapping Jett to attention. "Stop here," she told the driver.

"You sure? Chinatown's not for a few more blocks. This ain't such a great part of town, lady."

"I'll be fine." Quickly, she completed their transaction, handing him the unfamiliar green money and hoping she'd done it correctly. She must have, since he didn't protest when she stepped from the cab.

He drove away while she stared at the humming sign on the building before her. *Sleep and Things Home-tel.* Excellent. The magic was strong here. It was a perfect place to stay.

The perfection started to recede immediately. The door to Sleep and Things stuck when she tried to open it, its handle coated with something black and bumpy that partially obliterated the dull metal beneath it. Okay, she'd be careful to touch as little as possible. Once she'd muscled herself inside the place, a faint musty smell combined with a much stronger smell of pine and smoke assaulted her.

She'd breathe as little as possible, too.

If she wasn't desperate, and if she didn't believe this was the last place on earth anyone would search for her, she would have pivoted and run. But she didn't. She tried not to gag or wrinkle her nose as she approached the portly man at the desk. With the thick, brown stick hanging from his mouth and his slicked-back brown hair, he fit right in with the place. She wondered if perhaps it wasn't his duty to clean the front doors. Perhaps he did that on the same day he bathed.

He leered at her when she approached, lingering long enough on her breasts that she crossed her arms over them.

"Ya lost?" he garbled around the stick in his mouth. A clump of ashes fell from the end onto a dog-eared book on the desk. Unconcerned, he thumped out the smouldering result with a beverage can.

She shook her head. What was she doing?

"What can I do for ya, sweetheart?"

Look away from me when you speak. . .

"I need a room."

"By the hour or by the day?"

"A few days."

"Whatever floats your boat." He reached for a key hanging from a rack behind him and handed it to her. "Room 412."

He pushed the previously smouldering book at her and lifted a grimy pen from a wire holder. Recklessly, he scratched an X on the page. "Sign here."

She stared at it. "Sign?"

The man gave a long suffering sigh that nearly knocked her over with the odour. "Write your name," he clarified. "Ya okay, honey? Ya understand American, doncha?"

She nodded jerkily. Gods! She'd never written her name before. Would he refuse to let her stay here if he knew she could not inscribe his language? Should she worry about that? It might be a blessing.

She had to stay. It was a good hiding place. This place was rife with energy, no one would notice if she used a little of it to mark her name. Hurriedly, she magically scrawled "Jett."

"Your last name, too," the man instructed.

"Last name?"

Last name! She didn't have a last name.

"Sweetheart, I don't got all day."

What else did he plan to do? Her lips pressed together. It was foolhardy, but she knew what she'd use. It might be a false sense of security, but it comforted her.

"So..." He looked at the page when she'd finished. "So, Miz Pennington, be sure to keep your *visitors* quiet and be sure to check down here and pay each day."

She nodded, tempted to tell him she wouldn't have any visitors, but as he eyed her again, she quickly determined that might not be a wise move.

Room 412 was small. Miniscule in comparison to Thad's home and not nearly so clean. Actually, clean didn't come close, but it was cleaner than the lobby.

She looked around for a place to drop her pack and purse. How could she sleep in this filth? She'd ask for cleaning implements at the desk, but she feared they didn't have any. She wouldn't know how to use them, anyway. Dealing with the smoking man ranked low on her list of things to repeat, too. With her luck, he'd offer to help her.

She glared at the squalor surrounding her.

It would really be a small feat to use her power to make this room inhabitable. Far under anyone's scope.

She looked around. "Gods, please don't let the lumps in the bed be creatures," she whispered. A thick layer of dust covered the shabby dresser and the table set in the corner. She pretended she didn't see the bug on the table top. And then she couldn't. Almost reflexively, she shot a small bolt of energy that spattered charred insect remains on the wall.

Well, that was that. Now she'd used her abilities. She might as well go on and get this over with. Closing her eyes, she pointed at the bed. It was time to smite the mattress.

* * * *

Thad woke on the floor. Carpet fibres tickled the inside of his mouth and made uncomfortable impressions on his naked chest. With a groan, he pushed upright. What the hell had happened?

He dropped his face into his hands. His head hurt more than his worst hangover. Staggering a little, he stood and the room spun away from him. The carpet waved like huge drifts of newly fallen snow. Or rolling wheat. Rolling snow.

His stomach protested, wooziness making it roll instead.

Not good.

He stumbled for the bed, which he assumed was the large object looming before him, and landed face down on the sweet smelling pillow. What on earth had happened to him? A party? Why didn't he remember going? Or anything that had happened yesterday. Or for the last—

Two hundred years?

No, that couldn't be right. He rubbed his temples, trying to remember his past. He rolled onto his back, staring at his reflection in the cracked mirror overhead. *I'm a lot older than I look*, was his first thought. *But I look good for two hundred and thirty.*

Great. Not only couldn't he remember his past but he was crazy.

"Think Thad. Think!" he commanded. His memory was there. He felt it lurking on the edges of recognition, just beyond grasp.

"Where am I? New York. Okay. Name? Thad Pennington. This is so stupid." He cursed. He had things to do yet he indulged in this asinine dialogue. With himself.

How old are you?

"Two hundred and thirty."

Well, damn it.

His fingers tapped on his thigh, drumming out his agitation. This was all Jett's fault. If not for her, he'd—

Jett!

His missing recollections, mish-mashed and tangled, slammed through him stronger than a category five hurricane. He'd know, he'd fought a few. And she'd tried to erase that too...just like...

Jett standing over him.

That net.

His memories.

What the hell had she done? Left him. He guessed that in one. How could she do this to them? Anger buffeted him with a stronger intensity than his realisation had. It was amplified by stark fear. She was out there alone in a world she didn't come close to understanding.

With a maniac searching for her.

He sat up, thankful his vision was clearing.

Everything slid into focus. He had to find her before Airyon did.

She wouldn't be happy about it, but at this point, he didn't give a damn. And she'd be very sorry for this. She'd thought him tyrannical before? *Just wait, baby.*

Her plan had failed. Something had gone wrong. He knew as well as he knew his name, he wasn't supposed to remember *her* zipping away his thoughts. He wasn't supposed to remember her.

But the memories remained. Nice and intact.

Including the tears that had streamed down her face.

He shook his head, pulling on the first shirt that levitated to his hand. "Baby, why'd you think you had to go and do this?"

* * * *

Scouring New York City for a missing goddess was a lot like looking for Santa on Easter day. Jett was no where to be found. And the more Thad searched, the harder anger boiled in his middle.

He clenched the arm of his wing chair, trying to calm his thoughts. His other hand tangled in the terrycloth robe she'd worn after they'd made love. He figured to the outside person, he'd make a pathetic sight—the deserted lover clinging to a vestige of lost passion. Too much was at stake to sink into that morass.

Using the latent vibrations still lingering in the cloth, he reached out mental feelers for an identical signal. Methodically, he scanned for her energy. He'd looked for two days, searching for her in much the same way he was sure Airyon did. But only Thad knew the energy to hunt.

It had been two days of pure Torment.

The clock in the hall chimed midnight just as he sensed the weak resonance. Tentatively, he probed it, the sensation growing stronger the closer he got to her.

"Yes!" he exclaimed. He jumped to his feet. He'd found her! There she was—he probed a bit more—alone. In—*oh my gods!*—how had she ended up in such a seedy part of town? What was she thinking? Without delaying or considering the consequences of appearing out of the blue on a New York street, he transported to where he'd sensed Jett's presence. In a moment, he stood outside the rundown excuse for a hotel. It looked more like a halfway house for cockroaches than like a place for humans—or goddesses—to sleep. Gods, he'd have to give her a flea dip before he took her home.

The man at the desk had no problem letting Thad look at the guest registry—after the chokehold and the threat of shoving his cigar so far up his ass that surgical retrieval would be impossible.

And there she was. Plain as day. His heart swelled. She bore the name he'd given her—Jett. She bore his surname.

As it should be. He tensed. It didn't matter what he wanted. It would never happen, especially now that she'd shown him how expendable she considered him to be.

She'd try to erase him. Or at least erase herself from everything that had mattered to him for the last two hundred years. Hadn't she thought he might wonder how he'd lived that long? Obviously her thoughts weren't in it. But that was little comfort.

Without bothering to be discrete, he transported himself to her room. The sight there sickened him. The room was filth from one end to the other, the bed, where Jett curled into a ball, the only clean thing he could see.

She'd lived like this. His goddess had lived like this? Gathering the belongings she'd piled neatly on a small clean patch of dresser, he went to the bed. Carefully, he sat on the edge and reached for her shoulder with the intention of transporting the two of them back to his bed.

Wouldn't she be surprised when she woke beside him. In his clean apartment. Trapped in his arms.

Before he could touch her, she tossed away from him, caught in her troubled dreams.

"Airyon, no!" she muttered. "Don't hurt him. No! Stop!"

Thad dropped her things at the end of the bed and lay beside her.

"Jett. Baby, it's okay. Wake up. Jett, *wake up*. Look at me."

"No! Stop! Stop! Don't hurt him. Whatever you want!" Her arms flailed and narrowly missed his eye. A sizzle sound above them told that a black eye wasn't all he'd dodged.

Quickly, he doused the smouldering ceiling. He shook her. "Jett, wake up! Wake up now. I'm fine."

Her eyes popped open, wild and afraid. He wasn't sure she wasn't still dreaming. "Thad?" she whispered.

"It's me, baby."

"You're a dream. You must be." She reached out and stroked her fingers over the stubble on his jaw.

"I'm real," he promised, falling over her. He kissed her until she moaned and writhed beneath him while he ran his hands over her to assure himself that she was well and whole and real. He lifted his head, and he knew she could see his eyes glittering. "And I'm so angry with you, you'll be lucky if you sit for a week after we get back to the penthouse."

"You're threatening me?" She sat up, accidentally thumping into his forehead which still ached from her magical surgery.

He rubbed his temple, hoping he didn't get a lump. All he needed was a deformity to go along with everything else. "Yes, I'm threatening you," he growled. "More specifically, I'm threatening that cute little ass of yours with the first spanking of your life."

"You wouldn't dare! I'm a goddess."

His eyes narrowed. "I wouldn't dare? Just try me."

Excitement shimmered in her eyes though she looked a tad frightened. He glanced away. He didn't want to see her fear or even anything faintly resembling arousal. His body would respond in kind. Then where would they be. Screwing in this filthy room.

He didn't want to want her. He was pissed.

Saying he didn't want her was like a dehydrated man standing next to water and claiming not to want a drink. It didn't matter what either said. They would both get what they needed, whether they wanted to admit they needed it or not.

"This place is a dump," he said finally. His hand clasped hers to be sure she didn't move while he looked around.

"So I noticed." She sounded weary.

Thad turned on the light. An immediate power flux set his nerves on end. *It's just the dicey electricity here*, he told himself and looked back at Jett. Dark circles marred the creamy skin beneath her eyes. She looked so fragile. He wondered if she'd slept in the time they'd been parted. Had she just drifted off when he'd arrived?

The power did another momentary downshift.

"Why did you choose this place?"

"Can't you feel it?"

He sat up, reaching for her purse and backpack. He strapped them over his shoulder and reached for her. "Feel what?"

"The vibrations. This area is teeming with magic."

Thad snorted. "It's teeming with cockroaches. The vibrations you feel are billions of tiny bug feet."

She gave him a dirty look. Her eyes went wide as the power dimmed again.

"He's coming," she announced, her voice surreally calm. It reminded him of a horror movie where every one was in a state of panic while one person was in a serene state of acceptance. He wanted to shake it out of her. They weren't accepting a damned thing. Except possibly Airyon's surrender.

"I'm taking you home." His arms tightened.

"No!" she cried, tearing away. "You can't use your power. He'll be looking for a sudden transport. He's pinpointed his search here." The lamp flickered as if to underline her statement.

Cold determination poured down Thad's spine. Judiciously, he didn't mention all the energy he'd used to find her. They were out of here before Big and Wrathful showed up.

"Fine." He pulled her to the door, glad she'd chosen to sleep in her clothes. "We'll have to get there the old-fashioned way."

Thad didn't like the thought of being in this neighbourhood after midnight, especially without the use of his powers—whether she agreed or not, he'd blast whomever necessary to protect her.

He had few choices.

The way the power was bumping and grinding, Airyon would appear any second.

Jett didn't argue with him as they went. Her relief radiated to him in silent waves. She'd been afraid to be alone. He wanted to reassure her, tell her he was there now. He'd protect her, but she'd left him. She'd left his protection to be on her own. He wasn't sure anything he said would reassure her.

To his relief, the street was vacant, without so much as a stray dog making shadows in the few street lights that weren't broken. Of course, there wasn't a taxi in sight either. He wasn't surprised. Lingering here posed a threat to drivers. A cabby waiting for a fare could be robbed or killed.

Unfortunately, that left one option if they didn't want to wait around for Airyon.

The subway.

Personally, Thad didn't mind the subway. He used it frequently and wished every major city had one. But, it also wasn't the brightest place to be late at night.

As he guided Jett down the steps into the station, he watched her from the corner of his eye. She'd fallen inside herself after her announcement of Airyon's arrival. It pissed him off that she'd seemingly given up. On them, even on herself. She was going to let that bastard win.

The white tile of the station tried to gleam under the blue-white glow of the fluorescent lights but failed. They ended up a dingy grey—much like everything else in this part of town. Much like his life felt at the moment.

It still scared the shit out of him that Jett had

been *here*. *Alone*. If anything had happened to her...

He swiped the thought from his mind, focusing instead on her as the train sped to their platform. Hot, stale air whooshed over them as air-brakes engaged.

Jett hadn't said a word since she'd bellowed for him not to use magic. He hated it. The last time she'd gotten all quiet, she'd hit him over the head with a two-ton, magic sledge hammer. So to speak.

"What's going through that mind of yours," he asked. He pushed her into one of the seats by the wall of the train while he took his own on the aisle.

She shrugged. "I'm confused."

Confused? "About?"

"Why are you here?"

"Where else would I be? I'm pledged to protect you."

Pain flickered in her eyes. He hated to see it, but it bolstered his confidence in the feelings running strong between the two of them.

She looked away. "I released you from that."

"You can't release me from what's between us. Don't you realise, I'm not letting you go."

"It's not something you can stop or something you have a choice in."

"Like hell it isn't!" His exclamation echoed in the empty car, despite the scream of the train over the tracks.

"I've used the memory removal before. It's never failed."

"It did this time. I swear you will regret ever doing something like that to me again. It hurt like hell."

She smiled wanly. It was the closest she'd come

to actual emotion since he'd pulled her from the hotel room. "You are threatening me? Again?"

"Damn straight."

"I'm sorry." She stroked the side of his face, her thumb running down over his nose, catching on his lip. He nipped at the pad. He sucked the tip of her thumb into his mouth, loving the choked gasp she took.

Her breath ragged, she leaned her forehead against his. "I'm sorry. It's never hurt someone before."

"Maybe my memories just refused to go."

"Maybe I'm losing my powers. Maybe Airyon's done something to them, or being on earth this long is sapping them..."

She threaded her fingers into his hair, closing her eyes. Her face pressed to his, her nose nudging into his. Tenderness, wove through him. He gently sucked her bottom lip between his. She needed the reassurance of him. He could feel it.

"I'll take care of you," he whispered against her mouth.

"How? If I lose my power, you'll lose yours. All my pledged overlords will."

He remained silent rather than tell her he wouldn't need powers to protect her. A god against a mortal? He'd be a fool to believe he'd win. But by the gods, he would try.

They switched trains a few stops later and within a half hour were outside his building.

"Something's not right." Jett pulled him back as they were about to enter. Her fingernails bit into his biceps and the air around her shimmered.

"What is it?" He froze, ready to push her behind him if necessary. The danger must be high if she'd allowed her vibration to rise above the human level.

His brow furrowed. The last time she'd touched him at this level, he'd nearly passed out from the pleasure. Her touch was still pleasure, put passing out didn't figure into how he felt when her divinity touched him now. He had plans for the next time they were alone and Wrath wasn't banging on the bedroom door.

He felt a loss as Jett dropped her hand and her energy left him. She looked towards him, her eyes distant as if she were seeing another place.

"Airyon's been here," she said in a flat, disconnected tone. She straightened, tension drawing her taut. The light in her eyes shifted. "He's gone now."

"Are you sure?" The guy was getting to be a damned nuisance. He'd been instrumental in pushing Jett into Thad's arms, and the way Thad saw things, it was the man's only good point.

Jett's expression hardened, ready for any battle they encountered. He felt her mental energy as she canned the area.

"He's gone," she asserted.

But not for long. Thad sensed her unspoken words as clearly as if she'd spoken them aloud. They needed to hurry. Get in, get out. Hide. It seemed cowardly to him to run, but he'd rather be labelled a coward than see Jett hurt. Her only protection was to stay out of harm's way. Remaining here wouldn't be brave, it would be stupid.

He wasn't stupid.

Cautiously, he led her into the lobby. He could tell Jett wanted to go in ahead of him, to fight if necessary. But damn it, if anyone was taking a bolt of lightning, it would be him. She was his goddess. His woman. He would protect her with his life.

Intent on getting them to the elevator, upstairs, then out, he nearly missed seeing the fallen man beside the desk. Horror tore through Thad. The security guard lay partially obscured by the counter, his stunned eyes staring sightless into the ceiling. A dark scorch mark blackened the centre of his forehead.

Thad's horror blazed to rage in a red-hot moment. That bastard, Airyon, had killed an innocent man as if his life didn't matter, as if he wasn't important to anyone. The guard had a wife and two small children at home.

He stepped towards the corpse and Jett caught his arm.

"Thad."

"What?" he bellowed.

Her eyes darkened. Didn't this faze her? Didn't this death mean anything to her? Were mortals as expendable to her as they were to Airyon?

"Leave him," Jett commanded, her voice took on a different tenor. It was the tone she used when she sat on her throne of power and ordered him to carry out her dictates. The Goddess of the Zodiac stood beside him. Not the woman who needed him. Not the woman he desired more than air.

Her jaw softened slightly as she glanced at the fallen man. And Thad knew. The goddess and the woman who needed him and he desired were one in the same. She'd pulled her emotionless façade into place, her failsafe, her power.

She wasn't untouched by the events. Duty bound her. It compelled her to do what was necessary to protect mankind. Whether it was her first instinct or not.

Her small fist clenched as she stalked to the elevator bank. "You must retrieve whatever is necessary from your home and leave. Quickly. You cannot stay here."

Thad followed her. He didn't want Jett more

than an arms reach from him. If Airyon arrived, he'd take her from here so quickly neither of the deities would realise what had happened.

He could only imagine the devastation the guard's wife would feel when she learned of her husband's death. He'd be ground into the earth if anything happened to his goddess.

"You're coming with me," he growled.

She ignored him. "We'll get your things. I'll watch for Airyon. I can sense his approach and can hold him off while you escape."

He grabbed her arms. She was the most infuriating woman. He wanted to shake her. "Jett, listen to me. I am not leaving without you. Wherever I go, you will be."

"No. You must go alone. It's safer."

"Not in this lifetime, baby."

Her eyebrow rose. "I order you!"

"I'm your god. I command you," he replied.

Her lips pursed and her eyes narrowed, making it patently clear she was unimpressed and unamused by his joke. Okay, so perhaps his timing was off, but he wasn't backing down on the issue. She'd remain by his side, or he'd stay and face the same fate as the security guard.

"Get it through your head," he growled. "You come with me or I stay."

"You dare to defy me?" Fury flashed in her eyes.

She visibly struggled to keep her vibrations at an even level, and Thad knew he was due for a smiting. She was planning it even as she fumed. He had a feeling she wouldn't kill him. She'd set her blows to Hurt-A-Lot or Maim.

When they survived this, he'd take whatever she dished out. He raised an eyebrow to further enflame her ire. The angrier she became the more easily he could bend her to his will.

"Aren't you used to it by now," he said. "You don't bother to listen to my commands. Defiance and threats are the only means to gain your attention."

Her scowl could flatten a small country. Angrily, she stabbed the elevator call button. Her foot tapped as she waited without continuing their argument. A bad sign.

Her silence usually indicated a plan forming inside that complicated mind. Another argument lay on the horizon, waiting to entangle him into impotent compliance.

She had another thing coming if she thought she could make him leave without her. He hadn't waited this long to have her in his arms, only to lose her.

He dreaded what they'd find in the penthouse, and as it turned out, with good reason. His home was in shambles. Apparently, angry gods weren't neat gods.

Jett scowled at the overturned...everything. "I'll help you repair your home when this is over."

He shrugged. "Don't worry about it."

He pulled her tight to his chest. Relief overrode everything else. He didn't care about the destruction. Jett hadn't been here. He was almost glad she'd fled and they hadn't been here when Airyon and his cohorts arrived.

They wouldn't be here when the trio returned, either.

It took less than ten minutes for him to gather enough clothes for their trip, and most of that time was spent opening the boxes of Jett's clothes and dumping them into a suitcase.

She zipped his suitcase as he went to the closet to grab the dress he'd shoved in the back.

He groaned and slammed his palm into the wall. The dress. That had been his mistake. "Damn it!"

"What is it?"

The garment, of course, was missing. "Your dress. The one you wore here. It's gone."

Understanding dawned in her eyes. She pressed her fingers to the crease that formed in the centre of her forehead.

"Airyon took it. That's what drew him here—the remaining inkling of the virgin energy clung to the garment. I should have thought of that." Her fist pounded onto the dresser and the cracked mirror above it rattled in dire accompaniment to her ground out curses.

Thad moved the boxes to be completely sure the dress was gone. Only Airyon's residual rage remained now that he realised why he'd been unable to find Jett through her virgin energy. Who could blame him? Thad knew he'd have the same primal feelings if Jett had given herself to another.

But she hadn't. She was his.

And Airyon wanted her for another purpose.

Thad's jaw locked into a grim mask as he zipped the other suitcases. It would be doubly hard to protect her now. He didn't think His Wrathfulness had a lock on Jett's new vibration, but it wouldn't take much to discover it now that it was known to have deviated.

"Let's go," he said. Urgency built in his limbs. He needed to get out of here. Jett claimed to be able to sense Airyon's approach, but what if she was wrong? What if she was no better at sensing his energy than he'd been at finding hers.

She dug in her heels. "I have a plan."

"Oh, you do, do you?" Couldn't she let him be

in charge for fifteen freaking minutes? He had this under control.

He set down the suitcases in the hallway and pulled her to join him.

She tugged away her hand, crossing her arms over her chest. "Of course, I do. I'm not an imbecile. I'm a goddess."

The way she eyed him made him think that perhaps she thought *he* was the one short a few brain cells.

"We already have a plan," he growled.

She glared at him. "What is it?"

"Right now? That we're leaving. The rest is on a need-to-know basis."

"I need to know."

"No, you don't." He glanced around. "And neither do any of the ears that might be listening."

"I would know if Airyon or his minions were listening. Regardless, it does not matter where we're going." Wasn't that just like a goddess. She had all the answers. She was automatically right.

"Jett, I don't have time to argue with you."

She shook her head and sighed. "Look, hard-headed mortal, listen."

Hard-headed mortal? He'd introduce her to something hard as soon as they were safe. She'd pushed him too far. She needed to learn who was in charge and when she did, she'd pay his price.

"Airyon is as unfamiliar with modern technology as I am," she continued. "I will do what needs to be done and confuse him when he attempts to follow."

Thad tilted his head. Besides dwelling on her insult, he was having a difficult time following her in a way that had nothing to his intelligence level. It would help if she hadn't skipped from A to C in her logic. And if she stopped speaking in Jett-code.

"Do what needs to be done" stuck out in his mind. She was going to do something stupid and there wasn't a damned thing he could do to stop her. The human-goddess boundaries of their relationship chafed him.

He wouldn't be bound by them. She had to understand and accept that. He'd make her understand, even if he had to keep her in bed until she begged for mercy. It was the one place she hadn't yet tried to usurp his power. He knew that attempt was coming. She'd see then.

Chapter Seven

As soon as Thad and Jett entered the lobby, she strode directly to the guard. Her intention showed crystal clear. This was the stupidity he'd worried about upstairs. The brave, noble, *stupid* action.

"This is my holding," she declared, her voice ringing in the deserted entryway. "Airyon has no right to take the lives of those who live here."

Gods! She'd draw out Airyon in a heartbeat. They wouldn't even have the chance to get through the doors and disappear onto the New York streets.

"No. You can't use your powers," he protested.

She shook her head, wild locks of crimson-gold swinging around her face lit with a fire that seemed to snap along the strands. The same fire blazed in her stormy blue eyes.

Suddenly her plan became clear. She'd plotted to do this from the start and only intended to buy him enough time to escape. Only him. She wouldn't accompany him.

Thad scowled, planting is feet. Once she decided he'd safely escaped, Jett planned to reanimate the guard and face Airyon when he arrived. Alone.

How had she come to be so brave? Selfless?

He'd always thought bravery and selflessness

to be good traits. Now he cursed them.

I am a goddess, the laughing, often repeated words echoed in his head. This behaviour, the bravery, the selflessness, was her immutable makeup. If she died, then she'd die for what she believed was right. If she won the battle, she'd ensure her people were safe. The insight didn't comfort Thad in the least. He didn't want her to shoulder the fate of, well, everything.

Facing the enemy could be foolhardy. Sometimes it was better to run. He'd thought she'd known that. Hadn't she been running from Airyon? Hadn't she been hiding, the knowledge that avoiding the battle would keep her people safe? Apparently, she'd decided to work by another plan.

He'd be damned to Torment before he let her face Airyon alone.

She crouched over the guard, her hand hovering above his chest. "It was not this man's time. And...he is loved very much."

A bemused look crossed her face as she looked up at Thad, a mix of confusion and delight. She smiled as if seeing him for the first time. A quiet peace seemed to have slid over her. "Airyon will return when I do this."

"I figured he might."

"But he will not catch us, will he?" she murmured. "You will keep him busy chasing us."

"Chasing us will be *so* much better." *Us*. Yes, "us" would be better.

She smiled serenely at him. "You will evade him and protect us from immediate detection. Do not worry. Airyon will not win this battle."

It was about time she recognised his intention and position in her life. Her out-of-the-blue blind faith punched him in the solar plexus, packing more power than a championship kick boxer. It did little to calm Thad. Somehow, he didn't believe her new attitude would make *his* life any easier.

"Wait," he ground out. "What is this grand plan of yours?"

Jett was placating him. She had to be. Nothing had changed since she'd tried to leave. And she'd done that to protect *him*.

She smiled. "Need-to-know basis."

"Jett…"

"Do this with me," she said, drawing him from his irritation and throwing more confusion in his path.

"Do what?"

She jerked her head towards the dead guard. "Help me bring him back. Kneel on the other side of him and give me your hands."

Power awakened within Thad. It surged through his veins, manifesting in intense spirals of strength. What new gift had she bestowed on him? The energy shimmered around him, nearly as strong as the divine vibrations radiated from her.

He dropped to his knees. Confidence filled him as he took her hands. She nodded, and he knew she'd given him the knowledge to complete this task.

She squeezed his fingers. "As soon as we are finished, you will transport us to safety. Waste no time. After the guard is healed, there will be but moments before Airyon appears. I will mask and divert the trail as I did when we first fled."

Jett focused inward, her eyes shading as she meditated. Bands of gold energy circled their hands. They sparked with magical vigour, building in magnitude the longer they waited.

They were one unit, joined as fully by the

power as they were when he plunged deep inside her. Similar sensations churned along his limbs.

Her lips parted as she sucked in deep, rolling breaths. Her glazed stare seemed to burn into him. This was the goddess exercising her power. He knew he too should fall into the same sort of meditative state, but he didn't want to miss a moment of Jett like this. She seemed to recognise his reluctance and fed her knowledge into his mind. He had no question on what to do.

Slowly, he pushed their joined hands downward and swiped his palm over the char mark on the guard's forehead. It disappeared as if it were no more than dust.

Striations of power tugged from his centre to feed into the fallen man. The pull sucked along Thad's nerve endings heightening his awareness of the vortex of energy swirling around them. He realised suddenly, the energy wasn't swirling around them. It came from them.

His body bowed towards the guard. Without adjusting her focus, Jett gently disentangled her hand from Thad's. She splayed her fingers over his navel and pushed his body back into natural alignment, her touch a burning-cool brand straight to his groin.

Gods, he needed her in every way a man needed a woman.

Never breaking her concentration, she reconnected their palms and swept them over the guard.

"Reenter your temple," she whispered.

"Soul and body rejoin," Thad intoned. The words sprang to his lips, born of the divine knowledge she'd bestowed. He had no idea where else they would have originated. The ritual flowed as naturally from him as if he'd done it hundreds of times.

"Return," they said in unison.

Their joined hands pressed over the man's heart. Immediately, he jolted. Shaking breaths refilled his body as his ashen colour faded and life restored his flesh.

Thad straightened and pulled Jett to her feet. Instinctively, he knew they had to depart immediately.

A roar filled the air, counterpoint to their urgency.

The Wrath cometh.

Jett grabbed a suitcase. "Let us go."

He grabbed the other bag while she wrapped an arm around him, looping her fingers into his belt. Her head pressed to his chest as she hugged her other arm around him, the case banging the back of his legs.

"The guard?" he asked.

"I have protected him."

Satisfied the man would be safe, Thad pressed his face into Jett's honey-scented hair. The air roiled around them, buffeting their clothes and tearing at their bodies. From the corner of his eye, he saw the guard crawl beneath the counter.

"I suggest several jumps," she yelled above the noise. "Make sure they are to busy locations, but quick enough that no one sees us."

Thad's transport tunnel opened, pulling them inside and slamming closed before anyone followed. Energy whirled around them as they rocketed though it.

He took them first to Grand Central Station. The cavernous space was busy with people deep in their morning commutes.

In a breath, they zapped away and onto one of the trains on the other end of the subway line.

To a busy coffee shop.

To a ferry.

"Where are we?" Jett asked as he led her through a throng of people. He hadn't slowed his pace since the tunnel dumped them onto a moving walkway. And no one had noticed.

"JFK. The airport," he added when she looked at him in confusion. It struck him once again how places that were part of the fabric of his life were foreign to her.

"What is an airport?"

"People come here to get on vehicles which fly them to other places."

"We're going to go on one of these things?"

"No. We're renting a car." Much as he'd like to join the mile high club with her, driving seemed the safest route.

"It's like a taxi," she commented when they got into the rental, a small SUV. It was a larger vehicle than he would have liked, but if necessary, they could sleep in it.

Everything about the SUV fascinated Jett, and he had to push her back against the seat to help her on with her seatbelt. He supposed he could have merely shown her how to work the simple mechanism. But after coming so close to losing her, twice in the last few days, the contact, however brief, reassured him. It soothed his protective instincts to see to her safety.

A tingling surrounded him as he leaned over her and drew the belt across her tiny waist. His fingers intentionally brushed the skin exposed by her short blue sweater. Gods, he needed her soon.

The tingling sensation intensified, brushing over his skin like a soft-bristled brush. While blood rushed to his groin, the new stimulation was unrelated. He looked up to find Jett's hands hovering barely an inch above his head.

"What are you doing?" he asked.

"Changing your vibration."

The side of his mouth lifted. "I like my vibration the way it is, thanks."

Whatever she was doing, it pricked the restraint he held over his arousal, taunting it to action. His hand slid beneath her shirt to cup her breast. Jett made a soft content sound as she pressed into his palm. He flicked his thumb over the cloth enclosed nipple.

"It is only a temporary mask to hide you from Airyon." She slid a hand behind his neck, to pull his mouth down to hers. Anxiously, she rained kisses on his face while he worried the nub beneath his fingers. It pearled to a hard little bead, rolling beneath his fingers. He wanted to push up her sweater and bury his face in her cleavage. He wanted to take a bite from that succulent fruit, lick the bud in his hand until her body bloomed in the giant explosion that would have her screaming. He wanted so much, but mostly he just wanted the unity of her coming unglued in his arms again.

She kissed him wildly and he stabbed his tongue between her parted lips, taking satisfaction in her sweet taste. The dark recesses of her mouth offered promises she couldn't claim. Not right now. Or here.

Jett moaned, her hands splayed on his chest.

He realised suddenly that she'd unbuttoned his shirt. Anxiously, he looked around. This was progressing far quicker and farther than he'd expected. Thankfully, their vehicle was on the far edge of the lot and in the grey-dawn light there wasn't a soul in sight.

She leaned back, looking much the satisfied

cat in their cat-mouse game. Her finger trailed the crease between his stomach muscles, then the sharp curve of his hip bone. "It is a wondrous thing, the male body," she commented.

Her nails rode the thin trail of hair that widened into his waist band, before she slipped her hand inside the straining fabric to squeeze him.

He'd never be able to drive like this. Convulsively, his hand fisted in her thick, silky hair. He plundered her lips, his only focus her hot mouth and her cool hand on his burning flesh.

"Jett," he groaned.

"I need you to fuck me. Please I need you." Desperation showed in her eyes, no doubt the same that rocked through him. She needed to know they were together and whole and safe.

He stroked his thumb along her cheek. "I want to, believe me. I want to."

Oh gods, he needed to fuck her, too. His cock jerked in her hand. How soon before they could stop at a hotel? She wouldn't know what hit her when he pounded her into the bed. Oh, yeah, she'd know what hit her. She'd be screaming with the pleasure of it while he extracted payment for every minute of agony he'd endured the last few days.

The picture of Jett writhing beneath him, begging him for another release, soared through his blood.

"Baby, it can't be soon enough," he managed, telling her more than she knew. He carefully pulled her hand from his pants before he lost himself on her wrist then kissed away her disappointment.

She gasped when he pulled his hand from her breast only to unfasten her pants. No panties as usual. He'd forever think of her as the commando goddess, his naked-assed warrior princess. It worked well for his purposes as she moaned into his mouth.

She was so damned wet. Perfect. His mouth watered for the cream that coated his fingers as he rubbed along her cleft. When had he become addicted to her taste? He wanted to sink to the floor and bury his face in her pussy. Jett shuddered as he told her as much.

"Yes," she cried as his finger pushed deep into her clutching folds. "Thad, Thad...more," she panted, her hips lifting as far as they could while locked into the seatbelt. He introduced another finger, thrusting into her like he'd like to do with his cock. How could he bear the wait? It would be an early night. It needed to be, for his sanity alone. The scent of her arousal filled the car.

He breathed deeply, never pausing in his foray into her molten passage. When the tremors began, he pulled away his hand.

It took her a moment to realise what he'd done, before a tirade of swearing singed his ears. He grinned at her.

"I want you to think of what I'm going to do to you as soon as I get you alone. All day." He licked his fingers. She wouldn't be the only one tormented.

"Thad please," she begged. "I need you now."

She squirmed, and he knew even the thick seam of her jeans rasped her exposed clit. Her face flushed as she moved, her eyes closed. Her own hand inched towards her open fly.

"Please Thad."

Much as he wanted her to wait, to need him as much as he'd needed her all day, he couldn't deny her. He'd never been able to deny her anything. Now didn't seem like a good time to start.

His hand was back in her pants so fast, her eyes

flew open. She smiled and leaned back.

"You realise you're gonna pay for this, right," he said against her ear.

"Oh yes." A spark lit in her eyes every time he said the word 'pay.' Whether it was excitement or the need to smite him, he wasn't sure. His own desires warred within. He needed for her to understand what she'd done to him when she'd taken off—even if it was for a 'good' reason. He needed to be one with her again as they sated desire zinging between them.

He'd settle for her pleasure, as incomplete as it was when they weren't one.

She whimpered as his fingers sank into her slick channel once more. Her tremors started immediately, pulling at his fingers, clamping onto them so strongly he could barely move them. But he did, easing them forward and back while his thumb pressed and released at that tiny button at the front of her cleft.

Her legs pushed further apart, tightening the denim across his knuckles and holding his hand firm to her throbbing flesh. Her climax flooded around his strokes as she clawed at his shoulders, her head thrown back in unbridled ecstasy as he drove her over the edge.

"Mine," he rasped into her neck. He was never letting her go. Gods, please, she had to figure that out soon. She was his goddess. His universe.

"Yes, yes. . ."

"Don't leave me again."

She kissed him then, her hands on either side of his head as her chest lifted to his, and her cunt continued to milk his fingers. Her body was under his control, his mouth was hers. She took it as if his lips, his tongue against hers where the most cherished part of her life. He sank into it and her fingers buried in his hair.

Her urgency passed, she was in no hurry to rush the caress of her tongue into his mouth. She leisurely licked the recesses of his mouth. She'd have taught him a new religion with that kiss, if she hadn't been his religion already. And he was thankful. He'd worship at her temple all the days of his life.

She sank back against the seat as he pulled his hand from her folds, this time a content smile on her lips.

"I can taste myself in your mouth," she said without opening her eyes.

A flame tore through his groin, to the end of his cock.

Gods! And he was supposed to drive now?

* * * *

"Where are we going?" Jett asked when they diverted onto highway 80.

"My other home in Michigan. It should be somewhat free from my vibrations. I haven't been there for more than a day in over a century. I have caretakers who maintain it for me."

She nodded. "The home near your friend's estate? Bram, is it not? The one you just freed from the curse?"

"You're not going to let that go, are you?"

"You broke the code of interference."

"Bram suffered for two hundred years." Thad stared straight ahead, a bead of tension throbbing at his temple. "I know how he felt," he muttered.

His thigh went taut when she placed her hand over it. After a moment, he covered it with his own. He hadn't suffered alone. She'd wanted him, too.

"I couldn't visit there, let alone live there," he confided. "I felt guilty for cursing him in the first place."

Jett refrained from mentioning the curse had been yet another example of his interference. His friend had been well on the way to death when Thad had stepped in and chanted the incantation.

She hadn't stopped him. As her new pledge, she'd chosen to let him learn the lesson on his own. He'd suffered for years, a dark shadow over his soul. The shadow had been gone when he'd come to her days ago—had it been so recently that they'd fled the portal room? She'd known immediately that the curse was broken. It had taken a half-hearted probe to verify the truth.

"But you did go to see him," Jett said.

"I stayed in my lab."

The cave. It laid on the border between his estate and his friend's, its numerous chambers furnished like a home. Of all his holdings, she knew the cave was his place of refuge and regeneration.

He'd gone there the day after she'd bestowed his powers on him. She'd found him there, suffering from the aftershocks. Even then as deep pain ravaged his changing body, he'd stood up to her. His strength had impressed her. She'd made no mistake in her choice for warlock overlord.

Even if he'd been headstrong.

He'd matured immeasurably since then, but it didn't stop him from exerting his will. Often. Powerfully.

Her body clenched in awareness again.

The change in the man she'd wanted even then astounded her. He'd been an untried youth. Even near the age of thirty, his judgment had sometimes been halfcocked. Years in her servitude had hardened him into a formidable ally, wizened him to the immutable rhythms of life.

The road slipped beneath the tires of the vehicle as quickly as the years had passed. Now that the curse no longer bound Thad to his friend, he'd start to age normally again. How many years would she have with him before they were separated by the veil between life and death? Could she bear to give him over to her sister, the goddess who guarded the veil? She could curse him, again. Stop him from aging. The Higher Power, while giving her much leeway in her decisions, would never tolerate such a breach. It would not go unpunished. She could not put her holdings through the turmoil that would follow.

Still, her people would suffer when she lost Thad. Stoic acceptance would lessen the effects of the storm that would brew within her but wouldn't stop it. Remembering what had happened to Atlantis when her brother had died was a glaring reminder of what her unchecked emotions could do.

"Jett?" Thad's voice broke the silence that had fallen between them. She looked up expecting him to ask her if she needed to stop. He'd found a place for them to pull over about once an hour, fuelling the vehicle or getting food, letting her stretch her legs or run into one of those vile restrooms. The filth she'd seen in the last hours compared with that at the hotel. She hadn't wanted to touch anything. He'd realised her predicament and purchased her a supply of sanitary cloths and hand sanitizer, laughing about keeping his goddess untainted.

"If you could mask our trail when we went through the tunnel," he asked. "Why didn't you do that when we left the hotel? When you stopped me from using my magic to transport us?"

Thad was quickly learning the laws of the godly

realm. She wasn't sure if was a good thing, but she wouldn't keep the information from him. If he asked.

"It would not have worked. It was a direct path from a known to a known. The only reason a diversion will work now is that he has no idea where we will go. You were right though. Travelling in this...conveyance...is the best decision. It will make it harder for Airyon to trace our path."

She didn't doubt that Airyon would trace them but she didn't share her suspicion. When Thad glanced at her, though, the look in his eyes told her his thoughts mirrored hers. The time before battle was limited. Jett feared they'd have to fight before the starburst signifying the end of the Regeneration Festival occurred.

Somehow she'd have to keep Thad safe. Airyon had no regrets over striking her people.

"There's a decent hotel in the next town," Thad said, breaking through her worries. "I think we should stop for the night. Finish the drive tomorrow."

The battle would arrive... Tonight they needed each other.

She smiled at him.

"About freaking time," she muttered, stealing his favourite phrase.

He lifted her hand from his thigh where his cock throbbed inches away, much harder to disguise than her own arousal. He raised her palm to his lips.

The touch of his lips set off a tremble within her that she didn't think would stop until his manhood was lodged deeply inside her. And then it would only start again.

* * * *

The hotel suite rivalled Thad's penthouse in opulence, while not as large. It consisted of two rooms. A sitting area with heavy dark wood and maroon cushioned furniture and, through the doorway, the sleeping area was dominated with a high bed made of similar wood. Heavy curtains covered the windows, giving the illusion of evening though it was only late afternoon and the summer sun continued to burn bright in the western sky.

"Nice room," Thad commented, but his heated stare was on her as he deposited their bags on a rack at the end of the bed. "Much better than the average hotel."

Jett wouldn't know. Her only experience with hotels was the place where she'd hidden. This space was immaculate, the décor matched and soothing. It was intended to soothe, she presumed.

It didn't. Not for her.

Despite her earlier anticipation, now that she and Thad stood alone in the darkened room, the bed so near and the threat of Airyon momentarily so far away, anxiety shuddered through her. Nervously, she walked to the window and pushed aside the curtain to look outside. Misgivings bombarded her stomach as it twisted in knots.

She glanced at Thad from the corner of her eye. What did he intend for her? Her pussy clenched as it answered. Her body knew. It waited with gnawing hunger for the punishment he'd promised to dole out. The long smooth strokes into her body, his hands moulding her breasts, his mouth everywhere. Some punishment. More like welcome torment.

He'd possess her. He'd steal her will.

He'd fill her until he twined with her soul, making himself so much a part of her very fibre that she'd ache for the missing half of herself when he was absent.

Her teeth sank into her bottom lip as she stifled a whimper. How could she want him so much, yet quiver as if she'd never before been touched?

He hasn't touched you as he will today, a voice inside her answered. She felt him stalking her as she stared out the window. He'd made veiled threats ever since he'd found her. Now, they were alone. Now, they had time. Now he could follow through.

She stared out the window trying to pull her tattered calm around her. This side of the hotel overlooked a small lake. Pretty sailboats with colourful sails drifted on the calm waves in stark contrast to turmoil brewing inside her.

Thad came up behind her, his chin rested against her temple. He didn't say anything, his hands cupping her hips. In the window, she could see their refection. His taller, wider frame swallowed her smaller form. Arousal strained through the powerful body pressed to her back. His silent tension coupled with his promises from earlier stoked her apprehension.

The waves began to churn, tossing the boats like toys.

She took a deep breath to control the storm.

"Dinner?" he asked.

She blinked in surprise. "Isn't it too early?" Had she misread his intention?

"Not by the time it gets here. We can order then think of something to do while we wait." His hand slid towards her mound until his fingertips skimmed over her.

"Read?" she suggested. Soft spurts of cream flooded her cleft. Treacherous, betraying body. Already her breasts protested the fabric that now seemed to pull over them. Her clothes were suddenly too tight. She ached to rip them off.

He laughed, the rolling tenor, tumbling her to the deep sea of carnal need. Turning her in his arms, he devoured her with his gaze. "I don't think so. You know what I want—"

She braced her knees as weakness stole through them.

Thad dragged his hands along her spine. Slowly, he slipped them past her waistband, brushing the upper rise of her bottom. The ridge inside his trousers pressed against her mound. A weapon, unavoidable, threatening, lethal. "There's a particular goddess in residence who owes me big time and is going to pay up."

A thrill shot through her womb. Her tongue darted out to wet her parched lips but her mouth was too dry for it to be effective. She needed a drink. *From him.* Need battered her flagging resistance. How could she want this so much but want to avoid it?

"Really," she asked, attempting to brazen her way through the situation and show none of the fear buffeting her well-being. "And what is this 'big time' you speak of?"

His face darkened. "Shall I enumerate? I warned you that there would be consequences."

She swallowed, needing to be free of his arms, to run from the room. He'd chase and she'd be captured. Already his net wove around her. She couldn't take the intent burning in his eyes. It was too strong. Too determined. He'd blaze through her, ignite her own flame until nothing was left of her soul but the charred memories. And the sorrow of her loss.

It was the prospect of her loss, not of his seduction, that sent terror through her. When the Festival of Regeneration ended, she'd leave him.

She'd release him from his duty so that he could find fulfilment in another relationship, in a life without her, perhaps filled with another woman.

No! her being cried. *He wants you. Take as much as you can get.*

She wanted to heed the cry but knew she could not. For his peace, for her protection. The sooner the break, the less likely he'd be irrevocably scarred. She would go to the Higher Power, confess her feelings for her servant and ask for help. She might not be able to erase herself from Thad's recollection and life—perhaps because she wanted so badly to stay with him forever—but the Being would be able to do what she could not.

Next week, Thad wouldn't remember her existence.

This week, she'd make enough memories to last her an eternity.

"You are bluffing," she whispered around the emotion swelling in her throat.

"You get to take off a piece of clothing for each transgression."

"Maybe we shouldn't do this." He'd strip her to the bone.

His gait reminded her of a feline, as he sauntered to the bed. He leaned against the post, one foot crossed over the other, while he assessed her. "Maybe you don't have a choice."

"I do not commit transgressions," she argued, trying to put aside the thought of having his memory erased.

"Says who? The offender? I'm in charge here, and I say you've definitely transgressed."

Surrendering, she sighed. She could argue, but what was the point, she wanted him, over and over and over again. Agreeing was definitely the means to the end she desired.

"Oh, very well. What have I supposedly done?"

She could name a million things.

He raised a finger. "The brain wipe."

True. She had done that. She didn't argue that it had been as painful for her as it had been for him. She toed off a shoe.

Another finger. "Leaving me."

Leaving him had been the most agonising thing she'd ever done. Still, she toed off the other shoe.

"You let me suffer and worry for two days."

She grimaced. "Now really, that was part of the last one."

He raised an eyebrow.

With a long-suffering sigh, she removed a sock.

"It was two days," he prompted, pointing to the other sock. He appeared overly eager to divest her of the non-revealing clothes. Edginess ground through her, making her muscles hurt with her anticipation. Once rid of her footwear, she'd head into dangerous territory.

Her toes curled into the thick carpet. Taking her time, she pulled off the other sock. She balled it up and threw it over her shoulder.

His feral expression made it clear he wasn't playing. This was serious, and he was on the hunt, she the prey. His taut muscles flexed as they coiled and waited to pounce.

Jett tried to force air into her lungs as she realised how intense he'd turned since entering this room. She wished they'd remained on the road, dredging their way to Michigan and putting off the inevitable. This. This was as inevitable as her eventual departure and their imminent separation.

Her chest rose raggedly under the unspoken

promises he projected across the space separating them. He'd torment her until they both went crazy from the need. Until he drove endlessly into her and sent her out of control as he took the corporeal flesh that would only ever be his.

"Leading out Airyon by using your magic," he said finally, breaking the prolonged silence.

She didn't move.

"What are you waiting for?" he asked. A slow smile of triumph sparked in his eyes.

Slowly, she raised her fingers to her sweater's pearled closures. Button by button, she inched the garment open. With a shrug of alternate shoulders, it fell to her elbows and then to the floor.

Her breasts had hardened with her arousal, begging for him to fill his palms with them. The unfamiliar bra's transparent fabric was merely a gossamer veil over her painfully tight nipples. Its delicate covering chafed the sensitive buds.

She tried not to shiver in the cooled air as his heated perusal took in the newly exposed garment. He didn't need to know, before he'd found her, it had been plain white and not very pretty. She'd transformed it to this while he'd kissed her and she'd fervently wished he'd open her sweater and rip the flimsy thing from her body.

The animal in him turned her on. Her reaction to it frightened her. Her reaction and the unknown.

Goddesses always knew their direction. Goddesses were always in control. Thad made her feel disoriented yet unleashed, sailing wildly through the wind. Until he pulled her into his arms. Until he loved her with his body in a way that he could never express with his words. When he held her, she didn't feel lost anymore. She felt at home.

Right now, she didn't think she'd feel at home when he touched her. She was too agitated. He was too close to losing control. Even his limbs seemed to vibrate with the effort he exerted to hold himself back.

Secretly, she wondered what it would take to push him beyond that control. She fought back a smile. If she shoved him beyond that point, she could recover the upper hand. She would regain her dominion. After all, who was the deity here?

As if he could read her thoughts, light sizzled in Thad's eyes. "You made me wait two hundred years before I could touch you."

She crossed her arms over her chest, blocking his view of her breasts. Her head tilted to the side and her brows arched. "That is a truly desperate search for something to accuse me of."

It wasn't really a valid accusation, either, as far as she was concerned. The no touching command was a binding rule, and she hadn't created it. Normally, mortals could not touch gods or goddesses—it could kill the non-divine being—and a lower deity wasn't to change their vibration to facilitate contact without very good reason.

Lust was not one of those reasons.

His arms crossed his wide chest. "Well?"

"Well what?"

"Take off the bra or the pants."

She shook her head. "I think you've run out of transgressions."

"You don't think it's punishable to make me wait two hundred years for you? I think it's worth all your clothes."

"Oh very well. If you say so." Resistance left her. In any case, it only stood in the way of her ultimate goal.

It was time to take back control. She'd win this

game.

She'd make these hours last forever in her mind. She'd cherish the pictures of Thad driven over the edge of reason with his desire for her.

She lifted her hands to the clasp behind her back and released the bra. Her gaze never left his as the garment fluttered to the ground, leaving her small breasts bare to his sight.

Full of feminine power, she turned her back on him. Slowly, she unbuttoned her jeans and slid down the zipper.

One, she counted inside her head, sure he wouldn't make it to ten.

Two. Her head tipped back to the side, giving him a good view of her face as she closed her eyes and slipped her hand inside her open pants.

Three. Her lips parted as her fingers dragged along her slick folds. She imagined it was him, but it wasn't nearly as good.

Four.

"Oh yes," she whispered anyway, merely to incite him. "Oh, yes!"

Five—

Thad exploded into action.

"That's it!" he growled and vaulted to her side.

Panic stomped out her triumph as he swept her into his iron-hard arms. She'd underestimated him. He might go wild, but he'd never lose his control to her. Not here. Not like this.

His breath burned against her ear. "You've had your fun. Now, it's my turn."

Chapter Eight

Jett shrieked as Thad stormed to the bed and bounced her onto it.

He'd had enough of her teasing. Her mental resistance. Even now she was fighting his control. Jett just didn't get it. She still thought she could lead him by the nose. She didn't realise that here, he was in charge. She would bend to his will...and she'd like it.

The thought of plunging into her heat as she cried out her pleasure sent a rush of blood to his groin. Maybe he'd let her lead him around as long as she had him inside her that way. Fortunately, she couldn't go further than the bed like that—just where he wanted her.

A smug grin twisted his lips, and apparently, it looked as fiendish as he imagined. She gasped as he climbed after her, the mattress sinking beneath his weight. With a squeak, she twisted away to scramble off the far side of the bed.

Thad lunged over her. Knowing he wouldn't hurt her on the over-soft mattress, he sank into her, his body moulding hers. "You're not going anywhere," he growled, sounding more beast than man. Good. That's how he wanted her to perceive him right now. "You can't escape your punishment."

She looked over her shoulder at him, her fiery gold hair splayed around her. Fleeting worry clouded her eyes. As soon as it appeared, she hid it and tried for bravado.

Her chin lifted. "What are you planning?"

He merely lifted an eyebrow, letting that be his answer.

"Barbarian," she said through her teeth.

"That would be god Thad to you."

She squirmed, in vain, her struggle enflaming his erection. It pressed, rigid and throbbing, against her backside. The need to be inside her grew desperate, almost painful as urgency coiled inside him.

He skated his hands up her smooth, porcelain-white back. Goosebumps sprouted along the path as he traced the delicate curves. He loved her under him. He loved being able to touch her bare skin, touch her at all.

"You feel like silk beneath my fingers."

"Let me up."

"It reminds me of my favourite use for silk."

She said nothing. He sensed her attention, her excited anticipation of his next words.

He pushed aside her hair and pressed his open mouth to the back of her neck. Her tremble shot to his aching cock. He dragged his mouth, kissing and tasting with flicks of his tongue, up the slim column of her neck to her ear.

"I'd like to tie you to this bed with it. Leave you open to my every desire."

Her breath shuddered.

He pushed his palms along her sides until he grasped her hips. "But not now."

He yanked her tight to him so she could feel him hot against her ass. He ground his cock against her. Yes, like this when she was prisoner to his will. "This is my favourite position. I'm glad you thought of it."

She groaned and arched into him. Fire leapt through him. He took advantage of the gap she'd created between the bed and their bodies. When she'd slipped her hand into her jeans earlier, he'd gone onto full alert, his control flat-lining along with his heart. Inch by agonising inch, he worked his fingers inside her open pants, brushing over the crisp curls that hid the treasure he sought.

Her folds parted freely for him, giving him easy access to her slick heat. Her thighs clamped together as she again attempted to exerted control over the situation.

Ire raked through him. Why did she try to deny him, when here was the undeniable evidence of how much she wanted him, how much she liked what was happening between them? Why couldn't she accept she belonged to him?

He hooked his feet around the insides of her ankles and forced her legs apart. "You will take me," he ground out. His fingers worked over her exposed clit. "Contrition to your god."

Her body tremored as he worked the small bud. "Fuck you."

Apparently she'd picked up some language on her brief tour of New York.

"Oh you will."

"I will smite you for this."

"I'll look forward to it," he laughed, never ceasing his motion. She wouldn't smite him any more than she could give her virginity to Airyon. She couldn't. She belonged to *him*.

Jett clenched the bedspread, a torrent of swearing tumbling from her.

"Such language from a goddess," he chided,

delighted that he'd drawn such a reaction from her.

"Fuck you," she spat.

He rose up, careful not to hurt her as he continued to hold her legs apart with his knees. He bit the small of her back where it began its slope into her buttock. Idly, he swirled his tongue along the indentation.

"Just submit," he urged. He nipped her again.

Her hands fisted and she pressed her face into the blankets. His brow furrowed at her obvious tension. A battle raged within her. Was it that hard to surrender herself to him, to let him pleasure her, to reassure him that she regretted what she'd done to him? Even if she didn't want to admit wrongdoing, why did she refuse to be free with him?

Was it because he was mortal? A prejudice against him because he wasn't divine. He ignored the stab of hurt at the possibility. Jett wasn't like that. She didn't look down on him. Not as unworthy. He knew better than any that she found him very worthy.

So if it wasn't that, what? She didn't trust him?

She didn't trust him.

That was it. He'd been a loose cannon too many times in their history. In the last two hundred years, he'd gone against her will on more occasions than he cared to remember.

And now she didn't trust him. Not if it meant losing her control to him.

The pain that accompanied the revelation far exceeded that of the mind wipe. He nearly pushed away from her. Left her lying alone on the bed. Left the suite.

Determination quickly replaced the hurt. He'd

show her exactly what it meant to let him be in control.

Slowly, he eased her jeans past her hips. He pushed them the remainder of the way off, kicking them away. Jett moved to rise. He let her get to her knees, before he gently pushed her forward. "Stay like this," he told her, his hand at the back of her neck, the other under her belly to keep her hips up.

His balls drew upward as he eased from the bed and saw her ass high in the air, her knees parted to display her secret flesh. The sight of her glistening pink folds was a vice gripping his cock. He'd be lucky if he didn't lose himself inside his trousers before he managed to get his erection within inches of her.

"What are you doing?" she asked, her voice muffled.

He was tempted to tell her he was staring at the most alluring sight on earth. To tell her how her beautiful woman's flesh sent his blood speeding from his brain because it was all needed in his cock. How he planned to drive into her until she screamed her pleasure, how he planned to show her she could trust him to take care of her, soul and body.

Instead, he ran a finger over her drenched cleft and coated it with her ample cream. The entrance to her channel convulsed, trying to capture him within its grip. He lightly circled those inner lips. It was like dipping his fingertip into an active volcano. Her molten reaction threatened to erupt and engulf him.

He'd be ready.

Her supple thighs quivered as he tormented the flesh.

"Thad, please," she whispered, her words still

muffled by the bed.

"Don't move," he said. Without explanation, he pulled his hand away. To his surprise, she complied.

He reached for the phone and dialled the number beside it.

"Yes, I'd like to order room service," he said after someone answered.

Her toes curled, after a moment her fingers tapped.

Ah. . . impatient goddess.

Giving no warning, he eased his finger into her. Jett cried out in surprise, pushing her cunt against his touch. He slipped a second finger inside, holding it separate from the other as he spread the tight walls.

He smiled as Jett pressed her hand to her mouth to keep from moaning aloud while he spoke to room service. He had the feeling that she wanted to kill him right about now. He'd send her over the edge first. By his count, she owed him about four orgasms, in four different ways—losing an item of clothing for each transgression wasn't nearly enough.

Her stomach clenched as her desire twisted through her. His body had a similar reaction in gratitude for her need. *C'mon, baby*, he thought. *Come for me. Scream for me.*

Her head finally lifted from the blankets. "Take me," she demanded.

He shook his head, shooting his fingers in and out. He continued to speak on the phone, in a façade of inattention. It couldn't be any more untrue. His entire focus was on her. He almost forgot to hang up the phone when the room service person was finished.

The receiver dropped into the cradle a moment

before his pants dropped to the carpet, and he shucked off his shirt. He lay back. "Come here," he told her as he moved to lean on the pillows.

Her eyebrows pulled together.

He drew his hand over his cock to demonstrate his need. She immediately understood and moved to take him in her mouth.

"No, not like that," he told her. "Face away from me. Straddle my chest."

Bright red stormed up her chest to fill her cheeks.

"No."

No? Always vying for control. "You might need that spanking yet."

"You would not."

"Try me."

She rested on her elbows staring at him as if trying to see inside his head. He veiled his gaze to hinder her decision. She had to decide for herself, but if she decided to try for the power, she'd fail. It was his. She was his. She was in his power.

She was his power.

It was as simple as that. Jett was his power. Not the abilities she'd given him. No. It was the strength and determination she'd roused in him for the last two hundred years. The will that had grown stronger with each defiance of her. The emotions that surged out of check whenever she touched him or he touched her.

He had little doubt that combined with his abilities, he could defeat Airyon. He had too much riding on the victory. So much more than the God of Wrath possessed. Jett was his and she'd stay his. She'd drawn him into her body and given her virginity to him, the last link in his chain mail of power.

Today, in this room, it hung in the balance.

"Just take me," she begged.

Gods, he wanted to.

He shook his head.

Her eyes dropped and she sighed in defeat.

I'll make it good for you, baby. I promise, he vowed. *Trust me.*

Triumph surged through him as she turned her back to him, her hair falling to brush the top of her sweetly rounded ass.

"Wait," he said. Sitting up, he swept her hair into his hands and fashioned it into a clumsy braid. He pushed it over her shoulder so that nothing would obstruct his view of her body over him, even her gorgeous hair. "Now," he directed.

"You are going to pay for this," Jett said through gritted teeth, echoing his earlier thought.

"Baby, I've paid for two hundred years. Tonight is precious little to ask."

"This is all you want?"

Hell no!

"You're procrastinating," he said rather than answer the question that would reveal too many of his feelings for her. His feelings were too intense. They'd scare her away. She'd run even if it meant dealing with Airyon alone.

"I haven't made you pay for two hundred years," she said in a small voice.

He cupped her cheek. "Every night, I dreamed of holding you. I waited for you to finally come to me. To finally come for me."

She stroked her hand over him.

"I can't make it better," she said. "I can't take away those years." Her tongue darted out to flick the head of his arousal. He thought he might plough through the ceiling. A haze slid over his eyes.

"Try," he rasped. He twisted her braid around

his hand. "Dear gods, please try."

As she tongued his cock, she shifted sideways, stretching her leg over his chest. He immediately grasped her, drawing her exposed pink flesh to his mouth.

She whimpered as he drew her clit between his lips.

Wildly, she sucked him between her lips, drawing hard, lightly raking with her teeth. Her nails bit into his thighs as she angled her head to take him deeper. If he didn't know better he'd think she was shooting tiny sparks into him. Of their own volition, his hips bucked, seeking firm access to the warm recess.

"Gods, Jett..."

A hand slid from his thigh and she cupped his balls. Gently, she massaged the tight sac while she continued to work her mouth up and down his cock. Gods! If she continued...

Anxiously, he lapped at her folds, capturing the cream caught there. Satisfaction filled his chest at the taste of her arousal coating his tongue. He could drink of her forever and never tire of her flavour. Combined with the maddening sensation of her mouth engulfing him, he nearly slid off to another reality. A reality that consisted of only the two of them, forever, with no irate gods chasing them and no death looming in the uncertain future.

Pressing his hands into her upper buttocks, he held her to his mouth. It was all too soon that she cried out and climaxed against his lips. He pulled her from him. He didn't want to come in her mouth. He needed to be deep inside her channel when his seed spewed from him.

He drew her around to sit on his lap as he sat up.

"Have I paid enough?" she asked.

The ends of his hair dragged along her breasts as he shook his head. Her nipples peeking through the strands, begging to be plucked and devoured.

"Not nearly enough," he rasped.

"What will be enough?" she panted.

Nothing.

"I'll let you know when you get close."

"Give me something more solid."

He drew her hand to his cock and wrapped her fingers around it. "How's this? And I *am* going to give it to you. My tribute for my goddess."

Her eyes dilated and he knew she found his gift more than acceptable.

Her hand stroked up his length. "This seems a worthy and sizable tribute."

She shifted so she straddled him and her belly brushed his. Her breasts prodded his chest as he sucked at the indentation over her collarbone. Her touch lingering, she rose up and guided him to her entrance.

"I accept," she groaned as she slid down his shaft. Immediate, liquid heat immersed him, the true nectar of the gods, cherished and protected.

His.

She moved uncertainly, his precious, inexperienced goddess. He had no doubt she'd soon master this new position as she had everything else unfamiliar. Her supple walls hugged him tighter than a fist. Her teeth sank into her bottom lip and she lifted up, hands clutching his arms for balance.

Her eyes never left his. He knew she searched them for guidance and signs of his desire for this. If she found anything less than complete pleasure, he'd be damned. His fingers curled into her hips to help her to the perfect rhythm.

He nearly swore when a knock sounded on the outer door.

Gods bedamned! Well, except for Jett. He wanted her only in his arms. He didn't want anything to remove her, even the need to answer the summons of the room service delivery.

Jett groaned when the knock reverberated again.

"Room service," he said through his teeth as he guided her movements in smooth pistoning strokes. His lips found a taut nipple.

Who needs food?

"We'll have to stop," she gasped. She arched towards his mouth, her arms wrapping around his head.

No way! After two days, he was finally once again within the firm squeeze of her cunt. Rightness and connection filled his being. Nothing would prise him free. Not even the allure of food. He didn't want the aloneness of being separated from her, even for a few minutes.

He knew if he left her here while he answered the door, she'd retreat within herself again. She'd put on her armour and attempt to take control. She'd fight him. Every dominant gene in him growled at the prospect. She would learn. She would defer to him and bend to his will.

An exertion of his will and her bending to it entered his mind. It would forge and test her trust in him. The picture of her spread out on the bed, two men loving her, played in his head, a slow, passionate film.

"We could let in whoever it is," he offered. It wouldn't take much in the way of low level magic to control the person's mind. Jett didn't know he had the ability which predated his service to her. He'd make it so the delivery person never remembered seeing him and Jett in this carnal clench. At the same time, he'd ensure the man never did anything with which Thad didn't approve.

"He'll see us like this. I can't risk wiping his mind." Her husky groan sounded far less protest than excitement. Was it his imagination or was she suddenly more slick? Her inner muscles pulsed around him, throbbing with consent.

"We'll never see him again," he coaxed. He drew his hand over her curves, tracing her slim waist and concave belly, cupping her breasts. The great artists had never sculpted a beauty as perfect as hers. How could they have ever captured her luminescence, her grace? The rolling movement of her hips over him was a sensuous dance towards climax.

"Don't you want him to see?" He ground into her as her opened cleft kissed the flesh around his cock. "I want him to see you ride me. I want him to see how hot you are for me, how my woman takes me so willingly into her body."

Her lips parted slightly at his words while her eyes glazed with the sensations he knew flowed through her body. She teetered on the brink of her orgasm. If he timed it right, she'd fly over the edge as the door opened. It would take all his control not to sail right after her when that sweet clenching milked him.

"Should I let him in?" he asked. He'd take no for an answer, but he didn't think she'd say no.

Her body bowed, her nipples growing into tight pearls, thrusting towards him. She seemed to stop breathing as she nodded.

Thad used a slight, under-the-radar-amount of magic to open the door. It was so minute of an energy it was more of a parlour trick than magic. He nearly regretted his decision when the delivery person, a light-skinned black man with a build similar to his own and a multitude of long, thin braids, entered the suite, carrying a tray from the restaurant downstairs. The man's eyes turned immediately lustful as he stared at Jett. Thad thought perhaps the delivery person barely noticed that Jett wasn't alone, other than the penis disappearing as she writhed over it.

The man's mind was strong and Thad immediately knew, he'd have to split his focus between Jett and their visitor, in order to stay in control of the situation. He wanted to have all his attention on her, but he couldn't allow anything to go wrong as they played. Nothing would hurt her.

His jaw clenched. And no matter what the man did, he would not be allowed to take her cunt. No man would touch her that way, save himself.

The door to the hallway closed as the delivery person—Kale, divined from his probe into the guy's head—stepped into the room. He placed the food on the table in the other room then returned to lean on the doorway, watching them.

Thad pretended total concentration on Jett, allowing Kale to watch them, watch her cunt suck at his penis as the thought of being watched aroused her to new levels. Lifting up, she slammed down, riding him harder, pressing her clit into his pelvic bone.

"Yes, baby. Ride me," he urged.

His eyes met Kale's and the man looked slightly disconcerted to be caught stroking the bulge in his khaki trousers. Thad lifted an eyebrow and beckoned him forward with a flick of his fingers.

Kale was about to have the hottest and most frustrating dream of his life. Tomorrow, he'd never remember the faces of the two other participants, but he'd otherwise remember his 'fantasy' in explicit detail.

Jett whimpered as spasms thundered through her middle. She could hardly believe Thad had invited someone into the room while they made love. Perhaps the person had gone away before Thad opened the door. No sound came to her but those of her pleasure, Thad's moans and their bodies slapping together. He filled her so completely. If he thrust any further into her, she was sure he'd come out her navel.

With difficulty, she lifted so he nearly came free. She loved the way his fingers tightened, his breath hissing as he appreciated her unschooled efforts. Slowly, she sank down his shaft, each long heavily-veined inch stimulating her over-heated folds.

She wanted him to drive harder into her. To take her so completely, she'd forget that soon she'd leave him, that she'd forget eternity and only be in this steaming moment.

"Oh gods! Jett! I could fuck you forever."

Yes, oh yes. It was tight, so tight in fact that it seemed Thad had to use some effort to pry apart her slippery channel walls with his wide member. Not that she protested the invasion, she rocked forward and back, taking on a rhythm that shook the bed.

Thad praised her efforts, his voice growing deeper and darker with each phrase. Her heart filled with the emotion she held for him. To affect him like this, to know he wanted her as a woman, to know her pleasure gave him pleasure built the inertia of her thrusts.

He gave her a strange smile a moment before she nearly startled from his erection. In truth, she

would have come fully off him had he not yanked
her down. Her eyes wide as he impaled her, she
stared down at the two hands that cupped her
breasts from behind. Long, light brown fingers
weighed the small mounds, working the pointed
tan nipples. Lightning flung through her pussy as
the hands squeezed and pulled.

Her hair worked free of its braid and swung
wildly along her back as she turned to look. The
handsome black man smiled at her, his eyes
brimming with lust-filled intentions.

Thad turned her face back to him, "Relax,
baby. Relax," he murmured, shifting under her.
"Let Kale touch you while you ride me. I won't let
any thing bad happen to you."

She had few choices. Her body refused to do
anything but comply. Slowly, she began to rock
while Kale's starched button-down shirt abraded
her back. His breath was hot on her shoulder as
she undulated over Thad's larger than ever cock.
She knew at once that seeing her like this aroused
him just as much as being between the two men
aroused her. She wanted to arouse him further.
To please him. To give him a memory that would
stay with him as long as he remembered his time
with her.

She turned to Kale. His kiss pressed to her
shoulder as his odd textured hair tickled her neck.
One thin braid fell over her shoulder and fell
between her breasts.

She lifted his chin, and Kale moved forward,
covering her mouth with his generous lips. His
mouth was larger than Thad's, his tongue fuller.

Thad growled as Kale explored her mouth.
She drove her fingers into the braids, cupping
the back of Kale's head. She knew the sight she
must present, head turned to the man behind her,

kissing him, his hands moulding her breasts while her body gyrated smoothly over Thad.

Kale tasted of mint, and Jett sucked it into her mouth while she allowed him to claim her lips. He moved with her, as she fucked Thad, managing to shuck his shirt. Light chest hair grazed her back in sweet friction as they moved in near unison.

His hands left her breasts and smoothed over her ribs to her flat belly. Forming a vee, they pressed downward to her cleft. He massaged them over her folds, holding her further open, taunting her clit as she continued to kiss him and slam up and down Thad's staff.

While Kale continued to caress her with one hand, she felt his other go to the bulge that pressed into the small of her back. A moment later, his erection popped free. The hot, smooth cock rubbed against her as she moved.

How far would Thad let the man go? Would he let Kale fuck her? He seemed inclined to it at the moment as he didn't stop anything the man did. Breaking from the kiss, she stared down at Thad with wide eyes as the other man turned his mouth to the tender flesh at the base of her neck.

Possession filled Thad's eyes. He wasn't unaffected by the other's touches. His jaw was hard, taut with passion and fury. She bit her lip. Fury? Hadn't he called the man to the room? Hadn't this been his idea?

Anger slipped through her. How dare he be angry? Turning away, she again took Kale's mouth, opening her lips wide and sucking his tongue into her mouth. Her body twisted so that she half-pressed to his chest. His arms went around her, a vice as he held her tight and nearly lifted her from Thad's cock.

Thad grasped her hips, forcing her against him.

He set a relentless, punishing beat as he ploughed into her, pushed over the edge of his reason. The two men touched her everywhere, competing, it seemed, for her full attention. Each pulled her towards them, stretching her in new positions, neither surrendering charge.

Thad's emotions ran close to the surface. He didn't hide how this act strained his control or that the same control was ready to snap. He barely tolerated the other man touching her, but he allowed it for her.

At the same time, passion flared in his eyes as he watched Kale run his dark hands over her pale skin. Warmth from Thad's claim, surrounded her like a fine silk woven net.

Suddenly, the sensations meshed together. Thad, Kale, the well-being her warlock overlord roused inside her. Her channel fisted around him, an electrified tunnel of craving, and he exploded, shooting a fiery stream deep in her womb. Shattering frissons of ecstasy ripped though her middle and rocketed to her limbs accompanied by strange spirals of need. Need for what?

More. She wanted more.

Kale's engorged manhood still rubbed, strong and hard against her back. It begged for attention as her release milked Thad's cock.

He tried to capture her cries with his kiss, but Thad refused to allow the upper hand. He yanked her from the man's arms and pulled her down to him. Kale's braids tickled her back as he leaned forward.

Her ass pressed against his cock while his hands smoothed over her buttocks, spreading the globes as his thumb tested the bud there.

A ripple of excitement ached in her pelvis.

"You want him to fuck your ass, don't you?"

Thad rasped in her ear. The gentle slide of his hands on her back belied the harshness of his tone. Some time while she wasn't looking, he'd staked his claim. She was his and he'd only allow Kale to touch her with his permission.

Thad didn't wait for the answer before he continued, "He's smaller than I am. I'd hurt you if I tried to take you that way, but you could accommodate him." His eyes darkened with tormented fascination as he looked over her shoulder. She knew he saw what she felt—Kale dragging his tongue over her buttock.

"I want to see him take you that way," Thad conceded. It was obvious, he both desired to please her and to see her thus, but yet was reluctant to allow any man to enter her body.

Tenderness choked her. If he had not said he wanted to see it, she'd have refused. She'd tortured him enough in the past without knowing it. She didn't want to hurt him. Ever. A nagging voice in her head told her she'd do just that when she left him. She had no choice in that, but she had a choice in this.

She brushed her hand along his jaw and kissed him. "Yes," she whispered against his lips. "But only for you. Remember that."

He slipped from her body but remained beneath her, holding her and kissing her.

"How will you see?" she asked, as Kale pulled her ass higher.

"I'll see well enough," he told her. "And, I'll feel it. I'll share every tremor that goes through your body, every sensation." He kissed her tenderly, his fingers spearing into the damp tendrils at her temples. "I'm one with you, my goddess."

Reaching out he grabbed a tube he must have dropped on the bedside table earlier while she'd looked out the window. He handed it to Kale. Jett watched the transaction, thinking Kale looked a little dazed as Thad handed him the container. Surely, he'd never before experienced something like this when making deliveries.

Without direction, he opened it and smeared it over his dark cock, paying extra attention to the ebony head. But, of course he'd know what to do with it. He wouldn't need instruction.

Nervous excitement filled her as she watched. She worried a little. Thad's finger had felt so good, but Kale's member was somewhat larger.

He smeared some of the lube at her tense nether opening.

"Relax," Thad urged. He kissed her, making love to her mouth while Kale worked his slick finger inside her. Slowly, he wriggled the digit around. Wanton tingles pierced her reserve. She couldn't contain her satisfied moan as she dropped her head against Thad's shoulder.

He turned his mouth to her ear. "Yes, baby," he whispered. "That's right. Don't worry. It's okay."

She hoped he was right. Tumultuous feelings warred inside her. Fear. Excitement.

Kale's cock prodded at her, beginning a slow, insistent push. "Just relax, and sink into it," he instructed.

Her brow furrowed, and she lifted his head. Thad had said the same thing, at the same time.

"Relax," Kale repeated. This time, she saw Thad's lips move as he spoke simultaneously. His eyes were closed, his face mirroring Kale's expression when she glanced quickly over her shoulder.

She understood at once what her warlock had done.

Thought ceased when Kale pushed further.

"Thad!" she cried out at the burning, full sensation when Kale sank into her, aided by the lubricant.

"Gods! So tight. It feels so good," Kale-Thad gritted.

It hurt. She struggled against it, panic soaring up her spine. "Make it stop, Thad," she begged, even as the impression gave way to intense pleasure. Her cleft wept with obstinate arousal.

Thad clasped her hips, holding her as the other man began his in and out assault, driving her from her mind. She no longer cared who was who. The slight pain receded, then disappeared completely.

Kale reached around her and plunged several fingers inside her clutching cunt. Two, three, she didn't care. Combined with the experience of his cock making short stabs in and out, in and out, she'd left behind everything but feeling.

"Oh gods!" Thad cried as she began to quake.

Her entire body clenched, and she screamed as her release tidal-waved over her. The world dimmed, sound disappearing save for the blood rushing through her ears.

There was nothing she could do to stop the mirror over the dresser from shattering.

Chapter Nine

"My goddess, my perfect goddess," Thad murmured. He held Jett tight, stroking her tangled hair as she regained consciousness. Vaguely, she became aware of what had happened. Thad had taken over Kale's body. It was Thad who'd propelled the man. She'd never known he possessed such an ability.

Vaguely, she thought she should be irritated with him for hiding the information from her, but she couldn't muster the energy. She'd deal with that later.

Like a zombie, Kale got up from the bed and headed into the bathroom. She heard water as he washed himself.

She snuggled into Thad, barely noticing the other man getting dressed and leaving as if nothing had occurred. He didn't spare a last glance in her direction.

She knew Thad had taken no chances. The man never had the opportunity to hurt her. He wasn't even aware of what had occurred. Thad had had him under his control the entire time.

Though she wanted to get up and wash also, the tenderness of his embrace seeped into her, muting his words while he praised her for what she'd done.

As she drifted off to sleep, he murmured plans for the future, plans for when Airyon was dispatched and they were safe. Plans which he didn't know would not include her.

She wouldn't be there. She couldn't be.

She woke with a start some time later. Something wasn't right. A glance at the clock told it was early morning. Another muted noise, similar to that which must have woken her, thudded nearby as she sat up completely alert. Thad slept like the dead, not hearing the quiet sounds. Perhaps there was nothing to hear, and it was only her advanced sense of vibrations that perceived the unwelcome visitors.

Hastily, she slipped from the bed, tucking Thad's arm around her pillow as he murmured a protest at her departure. Pulling on his shirt, she headed for the sitting room.

The door shut securely behind her, cutting off her escape to the bedroom and Thad. She spun to find Preeto and Ghenton, Airyon's brothers, looming behind her.

"Preeto, would you look at this?" Ghenton said as he circled Jett. "She looks like the Goddess of the Zodiac Quad, but isn't the goddess a virgin?" He sniffed. His dark eyes raking over her and his lips twisted in a smirk. "Not anymore."

She backed away. The two made her feel dirty with their leering looks and nasty comments. Nothing was farther from the truth when it came to what happened between her and Thad. It was beautiful and right.

Unlike these two. Everything about them was ugly, except their looks. They were handsome and identical to Airyon except for hair colour. Airyon's was black while Preeto's was red and Ghenton's was dark blond. In all other ways, they shared the same features and body structure.

They were perfect.

But the cold harshness in them marred that beauty. What was once beautiful was now frightening.

"What do you want?" she demanded, scrambling in her mind for a plan. She needed to dispatch the two of them before Thad discovered she wasn't in bed with him. Or before they attacked him while he slept. They'd kill him with a single shot. She didn't think her sister, Nara, would be inclined to part the veil to return Thad. Actually, if she knew Nara, she'd do her best to keep Thad right there with her.

"We've come to return you to Airyon," Ghenton sneered. "Of course, you're lucky. He won't care that you've defiled yourself. He wants to join you only for your power." His chin went up a notch. "If it were me, I'd see you to Torment."

"Neither of you have any say," she replied.

"He's your mate."

"Not by any recognised ceremony." A band of horror squeezed her chest. Was she joined to the God of Wrath? Had he joined with her in some twisted ceremony during her absence? It wouldn't be binding. She hadn't spoken. Still, the thought that he called her his own made her skin crawl.

Preeto stepped closer. "You are promised. That is ceremony enough."

"I have never promised. I would not join myself to that god of worms if he were the only male left in eternity." She rose to her full height and glared at Airyon's henchmen-brothers who still towered over her. "Why did Airyon not come himself? Why must I deal with his slime trails?"

Preeto sneered, seeming unfazed by her insult,

his laugh sending a chill clawing down her spine. "He's been busy. Don't you ever listen to reports on your territories? Haven't you read the Daily Deity?"

"Nothing he does would surprise me," she returned, dread accompanying the earlier chill. What was Airyon doing? "I would think after three millennia, you would stop doing his dirty work. Your holdings are in disarray...you have no time for them while you follow after him like dogs."

Both men immediately turned thunderous when she dared to besmirch them again. Preeto grabbed her, his fingers digging into the delicate flesh of her upper arm. Instinctively, she raised her vibration to full level to ward him off. Preeto might have divine responsibilities, but he was an even lesser god than she was.

Her mind screamed for Thad, but she knew he couldn't help her. It would be far worse if she saw him die by these cretins' hands.

Preeto's teeth gritted as pain flew up his arm, so strong she could practically see it.

Behind her, the door to the bedroom flew open, and Thad tore into the room.

She screamed as Ghenton sent a lightning bolt for his head. Thad raised a hand, and it deflected back at the sender. Taken by surprise, Ghenton didn't have time to counter. The smite hit him full force. He disintegrated as his divine form was removed from earth to return to the heavenly plains where he'd go directly to Torment.

Preeto fell to his knees overtaken by her angry vibration. A moment later, he followed as his brother had gone.

She turned to Thad, immediately lowering her vibration as he rushed towards her. He crushed her to his chest.

"Why didn't you call me?" he demanded as he hugged her so tight she thought her ribs might crack. "I could just kill you for taking them on by yourself."

"How did you do that?" she asked.

"What?"

"Deflect Ghenton's smite. I know of no mortal, gifted or not, who can do such."

He shrugged. "I just knew I had to protect you. I sure as hell wasn't letting one of them kill me so that they could take you from me."

It didn't make sense. His determination alone wasn't enough to save his life. Was it something to do with his prolonged exposure to her? Had she somehow wrapped a blanket of protection around him when he'd become her consort?

"Don't ever do that again!" he ordered.

"Fight them? They will not be back. They are—"

"Fight alone!" he roared.

"I have been fighting my own battles for several millennia. I never expected you to fight with me. I do not need you to. I only asked that you help hide me."

Hurt wiped across Thad's face before his expression hardened, his jaw tight as granite. "Get your things together. We're leaving. We can't stay."

"I need to shower."

"There's no time. Get dressed."

* * * *

I don't need you.

The thought repeated with sadistic regularity though Thad's thoughts as he stared at the road, trying to navigate through the torrential rain that hammered the SUV.

He'd never been in a storm as bad as this. He must be driving in its path, he decided. The rain never let up, the thunder and lightning nearly constant. The deluge forced the vehicle to a crawl.

None of it seemed to faze Jett. She didn't seem to notice as she stared with detachment out the side window.

She didn't need him.

His jaw locked. What kind of a stupid-assed thing was that to think? Of course, she needed him. They needed each other. How could she throw away what was between them with such careless ease? He was ready to commit forever to her, to cherish her, his precious goddess. Obviously, she was ready—

For what? To abandon him.

She'd already tried to do it once. How long before she left him again? How long before he had to stand before her throne and pretend he'd never touched her intimately? Was he supposed to pretend to forget he'd plunged inside her while she cried out his name, too?

He couldn't do it. He *could*. But he refused to. He wouldn't. She could smite him, send him to hell, turn him into a germ, but he wouldn't bow to her and forget it all.

His fingers clenched on the steering wheel, his knuckles turning white. A grim protest rose in his chest. He'd never forget.

She'd fight and protest, but he was keeping her by his side. She wasn't going anywhere. She was his.

Beside him, Jett squirmed in her seat. He wondered if her body still burned with reminders of last night. More likely, she wanted to shower, although she didn't complain. She'd been completely quiet since they'd left the hotel, merely murmuring her thanks when he'd gone though a drive-thru to get food. He found once again that he didn't like her silence. He sensed it was different this time than the other occasions. It wasn't brooding. This time, he couldn't almost hear the wheels whirring in her mind as she planned.

She was listless.

Was he terribly wrong about the rightness of their being together?

"Jett," he said, gaining her attention and taking her cold hand. His heart cracked when she looked at him. Dark circles shadowed her pained eyes.

"I have never sent one of my own to Torment," she murmured.

"You had to protect yourself."

She shook her head. "I should have gone with them to Airyon."

"No!" he exclaimed. "That's not happening! I won't allow you to go to him."

"Allow?" She didn't elaborate. The ice in her tone said everything. She was a goddess. He couldn't stop her from doing anything.

If she wouldn't put value in their relationship, he'd stand on the one nearly microscopic thread he had. "You promised to obey me as your god. You don't break promises."

"You were almost killed," she protested. Her apparent ire over "allow" dissipated, and he saw the heart of the problem. Jett valued life, whether it was a god who tried to steal her back to Airyon or if it was her pledge. She hated senseless death. She was plagued by worry about *his* death.

"But I wasn't killed." He squeezed her hand. "How did he find us?"

"I do not know." If possible, her hand grew

even colder. She tightened her fingers. A faint tingle from her slightly raised vibrational level ran up his arm. The pleasant buzz didn't make him woozy. Instead, an arrow of pleasure shot to his groin.

He wanted her. His body didn't care that now wasn't the most opportune time. It didn't care that they'd held each other long into the night. He needed to hold her again. Soon. Perhaps he should find a place to stay for the night. It didn't seem as if the storm that lashed the SUV was going to let up anytime soon. Even if they didn't stop for the night, they should pull over until it cleared slightly. It poured so heavily, he could barely see beyond the front bumper of the vehicle.

The thought that Airyon had found them before and would probably find them again forestalled that idea. Thad preferred to be on his own turf when he faced the God of Wrath.

"How long do you suppose it will be before Airyon tries again?" he asked, though he hated to mention the god's name to Jett. Every time she heard it, she got a look in her eyes she hadn't had when she'd run away from Airyon, a look Thad knew was directly related to sleeping with him. She wanted to put an end to this even if she had to confront Airyon.

The look was there again. Sad but determined. Committed to her fate. It was a fate Thad wouldn't allow.

Jett pulled a hand over her face and pressed her fingers to the bridge of her nose—an age old gesture of stress, obviously not confined to the mortal world. "If he found us so quickly, he will find us again. I will have to fight him."

Why did she feel like she had to do this alone? Didn't she remember that he had abilities?

"And I'll be with you. I won't let you face him alone."

"No. He will kill you," she protested.

Not in this lifetime. "I'll stop him, like I did the other one."

She frowned, her fist hitting the armrest on the door. "That was an anomaly. You should be dead right now."

"That might make things easier on you."

"Do not say that! Do not ever say that! I do not want you dead, do you not understand that? If I could, I would see you live forever. I cannot do that. But I can do whatever I must to see that your time is not shortened."

Her anguish sliced his soul. He pulled to the side of the road and gathered her into his arms. "Nothing's going to happen to me, baby. I'm okay. I'll be fine."

A sob shook her body. Powerless to help her, he stroked his hand over her still tangled hair and held her while she cried.

She pressed her face into his shirt. "I will be glad when the next two days are over, and I do not have to worry so much."

He pulled back, eyeing her warily. "Two days? Why is that?"

Did he only have two days left before she'd slip through his fingers? He knew before she answered that she'd confirm his worst fear.

She looked surprised by his sharp tone. "That is when the Festival of Regeneration is complete," she said as if it were something he should have known all along.

It would have been nice if she'd passed along the information sooner and given him a timeline. Not that it would have changed anything he'd done. He'd still want her in his life as long as possible. Somehow he'd have to convince her to stay. She could perform her goddessly duties from his side, just as easily as somewhere else.

As much as he'd like to order her to remain with him, he knew it would never work. She had only to have the faintest of thoughts of someplace else, and his arms would hold air. He could try to follow, but there were some places from which he was barred.

"What will happen after this Festival?" he asked.

"Airyon will be quickly brought into line. I will not have to worry about him until the next festival in another five hundred more years. I will likely be reprimanded for some of my choices." She frowned. "Once I explain, I am sure it will be nothing too harsh."

"Why would you be punished?"

"I have neglected my duties. I have sought pleasure with you."

"To protect yourself," he argued.

"Every time?"

Confessing his commitment to her now wouldn't ease her mind. She'd put it down to misaligned duty, a warlock overlord going beyond his obligation. "Would it help if I spoke for you?" he asked.

"A mortal cannot speak for a goddess. Do not worry for me. I will have justification. This will be between the Higher Power, Airyon and me. Airyon will be required to account for his actions, as well."

He frowned. He was more concerned with the two of them than with Airyon. As he saw it, they had only to evade His Wrathfulness for a few more days and they'd be safe. It was his future that was in jeopardy.

Jett didn't share his feelings. She'd blithely go along as if nothing monumental had happened. As if she hadn't smote his heart into the dust. If she kissed him on the cheek with a quick "thanks" before skipping away, so help him...

A growl built in his chest. "And who will help you *then*?"

She tilted her head, her eyes narrowed slightly, and he realised he hadn't bothered to disguise his fury.

It had taken root this morning when he'd woken to discover he was alone. Every possessive cell in him had clenched as he'd leapt from the bed. His anger had been temporarily muted by fear when he'd realised there were two men in the sitting room with Jett. He'd known instinctively they weren't mortal.

He hated that she hadn't trusted him to help her and that she'd chosen to fight on her own. His anger had festered behind his wall of control ever since then.

This new development was the tipping point.

"Who's going to protect you from Airyon or someone like him when this festival rolls around next time?" he demanded. Futility stoked his furore. It wouldn't be him. She'd go on while he'd die. She'd stay young and graceful while he grew feeble.

His jaw clenched. Who could beat such an impossible situation? Try as he might, he could see no way to fix this. There had to be some way. Fate wouldn't write him into this corner without a plan. If he ever got the chance, he and Fate would have words.

Jett looked away. "I do not know. Should the need arise, I will find someone. It is a long time from now—"

"The way time flows for you, it's not long." The thought of someone else protecting her, some other faceless man perhaps holding her, was as painful as having his skin flayed from his body. It was a wonder to him that she couldn't see his soul's open wounds.

"Thad, I cannot stop reality. We can only make the best of the time we have. I wish only to act for your best benefit. To do what I must to protect all my people. Including you."

He pulled back onto the road. "I don't need or want your protection." He wanted something far more important that she could never give.

"It does not matter what you want—"

"Doesn't it!"

"Not when it comes to protecting you."

Rain slashed across the windows, the wipers barely able to accommodate the torrents. Just like his life. He fought to keep order while everything spun out of control. He couldn't keep up with this. He wanted to grab hold of it, but it slipped away like fog in the bright morning sun.

"There's a place up here where we can stop and eat," he told her, changing away from the futile subject. There had to be a solution neither of them was seeing. He had to believe if Jett knew a way for them to go on together she'd grab it just as quickly as he would. Her sadness was palpable and just as deep as his.

He hated for her to be unhappy. It made him angrier that he couldn't wipe it away and make everything all right. He was her man. She was his mate. He should be able to fix this and put the laughter back in her eyes.

He refused to give up on them. Right now, he'd take care of her. When they got to his home, he'd start digging for ways to keep her with him. "The truck stop should have showers available if you want to use one, too."

She gave him a smile that didn't go farther than her lips before it faded. "I would like that."

He concentrated on the road, hoping none of the lightning that flared around them hit an overhead wire or a tree. That would be just what he needed to round out his day. Stranded in an SUV with his goddess and unable to do anything about it.

"Can't you stop this?" he asked as a new blast shook the vehicle. Since she was technically Mother Nature, she should have no problem controlling the storm.

"I have nothing to do with this. I have been trying to stop it for hours, but Airyon keeps changing the storm cell. Wrath is often deceitful."

Oh hell. "He knows where we are?"

"He has a general idea. It is a huge storm."

Well, that was just fantastic, wasn't it? Was it possible to evade Airyon? Would he catch up with them?

They lapsed into silence again until they reached the truck stop diner. It worried Thad that Airyon knew their location, not for himself but for Jett. He'd have to be extra vigilant.

As he pulled into the parking lot, she removed her seatbelt and climbed over the seat to fish out what she needed from the bags. After he'd parked, she handed him a change of clothes, as well.

She seemed to have easily settled into the human life. Not using her magic didn't seem to be too big a deal. And most of the time she seemed completely content, even happy.

An idea hit him as quickly as the lightning outside shot around them.

"Can you become mortal?" Thad asked

suddenly.

Her eyes widened with shock. Suddenly, joy bloomed across her entire being. "Yes," she breathed. "It has been done. Yes, I could become mortal."

He pulled her towards him. "Would you? If you could stay with me, would you become mortal to give us a chance?"

She didn't hesitate. "I would. When the Festival ends, I will request the Higher Power appoint my successor. It is unlikely that I will be denied." Excitement radiated from her. "And I will leave behind my divinity."

"And be my wife," he pushed, willing her to agree.

Jett smiled. "And be your wife."

Chapter Ten

Hesitant euphoria bubbled through Thad's veins as he left the showers and entered the restaurant area of the truck stop. Jett was going to stay with him. She'd be his.

They still had the problem with Airyon. It poked at his happiness, but he told himself over and over that they would defeat the overblown god. After all, Jett was more powerful. She hesitated in defeating her nemesis from concern for her people's safety. Thad frowned. And his. He wished she'd stop being concerned for him. For the love of the goddess, he wasn't helpless. He was certainly more than capable of protecting them both.

Sure Airyon was a god. Thad wasn't convinced that the man was more than a spiteful child. Leveraging a few brain cells would likely outwit that petulant deity.

He frowned and ran his fingers through his damp hair. Jett put far less credence into his abilities than she should. Of course, if she realised all of them...he'd have thought that after last night, she'd know there was more to him than she'd ever guessed .

Surreal silence greeted him as he headed

for one of the restaurant's booths. He'd been so caught up in his thoughts, it had taken him several moments to notice everyone in the diner had gathered around the television suspended above the counter.

Dread knotted in his chest.

"The apocalypse is upon us," a reporter said dramatically. Destruction surrounded the man. "Yesterday, freak storms began to ravage the world. Landslides, tsunamis, tornadoes, blizzards, wind storms, hurricanes. Nowhere has been left untouched as Mother Nature has flown into a rage. Many are confident the end of the world is at hand..."

The news report flashed to a woman speaking about her notion of the end of the world and the reasons she believed it was here. Pictures of world-wide devastation filled the screen.

Thad's eyes narrowed.

Speaking of petulant deities...Airyon. Thad knew beyond a shadow of doubt that Wrath was behind this. With two days until the end of the Festival, this was a last ditch effort to pull Jett from hiding.

And it might just work. She'd go ballistic when she saw the news reports. She'd do whatever was necessary to stop the devastation of her worlds. Even if it meant sacrificing herself to Airyon.

As much as Thad wanted to arrest the havoc destroying the earth, he had to stop her. Airyon would do this and worse, if she went to him and he took control. The world would be at the constant mercy of his whim. His wrath.

Bile boiled in Thad's gut. Was he being selfish? Did he want to protect her just to keep her with him? Should he let her go? A protest twisted though him. He couldn't surrender her. She belonged with him.

If he kept Jett with him, kept her from discovering Airyon's activities, thousands might die. Thad's eyes squeezed shut. He, the warlock over this territory, would also be responsible. He'd share Airyon's blame.

But if he let Jett go to Airyon...if Jett wasn't protected from the god, countless millions would suffer and die in the millennia to come.

It was a vomitous choice.

There was no choice. He had to hide her, not for himself, though everything in him screamed to protect his woman. He had to hide her for the generations to come. The world would return to balance in two days, and Jett along with her four overlord warlocks would right the destruction.

Spinning on his heel, he headed towards the shower area to keep Jett from entering the diner.

* * * *

Jett left the showers, carrying a plastic bag with her damp towel and dirty clothes shoved inside. She'd donned some of the clothes from the boutique. She liked the flowing sapphire-coloured pants and wrap-around halter shirt. The pants swirled around her like a long skirt as she moved, brushing her legs in a gentle caress and reminded her a little of the flowing garments she wore at home. The shirt hugged her and emphasised her curves. She couldn't wait to see the look in Thad's eyes when he saw her.

She also couldn't wait to see the look in his eyes later when he saw her in the undergarments Anya had selected to go with the purchases. Jett had to admit it felt foreign to wear the lacy thong and specially designed bra. But, it felt even more sensuous.

Her long locks fell in smooth, gentle waves to her waist. She'd combed them straight—well, straighter—somewhat taming the unruly curls. Overall, she felt far more feminine than she'd felt since her creation. It was the thought of Thad's reaction to her that awoke it in her. She couldn't wait for tonight.

And in a few days, at most weeks, she'd be mortal. She'd be with him forever. If she remained a deity, they'd be separated forever. Even in his death, the veil would forever part them. Gods never breached the veil, even when they died. But as a mortal, she'd age with him. She might be parted from him briefly when one of them died, but in the end, they'd be together for an eternity beyond the veil.

She smiled. An eternity with Thad. She couldn't have come up with a better ending for them. Because it wasn't an ending. It was never-ending. It was forever. And she knew she'd love him that long. She'd loved him for two hundred years already.

She loved him...

She still hadn't come completely to terms with all the implications. When she'd knelt over the guard, knowing how deeply loved he was, and she'd looked up at Thad...she'd known. The feelings she'd harboured for him for the centuries, and that had kept her from turning him to dust when he blatantly disobeyed her orders, were love.

He might never return the feeling, but he filled her heart. She'd loved before, but never in her long life had she experienced what she felt for him. This consumed her, filled her with well-being and belonging. The thought of losing it had torn her apart. But now she wouldn't lose it. She'd do anything to ensure his happiness, to keep him safe, to care for him. She never wanted to be anywhere but in his arms.

Thad leaned against the wall, waiting for her as she came around the corner. He straightened and came to her side.

"Hey," he said, his gaze probing hers. He seemed to search her expression. Search for what?

She tilted her head, wishing she could see what he was thinking. His vibration was troubled. Had he changed is mind already? She pushed that thought away. He wouldn't change his mind. The tenderness in his eyes told her that.

"What is wrong?" she asked.

He pulled her flush to his body. His hands flattened on her back as his mouth opened over hers. She forgot to breathe, fire racing through her as it always did when he touched her.

She pressed against him as he lifted his head.

"The food's bad here," he said. "Let's go somewhere else."

She shrugged. "Whatever you think. I am not all too hungry anyway. I feel much better now that I have showered and changed."

A shiver of awareness skittered down her spine as his nose pressed to her neck. He trailed scalding kisses to her ear. "Let's go then," he whispered. "I want you in my bed tonight." His hand swept down to cup her buttocks. He pressed her tight to his turgid cock. "I want to hear your sweet cries echo off the canopy as you writhe beneath me."

A surge of heat flooded her cleft. Her breath stuttered from her. Urgent need for exactly what he described jolted to her toes, radiating from her womb. How could she need him again so soon?

She wanted the closeness, the oneness, knowing she was his and always would be.

His fingers twined through hers as he pulled her out into the rain and they dashed for the SUV. He opened her door, seeing her inside before he ran to his side.

She screamed as a bolt of lightning slammed down into a tree on the edge of the parking lot. The rain poured even harder, if that was possible. Thad dove inside the vehicle, slamming the door shut behind him before another bolt hit closer.

"Thad," she cried, hugging him tight.

He lifted his head and grinned down at her, his expression gleeful. Men! They thrived on danger and lived for the adrenaline rush.

He cupped her cheek and gave her a crooked smile. "You know, they say, the safest place to be in a storm is in a car."

"I find that hard to believe." She looked towards the truck stop, obscured by the deluge. "Perhaps, we should have braved the food."

"I can think of better things," he countered playfully.

One side of her mouth curved upward. "Really? Like what?"

"Climb in back and I'll show you."

She smoothed a hand over her breast, her puckered nipple poking against the silky fabric. She closed her eyes and leaned her head against the seat.

"I do not know, Warlock Pennington. That seems a breach in conduct." She circled the aroused flesh with her fingers.

"Get over it," he growled. "And that's god Pennington to you."

She shrugged. "Maybe I am an atheist."

"Maybe, I can make a believer of you." He

dragged her across the space separating them. "Or at least give you a spiritual experience you'll never forget."

"I thought that was last night. By the way, mind control? Since when can you do mind control? I do not recall bestowing that ability."

"Since forever. I was born with it."

So, he'd been keeping secrets from her. Usually, she'd consider smiting or whatever horrible thing she could turn him into. Given that she was going to become mortal, it seemed she'd have to come up with another suitable punishment for him.

She pushed against his chest, leaning away from his questing lips. Taking him by surprise, she was able to scramble back into her seat.

"What's wrong?" he asked.

"You have been keeping secrets from me."

Guilt and apprehension sped across his features, and he held up a supplicating hand.

"Jett—" he began.

"What other abilities do you have that you have not shared with me?"

Relief erased his previous look. Her critical senses surged to full alert. There was one reason for him to appear relieved by her question. He was hiding something else. Something big. If it wasn't hidden powers, then what?

She'd been teasing when she pulled from his arms, but now...she wasn't going back to his embrace until she had answers.

"I don't have any other abilities that you don't know about. Mind control, telekinesis, teleportation, all the other powers you've given me."

"I am going back inside," she announced.

"Jett...I'm sorry I didn't tell you."

But her hand was already on the door handle.

Thad reached for her as she exited the vehicle, trying to make her stay.

It happened so fast, she acted by instinct. One second she was evading Thad, the next she could think of nothing but saving his life.

Thad bellowed her name as a lightning screeched towards them—his cry more a reaction than a warning. A warning would have come too late. She'd already caught the bolt in her right hand, holding it away from his head. The power electrified her body and spiralled around her limbs. It shimmered around her like an ethereal veil. The force of the storm streamed into every tingling pore.

It enraged her already boiling fury.

"Damn you to Torment," she yelled at the sky. Her voice thundered through the storm as she hurled the bolt back to the heavens. "Damn you, Airyon! You will not win. I will not join you."

"Jett," Thad said gently, his voice almost placating.

"What!" she yelled. She took a deep breath, recognising she'd bellowed. "What?"

"Baby, get in the car." He said it as if trying to urge her away from the edge of a cliff.

She scowled at him. *She* wasn't in danger. Airyon couldn't hurt *her*. He could only piss her off. Thad was the one in danger.

"Please, Jett, get in the car. Let's go. The longer we stay here, the more chance there is of him showing up."

She wanted that slime to show up. She wanted to grind him into the dirt. He'd tried to hurt Thad!

She stared at the sky, the rain coming in sharp pinpoints against her skin. Damn Wrath. She hoped he hurried. She was sick of this game. It was time to end it. Time for her to show him who was the stronger deity. No one was killing her warlock.

"If we don't get out of here, he will find us," Thad continued, apparently sensing her inclination to battle. "I'll have to fight him. You realise that, don't you. I *will* fight him. I'll die before I let him take you."

She swung around to look at him, catching the desperate look on his face. He'd climbed across the seats. Now, he scooped her up into the vehicle before she could protest and slammed the door securely between them and the storm outside.

He pushed her damp hair from her face. "Let's go. I'll feel safer when I have you home."

She judiciously didn't mention that Airyon could easily send a tornado to flatten the house. Thad was already upset. And he wasn't stupid. He knew of the possibility.

And Airyon knew where they were. If the lightning bolt hadn't been intentional, her catching it certainly would have alerted him to their vicinity. Unless she missed her guess, and she didn't often, the storm was about to get far worse.

It didn't matter. She was done hiding. It was time to dispatch Airyon once and for all. She'd lost her temper outside the SUV. He knew she was angry now. If she knew him, and she knew him well, he'd disappear. Chasing after him would be fruitless. He was like a roach. He'd go into hiding, giving her signs of his presence without letting her see him.

She'd have to wait. And plan. It wouldn't be long. He couldn't afford to delay until the end of the Festival. He'd show himself in a final act of desperation. And when he did, she'd finish him.

"You're right," she said to Thad as a barrage of

lightning bolts sliced into the surrounding trees like the legendary fire-storm. "We should leave here. Now."

* * * *

The rain continued to fall in sheets for hours, the wind gusting around them and buffeting the SUV. Thad's shoulders ached with the tension of the constant vigilance of keeping the vehicle on the road when he could barely see through the torrent. Beside him, Jett slept exhausted from her own tension and worry. When the landscape became familiar about an hour from their destination, they'd driven out of the storm and entered another system that looked decidedly like snow clouds. In August. The temperature had dropped drastically, turning the wet pavement to ice.

Determination drove him. If he would fight Airyon, it would be on his home turf where there wasn't the possibility of innocent bystanders being caught in the battle. On the grounds of his home, he felt his power most strongly. For the first years after Jett had bestowed his gift, he'd secluded himself on the heavily wooded acres. She was far from his reach, but he sensed her most strongly there. It was only when he could no longer bear the guilt of what he'd done to his neighbour and friend Bram that he'd fled to another city. With his ability to transport he'd been able to easily come back and oversee the situation.

Much more easily than with this trip.

Jett had been right when she'd sensed that he'd released Bram from the curse that had held him in a ghostly state for two hundred years. If only the curse hadn't been the only way to save the man's life. Thad had endlessly searched for a way to help him. Still he couldn't stay at his home and endure his friend's hostility and his own blame in the curse. Worse, every visit drove home how much he wanted Jett. Every impression of her nearness had reminded him he'd never touch her. His anger had grown almost out of control. He reached out as drew the back of a finger down her cheek reminding himself he *could* touch her now. Forever.

Jett startled awake and looked around while he pulled off the main road and onto a well-kept winding drive that lead to an equally well-kept building.

"Where are we?" she asked, her brow furrowed. "Another hotel?"

He stopped the vehicle on the curved driveway in front of the sprawling three-story structure. It rose like a huge white glacier cutting across the manicured lawns. A dense backdrop of trees stood behind the house, their dark green leaves rattling in the howling wind. He cringed at the damage a snow storm would do.

As if to confirm his thought, fat snowflakes began to swirl intermittently around them. The fall immediately grew in intensity.

"My home," he told her. He glanced at Jett's sleeveless attire. Damn. He'd be willing to bet it was frigid outside.

She caught his gaze and waved away his concern. "Do not worry. I am a goddess. A little cold will not hurt me."

And he'd warm her quickly, once they were inside.

She glanced at the sky. "As Airyon rages like this he has not found us. I believe he has lost us once more."

Airyon had lost track of them and they were

momentarily safe here where Thad's power was strongest. His plan to warm her became more tangible. He had visions of Jett on the rug before a roaring fire, naked save for his shirt which he'd quickly remove from her. A snowstorm wouldn't be so bad, if one could ignore the source for long enough.

Jett looked at the hand which had caught the lightning bolt. Her fingers flexed into a fist, but not before he saw the black marks marring her skin.

"You're hurt!" he exclaimed.

"No. I'm not."

"Let me see."

"Warlock, I assure you, I am fine."

"Damn it, Jett! Give me your hand," he demanded. When she delayed, he reached across the space and drew it towards him. Gently, he pried open her fingers to see her palm.

She wasn't hurt. She yanked away and crossed her arms, burying her hand under her elbow. "I told you I was unhurt."

An injury might have been better.

"Were you going to tell me?" he asked.

Looking out the window at the storm which blurred the house, she shook her head. "It is not your worry, Warlock."

He didn't like that she'd stopped calling him Thad. He closed his eyes scrubbing away what he'd seen. Airyon had left a message on her skin.

Two days.

The meaning was clear in the pair of words. Airyon was giving her two days to come to him. Two days to make a choice. Two days before the battle where he tried to claim her.

Thad's jaw locked. He didn't believe the God of Wrath would stand by quietly waiting for her to make her decision. He'd do everything he could to make her believe she had no choice but to surrender to him.

To Torment with that. Airyon was not taking her.

"You lied to me. He knows where we are, doesn't he?" Somehow he'd have to shield her from Airyon's persuasion.

"You dare question me?" Her head tilted in an imitation of the haughty stance he'd seen for the last two hundred years.

Like hell was she going there. Without a word, he climbed from the SUV and came around to her side. Throwing open the door, he pulled her around in the seat and stepped between her legs as he yanked her against his groin. Despite the argument, his cock engorged at the position and her heady scent surrounded him. Gods! Would he ever stop wanting her with this desperation? He hoped not.

"This gives me the right to dare. Don't think you will fight him alone. I won't let you go. I won't let you face him alone."

Her face crumpled as her strength fell from her. Trembling she pressed her face into his neck. "I do not want you to die."

"Don't you understand? I'd die without you. We're in this together now."

Jett shivered as he lifted her from the vehicle. Who would be surprised? Though he would have liked her reaction to be from arousal, the snow landing on her bare shoulders was likely the cause. Hugging her close to his chest, he rushed towards the double black doors. They opened easily beneath his touch.

"Welcome home, Jett Pennington," he said as they crossed the threshold and he pushed the door shut. They weren't exactly married except in heart, but she'd taken his name. He'd legalise it with a mortal ceremony as soon as possible. He smiled. After all, they'd both be human. And safe.

She sighed and snuggled into him. "Perfect," she murmured.

Yes, it was, even if she didn't disguise the note of worry that captivated part of her senses. She couldn't truly forget Airyon or his attacks, either.

Thad hugged her closer. Airyon would not separate them. Thad wouldn't allow it. She was in his arms and his as it was always ordained to be. Wrath wouldn't destroy what Thad had finally attained.

He nudged her chin up with his and covered her lips. Her mouth opened in an invitation. He took it as a shudder shook down his frame. Her soft hands stroked over his hair. She was his benevolent goddess and she offered the reassurance she knew he needed. How much of that reassurance did she need for herself?

His tongue plunged into her mouth, claiming, demanding. With every stroke, every thrust he sought to tell her he'd stand before her. He'd fight this battle. She wouldn't face Airyon alone. A possessive growl built in his chest. She wouldn't face Wrath at all if he could help it.

Jett turned in his embrace, wrapping her arms around his shoulders and her legs around his waist. Desperation filled her hungry kiss. He cupped the back of her head and adjusting to gain deeper access to her mouth. Her mound rubbed the ridge in his trousers. Her thighs tightened as she undulated, seeking more pleasure.

He pushed his hands beneath her waistband, sliding against silk as he cupped her ass and pulled her snugly against his straining cock. She moaned in pleasure, locking her ankles behind him.

"Fuck me here," she urged as he pushed her against the door.

Within the false safety of his home, they barely heard the throat clear behind them.

Gods, he'd forgotten they weren't exactly alone. Though he hadn't been here in a lifetime, the manor was fully staffed.

Jett went stiff when she realised they were observed, but Thad refused to release her. He held her exactly where she was. He needed her scorching heat against him and her soft compliance pressed to his chest. Tension strung through her, but as she relaxed it was obvious she realised the presence wasn't Airyon. Proving it, she pushed her face into his neck while he looked over his shoulder to see who had interrupted them. His glare centred on a dark-haired man in his mid-thirties, dressed in khaki pants and a sports shirt.

He recognised Gregor from pictures. Though he wasn't formally dressed—Thad didn't require it of his servants, particularly since he was rarely in residence—this was the butler.

"Yes?" he growled.

The butler's eyes widened slightly before returning to their cool assessment. "May I ask your business?"

"No. But since you'll insist on knowing, I'm bringing my future wife home."

The man blinked. Recognition lit his gaze. "Mr. Pennington? I beg your pardon. I didn't recognise you at first." He frowned. "And you weren't expected."

Thad fought a smile at the man's censuring tone as Gregor made clear what he thought of the lack of notice. It amused him that a single man of only thirty-five could pull off the silent reproach so effectively. He'd likely learned it in buttling school.

"Exactly," Thad replied, without explanation. "Our bags are in the back of the SUV." He reached into his pocket, the back of his hand brushing Jett intimately as he withdrew the key ring. He tossed it to the man, who deftly caught it. "Please bring them inside."

"Absolutely. Is there anything else you require, sir?"

"We'll want to eat in an hour. Inform the other staff of our arrival so we aren't interrupted again. And call Bram Wingate. Ask him to join us for dinner."

"Yes, sir."

"We'll be in my chambers."

"Yes, sir." Gregor looked to Jett. "Welcome home...Miss..." he intoned, an eyebrow raising in wordless challenge. Jett lifted her head, and stiffened in Thad's arms. Her fingers clenched on his shoulders. Slowly, she slid down his body until she stood unsteadily within his embrace.

Her eyes never left the servant, her brows drawn together in question. Thad examined the man who held her gaze. Though neither said a word, he sensed silent communication winging between Gregor and Jett. His back teeth ground together at the intimate exchange. What was between her and this man?

Right that second, he didn't want to know. He wanted her alone. He needed more 'reassurance'. He almost laughed. More likely, he needed to do more claiming. Their time together before the battle was limited and her exchange with his servant made him uneasy.

He urged Jett towards the stairs which curved towards the upper level. "We'll be down later."

"All will be ready for you, sir."

Jett looked over her shoulder at the servant.

"You know him?" Thad asked, close to her ear, making it look like a caress and lovers words between them.

"No," she responded, turning back to him.

She was lying. He felt it to his core. She knew the butler. He'd never known her to lie, and this was twice in the space of minutes. It sent anger splintering through him. He nearly slammed the door as they entered his rooms.

The first time she'd lied, it was for his 'protection'. What was it about this time? Protection again? Something else? He knew it wasn't because Gregor was a former lover, unless he'd been piss poor at it and couldn't figure out what to do with his dick.

"Who is he to you?" he demanded.

She frowned not quite hiding the guilt from her deception in her eyes. What the hell didn't she want to tell him *now*?

"In truth, I have never met him."

He scowled, dragging her against him. "I don't believe you. Why are you lying to me?"

"You're being unreasonable." She shoved against his chest, but he refused to release her, even when her vibration level rose. Her hands grew hot with the power to smite him. He'd like to feel that power around his cock. Gods! It would be unbelievable.

He stared into her eyes, prepared to receive whatever she sent his way. He was confident she wouldn't smite him. This wasn't the first time the power had gathered in her hands when she'd grown angry with him. In their long history, she'd never before struck him. She knew...

"You belong to me," he ground out.

"I belong to no one."

He'd disagree with that. Later. When she was naked. Under him. Begging for him. Her thighs open and cunt weeping her sweet cream.

The heat in her hands diminished slightly. "I chose to be with you."

"Because you're mine," he insisted.

"As you are mine." She bit the underside of his jaw, trailing her tongue to his ear.

It was true. His heart belonged to her so fully that he'd never regain it. He never wanted it back. And if he wasn't inside her in about five seconds, he'd explode. Need greater than ever flooded through him, making his words and movements harsh when he wanted only to love her. It sent him flying wild and out of control. Again. He didn't understand how she made him feel this way over and over. No other woman ever had.

And still the threat lay that she'd leave him. She'd said "I chose to be with you" but what she hadn't said was that she'd chose when to leave too.

Damn Airyon. Damn him! Thad swore. Jett still thought she'd have to leave to protect him. To protect the world. Everyone but herself. She didn't want to, but she'd do what she believed needed to be done.

His only choice was to find Airyon and defeat him before the deadline he'd imposed. Thad wanted to fight the god here, but it seemed he'd have to seek him instead. He wasn't stupid. What kind of fight was there god against man, even if the man had immense powers which had been proven over the centuries and strengthened since he'd joined with Jett?

Airyon was still a god. Thad was still a mortal.

He was a mortal pledged to serve his goddess, and a lover who would protect her.

Even with his life.

Airyon wouldn't know he'd become prey until too late.

Thad closed his eyes accepting his fate. He and Jett might be separated after all. If he died...at least he'd weaken Airyon. He was confident he could delay the god's attack until the end of the Festival. It would save Jett. It would save her worlds. It must. How could they go on if their goddess was destroyed?

"Thad?"

He stared at Jett memorising her perfection. Her golden-red tresses had dried into a riot of curls after the rain and now framed her face like a wild halo. Appropriate. Worry flitted through her blue eyes. He'd been silent too long.

He drew a finger along her cheek, intrigued by the flush that followed in its path. Her creamy skin was soft as a rose petal beneath his hands. He'd never let anyone crush his flower.

Gods, he wanted her. Tonight he'd love her until she had memories to last eternities. "What do you want from me? Anything, just tell me."

She tipped her head forward. Her hair hid her eyes, but he saw the way her chin trembled then crumpled.

"Anything Jett."

She shook her head, finally looking at him again with shimmering eyes as she tried to smile. "Take away my power?"

His breath caught. Would that he could do that. Anything to ensure they'd be together. He'd remove her power in an instant if it was within his ability.

She dropped to her knees, her head bowing again.

"You are my god," she whispered.

Lightning tore across his groin, filling his cock. Now? She had to say that *now*? That was what he wanted, not what she wanted. Wasn't it?

He hesitated. "My goddess..."

"Please Thad..."

His body throbbed, desire lacing through his limbs. How could either of them go on without this? It didn't matter how wild she made him. As long as she fed the need, he didn't care how desperate he felt. He prayed she'd find someone to give her what she needed when he was gone.

His jaw locked as another sort of desperation swept over him. He knew how death worked. In an odd sort of segregation, the rewarded gods and goddesses retired to The Valley of Rest while mortal souls passed through the veil to another paradise. Gods...eternity without her.

He needed her now.

"Take off your clothes before I rip them," he growled.

Her eyes went wide as she stared up at him. She wanted him to take her power. This was the only way he knew how.

"You have no idea what you're doing to me. Take off your clothes."

She bit her bottom lip. Slowly, she reached for the back of her halter and its hidden closure. Her movements remained unrushed as if to deliberately incite him to action.

"You'd better hurry," he warned. "That's an awfully pretty outfit. I'd hate to ruin it."

She froze, her breast heaving with a shuddering breath. "I'm sure Anya would make me another."

"Je-ett!" he groaned, his agitation clear.

"Tha-ad," she returned in the same tone. There was no hurrying her. Despite her subordinate position, she seemed intent on torture, and he was her victim.

Any day, he thought. *Torture me any day. See what it gets you.*

Her hands dropped to her side without releasing the top.

"I apologise." She lifted a shoulder. "I am always trying to be in control."

"You have no control here," he asserted, his arms over his chest. He lifted a brow as he regarded her. "I suppose, I'll have to prove that to you."

He lunged for her, tugging her up into his arms. He tossed her onto the bed. Before she could respond and scramble away, he lashed her arms and legs with energy bands, splaying her spread-eagle across the bed as they were held towards the four posters. She could free herself immediately if she chose. But she chose not to. She pulled against the bindings, writhing sinuously, testing their tightness.

Her pearled nipples pressed against the filmy fabric of the halter and his mouth watered to taste her sweet treasures again.

Jett's eyes fixed on his. "Now, what are you going to do, my Warlock-god? I seem to still have all my clothes on."

He fought back a smile. Jett wasn't very good at being submissive. She was good in so many other ways. Perhaps, she'd appreciate a slow, sensuous 'punishment' that would have her screaming her pleasure for the entire household to hear.

"That won't be a problem."

He raised a hand, and her shirt split from collar to waist as if he'd drawn a blade down the delicate fabric. He used his mental power to push aside her shirt, laying her open to his sight—except for the filmy bra she wore.

Heat flared in her eyes. Her position revealed

the extent of her damp arousal while little quivers rippled across her flat stomach.

"I see we have abandoned the 'let us not use our powers and attract attention' rule."

His cock jerked as her sensual tone wrapped around it.

"Power? Do you have any idea what it did to me to see that lightning bolt hit you?"

She pulled against the restraints. "It did not hit me. I caught it. Besides, it was heading for *you*. I was saving your sorry life." She lowered her gaze and he got the feeling she stared at the way his cock shoved against his fly. "Please Thad. Let me go."

"My 'sorry life'?" he repeated, ignoring her request since he was sure she didn't mean it.

"You should be grateful to me."

Her sandals untied and went flying in opposite directions. The smacks against the walls accentuated his passion. "I would be *grateful* if I never saw lightning in your vicinity again. Stay out of trouble or I swear I'll take you over my knee."

"How medieval of you," she breathed.

She squirmed against her bonds. Evidently, the thought turned her on. Her nipples crinkled against the transparent nylon still covering them. Her hips lifted slightly from the mattress.

"I'd be happy to go medieval all over your cute ass if necessary."

Her lids lowered as she watched him. "Swear it?"

He heard the intent of her words loud and clear. *I dare you to do it.*

The temptation was almost too much. He sliced away her pants from waistband to crotch with his invisible force. Probing with his thoughts, he shifted aside the edges to stroke over her cleft.

His mouth went dry.

Panties! The remaining scraps of her pants sailed to the floor, leaving her in only an alluring gossamer thong that barely covered her curls. Nothing could top the sight of her naked flesh— except her naked flesh accepting him inside her molten folds. The sight of the goddess in lingerie was more seductive than he'd ever dreamed during his wettest dream.

He'd slide it aside while he buried his tongue in her sheath.

Gods! The thought sent more blood flowing to an area that didn't need a drop more. He was already too aroused. Much more and he'd lose it the second he touched her. She, who never wore undergarments, had put them on to provoke him. He realised that beyond a shadow of a doubt. She'd get what she wanted. He'd make love to her while she still wore them. He'd let her know exactly how much those scant pieces of lace did him in.

"Thad, release me so I can touch you," she moaned. She shifted under his stare, her hips twisting on the mattress, her breasts thrusting upward. "I am so hot for you. I need to feel you."

His hand clenched around the poster, the bed's canopy shaking slightly from the force. This was his goddess. His woman. She belonged to him, but she had no idea what it entailed. His protection, his possession, his care, his control, his cock. . .all belonged to her. She was his mate.

Please gods, let me live. Let us be together. Please hear me and help me defeat Airyon.

He sat on the bed beside Jett and drew his fingers up her thigh from the knee. Her skin was silk beneath his fingertips, her tremble a pulsation to his groin. He'd learned this torture from the best, and it was going to be good. Two hundred years of Jett's invisible touches and unfulfilled, unspoken promises had taught him well. He'd burned for her for two centuries. He wondered if she'd last twenty minutes.

A better question was, would *he*? The sweet scent of her cream beckoned to him, and an animal inside him begged to be set free on her to slake its desire. She'd tied him in knots. His clothes were too tight for his skin, painful to his over-aroused manhood.

His cock hummed with the pleasure he knew was to come. He wanted nothing more than to sink into her hot little passage and lose himself inside her. While his gaze raked over her body and he transmitted his thought to her, she writhed in tune to the desire boiling through him.

Jett's breath caught in frenzied gasps. Her thighs quivered as she attempted to draw them together, but couldn't because of her restraints. It pleased him that she didn't break the energy bands and gave herself up to that domination over her.

It was good.

He toyed with the edge of her nearly non-existent panties. It would be so easy to rip them away and his control was held by a taut thread, about to snap. It was frayed from years of waiting and though he'd had her now, it was irreparable. His control might never be mended when it came to her.

A moan tore from her lips, and she pushed towards his fingers. Her lace-encased curls brushed his hand. His palm covered her, pressing her parted folds.

She wanted him as badly as he wanted her. He knew she wouldn't be this way with another man. This was the heat that flew between the two of them alone. The realisation fired him. At what point, would he send them both up in flames? Slowly, he drew a fingertip along the crease where her leg met her womanhood.

Jett shifted and tried to make him touch more of her, but he refused. Her desire wasn't at a possessed level yet. He wanted her senses overwhelmed as they'd never been before. He wanted it clear once and for all who had ultimate mastery over her body. It was what she wanted. What she'd asked for.

Getting up, he left the bed and went to the dresser despite her protest at his departure. He grabbed a few archaic neckties and returned. She'd trusted him when she knew she could easily get free. Would she trust him if he bound her with these?

Her scent wrapped around him. He nearly fell on her before he completed his plan.

Jett's brow wrinkled in confusion. Good. He wanted to keep her off-balance. He trailed the end of one of the ties along her body until he reached her throat. Deftly, he tied the cloth over her eyes, effectively blindfolding her.

He released her hands from the energy band and bound them above her head. The position drew her shoulders together slightly and lifted her pert breasts to him, a luscious offering. He looped an end around a spindle of the headboard to hold her hands there.

"I need you," Jett whispered.

"You lied to me about Gregor," he countered. That took her by surprise. She stilled, her brow wrinkled, then she frowned, yanking on the ties.

"I do not know him! I have never met him," she exclaimed before she let loose a torrent of curses.

It wouldn't take much more for her to totally

lose her cool.

He edged the gusset of her panties between the outer walls of her vagina, teasing her with the same fabric she'd worn to provoke him. Carefully, he ran it back and forth over her flushed flesh. The plump pink lips closed around the narrow strip while he tugged to scuff it over her clit.

Her breath grew ragged. "To Torment with you Thad!"

"Now, you wouldn't really want that, would you?"

He had the feeling that if her hands and eyes were free that she'd smite him here and now. Perhaps he had her in more of a state than he'd thought.

"Let me go and I will send you there myself," she grated, confirming his notion. Good thing he'd tied her up or he'd be well on the way to the afterlife.

He gave her cunt a gentle swat. "That's not very nice, goddess. Behave." He bent and nipped at the exposed nub.

Her teeth gritted, and she lifted towards him. She had no idea how much he wanted to dive onto her. His muscles clenched in protest of his delay. His balls drew up to his body painfully tight. Razor-sharp tingles ran along his groin, threatening to spill him if he didn't hurry to get inside her.

The words. He needed the begging words from her. Her promises.

"I've barely begun," he pledged.

He crawled over her body to straddle her. Abruptly, he moulded her breasts in his hands, drawing a nipple deep into his mouth and flicking it through the nylon that still enclosed it. She cried out as his tongue curled over the stiff peak. He rasped the fabric over the nub, taunting the aroused flesh while his thumb showed equal attention to the other breast.

Jett flailed beneath him.

"Gods, Thad. Please," she wailed. Her pelvis thrust towards him in supplication. An offering to accompany her plea. To accompany the desire he'd needed to hear. His body cheered. Soon he'd be within the cradle of her soft thighs.

Reaching between them, he pushed his hand inside her thong to stoke her weeping pussy. She was so slick, so wet. Her body clenched around his finger as he slipped it inside her. His. She was his. Slowly, he added a second, thrusting deep. Her feet flattened on the mattress as she pushed into his touch. He imagined the feel of her once again milking him as he thrust inside her waiting folds.

Leaving her sweet, pawing flesh, he ripped off his shirt. Urgently, he pulled open his pants and shoved them down just far enough to free his cock. His thumb inched aside her panties while he again to thrust inside her with his fingers. Her cream flooded his hand while his penis nudged the entrance to her womb.

Slowly, he worked inside her while his fingers continued to also shove in and out of her molten channel. It was so tight, too tight for a moment before he pulled his hand free. And then it was only her inner muscles spasming on his rod. She screamed her climax almost immediately, her fingers clenching above her head. Her head tossed back and forth as she rode the waves.

Gritting his teeth against the deep pleasure of her cunt fisting around him, he continued to move, thrusting in and out as she bowed beneath him. "Thad," she cried. "Gods, Thad. Don't stop. Oh, don't stop. Thad!"

"Oh yeah. Oh goddess," he groaned against her

shoulder. His fingers twisted in the thin straps of her thong, dragging her up to his erection, pulling her up to him and moving her away. "Yes," he gasped. "Drain me."

Relentlessly, he pumped into her. Perspiration coated her body as her voice grew hoarse from her cries. Still, she writhed and begged and clenched for more.

His muscles strained as he pummelled into her, his arms burning. He reached up and grabbed her bound hands. In a blinding flash of light, energy leapt around them, rushing around their bodies. Sensations merged. He felt what she felt and she felt what he did.

Jett screamed as her release tumbled over them. He wanted to go on and drive her to more climaxes, bring her more pleasure. He needed to remain one with her forever. His body rebelled. His cock took over surging against the vice holding him. He relinquished his hold on the moment, pouring into her body.

Thad dropped his head to her shoulder. She'd given him power, but he'd lost half of himself within her. He'd fight the heavens to keep her by his side where she belonged. No one, Airyon, his minions, even Jett, would remove her from his life. As they collapsed in a tangle of limbs, he knew forever more she was completely his. She had to be. She'd stolen his soul.

The only question was whether or not he'd be around to reclaim it.

* * * *

Replete from their love-making, Jett lay sprawled on the bed while Thad dressed. She couldn't muster the energy to move. Even her brain seemed lulled. Gods the things Thad did to her. The world could go spinning off its axis and she'd be unable to lift a finger to fix it.

She yawned and burrowed into the pillows, dragging the comforter over herself to ward off the chill which was invading the house.

"Hey."

She turned her head slightly to look at Thad as the mattress depressed under his weight. How could he look so disgustingly chipper? He stroked his fingers over her cheek, sliding them into her hair as he leaned over her.

"You need to wake up," he murmured against her mouth.

"Why? Come back to bed." She wrapped her arms around his neck. Thad wouldn't let himself be so easily distracted. Groaning against temptation, he braced his arms on either side of her shoulders.

"We have company coming, baby." He nipped her bottom lip, then soothed it with his tongue. "Don't you want to badger me some more about releasing Bram from the curse?"

"No."

He tugged the blanket down to her waist before she could stop him. Goosebumps erupted along her arms. She yelped as he palmed her breast. Gods she'd known it was cold in here, but his hands were like slabs of ice.

Heedless of her squirming beneath his touch he continued to lavish attention on her mouth. All the while, he tormented her tight nipples, roughing them as he dragged his fingers back and forth over them. She bowed into him. More. She needed more of the sweet agony of his icy hands over her overheated skin. She needed his body heavy between her legs again, shoving in and out in dizzying rhythm.

Energy licked across her skin drawing her nerves taut. Her thighs parted.

Thad, damn him, didn't accept her silent invitation. He carefully kept his body free of hers though he did move to kneel over her. His hand slipped behind her head. Hungrily, he plundered her mouth with sharp stabs of his tongue each plunge more and more demanding.

With a small cry, she lifted into him. Heat gathered in her middle.

She closed her lips around his tongue, drawing out the sweet taste of him. Thad growled, his head angling over hers. Jett sighed, sliding her tongue along his while his mouth grew more urgent.

Any moment he'd shove aside the blanket and bury himself inside her. Moisture seeped from her cleft. The need was so sharp! Her head swam from it. She had to have him inside her.

"Get dressed."

Her eyes fluttered open, her mouth bereft from his absence. "What? Thad!"

He headed for the door. "Meet me downstairs."

Anger sliced through her. How dare he arouse her then walk away? How dare he!

"Thad!" she protested as the door closed, her fingers vibrating with power. Her hand drew back of its own volition and a blinding blue starburst lit the room.

To Torment with him!

She glared at the charring on his pristine white wall. Angrily she flipped the blanket aside. *Bastard!* If he hadn't burrowed himself into her being she'd definitely smite him. She could only hope this passion remained with them the rest of their days. She couldn't help but believe that it would. Her desire for him ran too primal for it not to be forever. Though a mortal, it was as if he'd been made exactly for her.

Her feet sank into the white plush carpet as she slid from the bed. White. Always white. What was with Thad? She'd have to question him regarding that when she joined him. She'd have to question him about several things.

Irritation made her movements jerky as she stomped to the closet and threw open the doors. Empty. A moment later, the drawers yielded no clothes she could wear, either. She had a problem unless she used her powers. Well, Thad had a problem, anyway. She glanced in the mirror, an assessing gaze taking in her firm breasts, smooth skin and the thatch of red-blonde hair at her vagina. She didn't mind being naked. He might object if she strutted into the dining room without a stitch on.

Another thread of irritation added to the shroud weaving within her. Since when did she care if Thad objected to her actions.

Too long, if she admitted the truth to herself. So, she *did* have a dilemma. Their bags hadn't been brought to the room, and Thad had destroyed her garments. What was a goddess supposed to do? Wear a sheet downstairs? That would appear awfully goddesslike. The staff ought to enjoy that.

Unless someone remembered to bring up her things, she'd have to improvise with Thad's clothes. A knock sounded on the door as she considered her options.

A handmaiden. The vibration was unmistakable. Just as Gregor's had been. He was an acolyte, the male version of a handmaiden. Whoever placed the acolyte and the maidens here had put them here to assist and protect her. Jett didn't doubt it was the Higher Power.

Why was she surprised? The Power knew everything. It didn't surprise her that her dilemma had been predicted. Still, she was startled when she opened the door.

"Anya!" she exclaimed at the sight of the beautiful jean-clad woman. "What are you doing here?"

"I've brought your bag, goddess." She laughed. "No doubt you need them after Warlock Pennington finished with the others you wore. I am here to assist you in whatever need you require. The Higher Power assigned me to your aid when the god I served before you ceased to need my service. Should you enter civilisation, I was to see you were cared for. My apologies, goddess, but the instructions for my current duties were delayed by the Festival. I did not know you'd arrived." She sighed sadly. "I feel I have failed you since I did not even realise you'd come here until Gregor contacted me."

"You have not failed."

It all made sense. Though she'd never required one here, there was always a handmaiden nearby for any desire a deity might have. In the upheaval of her flight from Airyon it was a comfort to have something of her home.

"Who did you serve before me?" she asked. She knew all the gods who had retired to their great reward in the last millennium. All had gifted their handmaidens and acolytes with the opportunity to retire with them as well.

Anya's head bowed but not before Jett witnessed the stark agony that entered her eyes. "Master Bannor."

Bannor. A similar pain pierced Jett. Bannor had been her mentor until betrayal had sent him to Torment for crimes he did not commit. Of course, he did not bring his servants with him.

"All of you served him?"

"All but Gregor. He…" The side of Anya's mouth lifted in a half smile she could quite hide. "He used to serve your sister."

Serve Nara? Jett could only guess—and probably correctly—what that had entailed. Before she could further question her, Anya gave a slight bow followed by a knowing wink, then left the room.

Jett shoved her hair back from her eyes and looked around. The house was filled with beings who'd served the gods for years. No wonder she felt a strange vibration around her whenever she moved. An odd sense of power. She'd noticed it at once when she'd arrived but had put it down to being in Thad's true home—the apartment was more of a hiding place.

Her evolved senses prodded at her. Was there something more?

Closing her eyes, she dropped into a meditative state and sent mental feelers through the house. The strange energy came from the east side of the mansion. Accompanying that were vibrations from several immortal beings—definitely handmaidens and an acolyte—and certainly nothing ominous. She'd be well protected here. If Airyon arrived with his minions she'd have a contingent to aid her, as well. From the energy, she deciphered, Thad's home was currently staffed by five handmaidens and Gregor.

Jett scowled, wanting to smite something. As a goddess, she shouldn't be the last to know things. She didn't like being undermined, even if was by the Higher Power and for her protection.

It didn't do any good to dwell on it. She'd only

get angry. The Higher Power sending people into her territories, Airyon stalking her, Thad ordering her around...!

Men.

Throwing open a suitcase, she hastily chose a green wrap dress, with a voluminous skirt that fell to mid-calf and a back that was fairly non-existent. Idly, she wondered if there were more of the scandalous panties in her luggage. She hadn't thoroughly examined the contents when she'd gotten clothes earlier at the truck stop. Moving around the garments she found there were plenty of the scraps of lace.

Thad would like that.

She fingered a pair. They were white and nearly transparent. They would do. Hastily she stepped into the panties, enjoying the silky slide of fabric up her skin before it settled snug against her cleft. They'd been designed to arouse, both her and her mate.

Perhaps dinner wouldn't be long and she could bring Thad up here again. This time she'd tie him to the bed. Her mouth watered at the prospect of taking his warm, pulsing cock between her lips and tasting him until he exploded onto her tongue.

Gods! She'd rather that be her meal.

All thoughts of pleasure froze as she turned to inspect the spindles of the headboard and ice splintered through her veins. A scroll lay nestled in the rumpled blankets on the bed. A scroll that didn't belong on earth.

The roach was making his presence known.

With shaking hands, she slowly unrolled the missive to reveal its crimson words.

Chapter Eleven

A clip fell from the scroll and bounced on the floor at Jett's feet. Thad's. She'd taken it from him the day she'd run. It had her blood on it mingled with a few strands of his white-blond hair. Instantly, she knew how Airyon had finally tracked them. The combined vibrations of the two.

He couldn't have found the clip right away or he would have been there sooner.

Her gaze dropped to the scroll. The meagre words emblazoned on it struck apprehension through her soul.

I'M COMING FOR YOU BUT FIRST FEEL MY WRATH BEFORE I COLLECT WHAT IS MINE.
ENJOY YOUR WARLOCK...UNTIL I KILL HIM.

Jett's stomach knotted, doubling her over with the pain. The scroll dropped from her fingers and incinerated it before it hit the carpet. The cinders disappeared.

Damn Airyon to Torment!

And gods, what did "feel my wrath" mean? What did he plan?

Urgently, she collected herself and tore through the house to Thad's side. She had to be with him. She'd sense Airyon's arrival, but the flash of a moment it took to get to Thad and protect him might be too long to save his life.

She tracked his energy through the unfamiliar maze of rooms and found him waiting in a spacious sitting room, devoid of colour. Carefully, more carefully than ever, she masked her worries as entered. Thad couldn't know of this latest intrusion by Airyon. He'd insist on hiding her, confronting Airyon or some other fool-hardy action that would get him killed. His insistence that he could face Airyon made this so much worse. How could Thad not know that the god could turn him to dust if he wanted?

Her muscles trembled as she walked and she was thankful the long dress disguised the way her legs wobbled. She'd never felt so terrified. Was this what love did? Created out-of-control protective feelings for another person? She knew it didn't but she couldn't lessen her fierce emotions.

Her feet tapped on the hardwood, announcing her approach, until she stepped onto the thick-piled rug within the circle of furniture where Thad sat in one of the deep chairs. He rose to greet her while she assessed the room as a potential battleground. It was like being caught in some odd indoor snowstorm. There were plenty of 'snow banks to duck behind if needs be.

What was it with him and the lack of colour?

"White!" she complained, indicating the room and its puffy white furniture with her hand. Discussing his obsession with the achromatic was a good distraction—not that anything could keep her from her vigilance against attack.

"Thad," she continued. "You are the most

boring man ever. This place needs colour to liven it up!"

He grabbed her around the waist, his voice an ominous growl in her ear. "Boring? I'll give you boring."

She shoved his chest as her body tightened at his scent enveloping her. She ducked out of his embrace. "Stop! You will not start again what you did not finish. I should smite you for that." She thought of the mark on the wall upstairs and looked away. "Your homes? Everything is white."

"Our homes," he corrected, and a warm sensation crept into her chest. This was why she'd let him take control when he'd demanded it. Belonging to him. Peace filled her at the prospect of being with him always. Thad was like the shadow they created in the room's artificial light. His shadow seemed to envelop hers, just like his dominance over her. In truth, it united with hers. They were united. Blended together.

Thad looped his arms lightly around her waist and this time she didn't pull away. His mouth opened against her neck, nipping the skin while he pressed to her back, a burning wall of man. Tingles zipped through her, shooting to her core. His touch was sent from the heavens.

"You can decorate however you like, now that you're with me. I've always insisted on white because it reminded me of you."

"Of me?" she asked, slightly insulted. Did he think she was boring?

"Perfect. Unstained."

Oh! Golden threads of pleasure worked through her. How could she argue with that sentiment? "You won't mind if I add colour here and there?"

He shook his head. "I've learned that you're not the untouchable perfection I'd always imagined.

You're bold and daring. Fiery. You're not at all similar to the cold this white also personifies. Some added colour would far better suit you. And us."

She liked that word 'us'.

They had to get through only a day and a half more before 'us' could become a permanent reality. She was determined it would happen. Airyon still waited just beyond sight. She didn't fool herself into believing she wouldn't have to fight him. But she would defeat him. She wouldn't allow him to harm Thad.

"You're worrying," Thad observed.

She lifted a shoulder and dropped it. "A bit. Airyon is still out there waiting to attack."

His arms tightened. "I'd never let him or anyone take you. You're mine," he grated against her throat, his harsh tone betraying his strong emotions. With him pressed so tightly to her back as he clasped her to him, it wasn't hard to imagine what his ferocity would be when he repeated those words in bed. Her cleft tightened as she responded to his possession.

It didn't mesh well with her irritation over his earlier desertion. She hadn't completely cooled from their last encounter and now he was stoking the fire higher. Arousal, ire and worry made a lethal mix of agitation inside her. She could only hope nothing more stirred the roiling cauldron in her middle or innocents would get hurt in the resulting explosion.

"Sir," Gregor interrupted, seeming blasé about finding his goddess with her warlock's face buried against her neck. "The Wingates have arrived."

Thad's groan was hot on her skin. He took a deep breath and collected himself. Little could be done about the ridge pressing her backside. He stepped slightly away. "Very well. Show them in."

Relief flooded Jett. The distraction of his friends might calm her taut emotions.

"Bram Wingate?" she asked. "Is that not the man you cursed?"

"To save his life."

"And he is speaking to you?"

Thad shrugged. "I saved his life. We were supposed to meet a few weeks ago but the earthquakes in the west and an eruption near Hawaii prevented it. This will be the first time I've seen Zora and Bram since the curse has been lifted."

The entrance of a raven-haired woman and a powerful dark-haired man similar in stature to Thad halted further conversation. The man made a beeline for them. Before Jett could intervene or Thad could react, the man's fist ploughed into Thad's face and he flew backward into the couch, blood streaming from his nose.

Weeks may have passed, but Bram Wingate was still enraged. Who could blame him? He'd been cursed for two hundred years. Jett stepped between the adversaries before Bram could strike again or Thad retaliated.

"Stop!" she commanded.

"Jett, move," Thad growled. "If the ungrateful bastard wants to fight, I'll be more than happy to comply."

"Ma'am, step aside. Believe me when I tell you he deserves every blow I'll land on his pretty face."

Jett ignored Thad and focused on Bram. Airyon wasn't the only one she wouldn't allow to hurt her man. "I know you are upset—"

"*Upset?*" Bram thundered. "He tried to sleep with my wife to prove she truly loved me."

Her brows drew together, the dizzying logic painting an ugly picture. Bram's rage was for a completely different reason than she'd expected to hear as well. Thad had tried to sleep with Zora? Jett was tempted to move aside and let Bram pummel her warlock. She glared at Thad over her shoulder while still holding Bram at bay. Temporarily.

"You did *what*?" she demanded as Thad rose. He'd stopped bleeding with inhuman speed. Obviously more hidden abilities. His transgressions just kept building...

He swiped blood from his face with his sleeve.

"I never actually planned to do it," he explained. "Bram makes a habit of falling for women who don't really love him. She needed to prove she valued him over everything in order to break the curse."

Zora grabbed Bram's arm as he lunged for Thad again. "You promised you wouldn't attack him," she said.

"Zora—"

"It broke the curse didn't it?" she asked.

He gave a long-suffering sigh that reminded Jett so much of Thad she might have thought they were brothers if she didn't know better.

Thad stepped around her, moving back into Bram's reach—both a brave and foolhardy move in her opinion. "I've only ever wanted what was best for you," he told his friend. "All those years ago, I couldn't bear for you to die because of some bitch's unfaithfulness."

Bram's simmer seemed to lower a few notches, though he wasn't free of anger by any stretch of imagination. His dark eyes flashed with barely leashed fury.

"You were my closest friend," Thad continued. "How could I let you die, when I could prevent it?"

"Thad was cursed, as well," Jett supplied. "He was pledged to serve me and I did not let him escape punishment for his breach of conduct. He was supposed to let you die."

"Thank goodness, he disobeyed then." Zora hugged Bram tight, and he wrapped his arms around her. His lips pressed to her temple. A faint arrow of jealousy pierced Jett's heavy heart. The couple looked so right and content with each other. She hoped to know them better, someday, when she became mortal and the nastiness with Airyon was in the past. Until then she couldn't afford any close ties. Airyon's note made it clear that every moment others spent in her presence put them in danger.

She'd find a way to get them to leave immediately, but Thad needed this reconciliation. She needed to see why he'd let the curse be broken—with his *obvious* assistance.

Thad pulled her against his side, evidently needing the contact as he also witnessed the deep love between the two. He pressed his lips to her hair. "Thanks for stopping him before he beat me to a pulp. In truth, I wouldn't have stopped him. I deserve his anger."

"We will talk on that later, Warlock Pennington," she promised. He wasn't beyond her recrimination by any means.

"I expected we would." He got the same look he always did whenever he spouted his I-am-your-god speech. It wouldn't serve him well now.

Turning, she raised on tiptoes and pressed her lips to his ear. "If you ever touch another woman, I will see you gelded." With a quick swipe of her hand, she removed the blood from his face and shirt, demonstrating her power for effect.

"You needn't worry," he replied. "You're in my

veins. You own all of me, whether you like it or not."

"Perhaps I should attempt to sleep with your woman," Bram threatened.

"Over my dead body!" Zora exclaimed at the same time Thad grated, "Touch her and I *will* kill you."

Jett felt Wrath's presence near the room's entry a moment before he spoke.

"So much death..." he laughed. His smarmy amusement clouded the room as his black eyes danced. He appeared like an angel of death in the mortal-wrought black suit he wore, his hair in a modern business-like cut. It didn't hide what he was. Not the angel of death, but a servant of Torment.

"Perhaps, I can assist," he offered.

She shoved Thad behind her as she aimed a thunderbolt for Airyon. It came a moment too late. Wrath's smite flew at Zora, and she fell dead to the ground before Jett could prevent it.

Wrath laughed, dodging her bolt by disappearing. *It's only going to get worse*, he taunted, whispering into her thoughts. *I'll take them one by one until you come to me. Feel my wrath.*

Agony shot through her as the emotions of the mortals assailed her.

"Zora!" Bram's anguished wail ripped Jett's heart. He caught his wife up into his arms.

My fault. This is my fault. This perfect love ended because she'd selfishly run from Airyon. How many more would die because she'd chosen not to supplicate Wrath?

She experienced every drop of Bram's pain. Her eyes burned as she fought to remain stoic and complete the task ahead of her. This action drew an indelible line between her and Airyon. He was daring her to cross it.

She knew she would. She had no choice. Even if Airyon's next target was not Thad, she couldn't allow him to attack any innocent in his quest to obtain her.

"Jett?" Thad asked urgently. "Can you bring her back, like you brought back the guard?"

"I will try." This felt different. With the guard, she'd never doubted she could bring him back. She'd sensed his spirit near-by waiting. Zora's should be nearby too, but Jett couldn't detect it. It was as if she'd been snatched away to prevent Jett reuniting her with the body.

Tears flowed down Bram's face, his grief fully encompassing him.

"You have to save her," Thad insisted. "We can't do this to him. He's been through too much already."

"*We* did not do this," she protested. She'd done this. Guilt formed knots in her stomach as she knelt across from Bram. "Lay her on the floor," she instructed.

"She can bring Zora back," Thad told Bram when he refused.

Slowly, Bram complied. Thad knelt across from Jett as he had with the guard and took her trembling hand. She focused inward, meditating on bringing the woman back. This had to work. She didn't think she could bear the guilt if it didn't.

Lazy bands of energy spiralled down her arms, starting in her heart, and circling her hands joined with Thad's. The bands sparked, their power building as she entreated Zora to return to her body.

She fought to focus. The realisation she might

never have forever with Thad sunk through her like a fiery sword of destruction. Before, when Airyon hid from them, she'd allowed her belief in the illusion of forever. It was not to be. She'd always wage this battle between the lives of her people and oppression by rogue gods such as Airyon. He was not the first and he would not be the last. History always repeated.

Thad squeezed her fingers. She wondered if he felt her veering thoughts. They'd become one unit. He was part of her, a part that would always be separated when she left him. A part she would never recover. Somewhere along the line, they'd become so entwined it seemed she'd split her power with him and she'd joined with him to reach full potential.

It was all her misguided fantasy of obtaining the desire that had always lain beyond her reach.

Tremors churned across her skin as their combined powers fully enveloped them.

Jett sucked in deep, rolling breaths as she stared at Thad, focused on him, focused on Zora. He blurred from her sight as she willed the woman back to the body. Slowly, their hands moved to the char mark on Zora's forehead. It disappeared.

"Reenter your temple," she whispered.

"Soul and body rejoin," Thad intoned.

"Return," they said in unison.

Jett pressed their joined hands over Zora's heart.

Zora should have jolted back into her body, breath re-entering her lungs as if the wind had only temporarily been knocked out of her. Nothing happened. She remained ashen and still. Her sightless eyes stared into the ceiling.

Dread filled Jett. Her sister Nara, keeper of the veil between life and death, had stolen Zora away. Jett would have to confront her to retrieve the spirit.

A nearly insurmountable task, unless Nara chose to be willing.

Jett glanced towards Bram where he'd sunk to his haunches against the wall a few feet away. Sorrow disfigured his features as he realised death had parted him from his one true and irreplaceable love.

Insurmountable or not, she had to try.

She released Thad's hands and rose. He also stood.

"It didn't work," he said in disbelief.

She shook her head. "I must go."

"Jett, no!"

She'd already turned to vapour and sought another realm. Thad's distressed cry echoed along her residual energy trail.

The howl could have been her own.

Chapter Twelve

Jett was gone. Thad sank to the ground in disbelief. A split second and she was gone.

I'll be back. The words whispered through his mind, but gave little comfort. He worried for her when she wasn't at his side. Airyon's display of power showed exactly how much danger she was in. She might be strong, but if Wrath took her by surprise, she might not be able to fight him.

Airyon wouldn't kill her as he had Zora. He didn't want Jett dead. Thad wasn't sure if it was even possible for Airyon, a lesser god, to kill her. But could he keep her captive? That was essentially what he wanted, wasn't it? To hold Jett against her will and bend her to his bidding. Airyon wanted her power only to double his. He didn't care for the woman at all.

He was the exact opposite of Thad. Thad cared for Jett's power only to the extent it protected her. She was the centre of all his cares. Not the universe. Not some power struggle. Not death.

To him she was only Jett. A woman. *His* woman. And he wanted her back.

He glanced at Zora's lifeless body, understanding fully why Jett had departed. She had something more important to see to. Truth be told, he'd never have tried to dissuade her from it—he would merely have tried to convince her to take him with her. Who knew what she'd face wherever she'd gone? He didn't want her to face it alone.

Returning Zora's soul was the top priority right now. He smoothed his hand over her eyelids to close them. Gingerly, he gathered her into his arms to move her somewhere more comfortable—though how much comfort did she truly need? She was dead.

Moving her was something to do, and in the midst of mourning, he needed to activity.

"No!" Bram bellowed. "Give her to me."

"I was only taking her to the couch."

"I'll take her."

Thad acknowledged he'd be the same way if it were Jett instead of Zora on the floor. Ice ploughed through his limbs with unimaginable pain. He wouldn't survive Jett's death.

That wasn't happening. He'd be the one to face Airyon first.

With great care, he transferred Zora into her husband's arms. Bram sank onto the couch, his wife hugged to his chest. Undisguised despair ravaged his features. Slowly, he took deep breaths as he attempted to control the emotion overtaking him.

He's stronger than I would be, Thad mused.

"Where did she go?" Bram asked, stroking his thumb over Zora's chalky-white cheek. Instinctively, Thad knew his friend referred to Jett, not his wife's soul. He sank into the wing chair opposite Bram, ready to pour out the entire story to distract the man. Wearily, he leaned forward, his arms resting on his legs while his hands dangled between his knees. He looked at them blindly before he met Bram's tormented eyes.

"I suspect she's gone to plead for Zora's return. There's no other reason she'd leave." Except to fight Airyon. He prayed that had not been her purpose.

"How can she?" Bram asked.

"She's a goddess. The one who gave me my powers."

"And you want to marry her."

Thad stared at him for a long moment. "It's that obvious?"

Bram pressed his lips to Zora's hair, absently smoothing it from her face, before he pierced Thad with a look he'd thought never to see again. "How long have we been friends?"

Thad didn't answer. His happiness at the silent declaration of reconciliation was dampened by the tragedy between them. He nodded at Zora. "She'll be okay. Jett will fix this."

"She has to."

Thad wasn't sure if Bram meant Zora had to be all right, or that Jett had to fix the situation. Either way, both statements were true. And the same.

He prayed Airyon didn't find Jett before she'd completed her task and returned to his side. While he was at it, he added his hope that the god of wrath would implode into cosmic dust.

* * * *

"Nara!" Jett bellowed as she appeared before the veil separating life from death. Before her rose an endless wall of black while equally endless plains of nothingness stretched behind and beside her. A short distance away, Nara, keeper of the veil, rested, surrounded by attendants. She lay on a chaise, one acolyte fanning her while another fed her grapes, and still another massaged her outstretched leg. Her eyes widened slightly at the sight of Jett's anger, and she waved away her men.

"Yes, dear sister? What brings you to my humble domain?" she greeted. "Are you lost?"

"Do not feign ignorance." Nara's casual attitude towards her responsibilities and the rules of their positions irked Jett. She would not play games to placate her sister's childish nature.

Sitting, Nara gave Jett a smug, knowing smile. "Why sister, I do believe you've changed." She tapped her nose. "What could it be? Your hair? No, just as long and uninspired as usual. Your clothes?" She eyed the toga that Jett had automatically donned when she'd transported. "Still as gauche as always."

"Nara, I do not have time for your amusements—"

"Oh, *I* know!" She clapped her hands. "You've finally given it up."

"Nara—"

"Who's the lucky guy?"

"You need to return the woman."

Nara examined her crimson-lacquered nails. "What woman? I have a lot of women come though here."

"You know the one I mean. You stole her away before I could return her to her body," Jett grated.

All pretence of playfulness left her sister's demeanour. She crossed her arms and her eyes narrowed. "Stole? *Stole!* She was *dead*, which means; She. Belongs. To. *Me*. Just like the man belonged to me before *you* stole him."

"Neither of them was supposed to die. You

know that as well as I do."

Nara materialised a mirror and examined her intricately braided hair. "Dead is dead. The dead belong to me."

"Not those that should not be dead." Jett snatched a scroll from the air. "Zora Wingate. Age twenty-eight. Destined...*destined*...age at death, ninety-three. She still has sixty-five years left on earth. Give her back."

"No. You know I am allowed to keep those who come to me by accidental death."

"This was not an accident. Airyon killed her on purpose. None of those he kills are intended for the veil."

Nara laughed, setting her mirror aside in mid-air where it disappeared. She reclined back on her chaise while Jett fought the temptation to strangle away her sister's smug look.

The goddess of the veil pulled another scroll from the air and unrolled it. She tapped a fingernail against her lips while she read the document she rested on her upraised knees, one gold-sandaled foot tapping.

"This could be messy," she finally commented. "Airyon's been smiting left and right. By your standards, you could have a host of not-supposed-to-be-dead people returning to their bodies. Who's going to sort out that mess? I frankly don't have time."

"And you are *so* busy," Jett interrupted sarcastically.

"Do you think it's easy to keep souls from trying to return to their loved ones? To keep said loved ones from breaching the veil to contact the ones who've passed on. To keep track of everyone who dies...or as you're trying to convince me, haven't died."

"Just give her back. The longer you delay, the harder it will be to reinstate her to her body."

Nara lifted a shoulder. "I care."

Jett glared at her. "I will take it before the Higher Power."

"When? The Festival doesn't end for over a day. It will be too late by then."

Jett closed her eyes and took a deep breath before pinning her sister with a glare. Nara had always been self-centred and difficult and this ordeal was no exception. Jett would have to bargain with her sister. A nearly impossible task.

"What do you want?" she asked.

Her sister rose and paced to the wall where a shimmering orb had appeared. Quickly, she pulled it from the air and turned it over in her hands examining it. Satisfied with the spirit's condition, she opened a rift in the wall with her fingernail, shoved the soul through and magically closed the tear. Turning she regarded Jett, her eyes twinkling while she smirked.

"I *could* use a new acolyte."

Nara wanted Thad.

"No," Jett answered firmly. "He's mine."

The Goddess of the Veil laughed. "It's good to hear you fierce about something. I thought it might never happen." She spun in a circle. Slowing, she pierced Jett with her sharp perusal. "I want Wrath. Airyon. Right here under my thumb. He's caused quite enough problems for me, and I'd like to revisit a few on him."

"Done," Jett agreed, her promise etched in gold across a scroll that appeared in Nara's hand. She'd kill him at the first chance, anyway. Why not send him to Nara instead of to Torment? "Give me back the woman."

"Fine, but I keep the child."

"What child?"

"The child the woman carried."

Airyon had taken not one but two lives. Rage built in her core. He would not get away with this. "You must give back the child, too," she insisted.

Her sister's eyes softened in understanding. Still she shook her head. "You know I cannot return an unborn infant."

"I will fully form the child. Give back the soul. I will take care of the rest."

Nara gave a long-suffering sigh. "Very well. If you do not follow through and give me Airyon, know that I will never cooperate with you again."

"Airyon is yours."

"By my trust," Nara murmured. She flicked her hand and the veil parted. Two golden balls of light emerged, the veil snapping closed behind them. She pointed to the slower shimmering essence. "You. Back to your body."

Envisioning, Zora and Bram's vibrations, Jett held out her hands to form the infant. A moment later, a beautiful but completely still child rested in her palms, the perfect dark-haired combination of his mother and father.

"Are you ready?" Nara asked her.

"Yes."

"You know he will have great healing abilities. Powers greater than most mortals can dream."

Jett nodded. "Such is the way with children who have crossed the veil. I will be his guide."

"You," Nara said, pointing at the remaining orb. "Into your body. Live well so that your days might end in Paradise, not Torment."

The soul leapt into the child, who immediately started squirming, arms and legs flailing. Jett raised him to her shoulder, patting his back.

"Be well, child," she murmured her own

blessing. Holding him tightly, she turned them to vapour and returned to Thad and Bram.

She stood to the side of the room as Bram hugged Zora. His shoulders shook as he pressed his face to her neck. Tears streamed down Zora's face as she murmured platitudes and endearments.

Thad saw Jett immediately. He leapt to his feet and rushed to her. "You did it," he breathed. He hugged her, careful of the fragile gift she held in her arms.

"Yes." It was all she could say as she stared at the joyous couple. The baby squirmed for attention.

"Who's this little guy?" Thad asked.

"Theirs. You can't return an unborn child." Leaving his embrace, she crossed to the couple. "You should go to your home before Airyon returns. It will be safer."

"Thank you," Bram said. "Thank you. How can I thank you enough?"

She placed the baby in Zora's arms. "Raise him well," she answered. "And name Thad his godfather. The child will have great power. He will need someone to train him."

They looked down at the baby. "How?" Zora asked.

"You were with child," Jett replied. "But an unborn child cannot return to the womb. He is yours as he would be had the pregnancy gone full duration."

Bram stroked his thumb along the baby's cheek. "Ours," he murmured. "Oh, Zora."

Thad pulled Jett towards him so that her back pressed to his chest. "I can't wait to make our child with you," he whispered in her ear. "Children, actually. I'd like several."

She crossed her arms over his, loving the

weight of his embrace around her middle. She could imagine her body rounded with his child. The thought made something jump in her middle. Yes, she'd like to have his child.

It saddened her that they'd likely never have the opportunity. Too great a battle lay between now and happiness. Too much responsibility rested on her shoulders.

His tongued swirled along the shell of her ear. "Want to practice tonight?" he asked, his hand dragging along her hip, unnoticed by their guests who were enthralled with their child.

"Always." she replied. She could forget her earlier irritation, though they would still discuss his role and method in the curse breaking.

She wiggled her bottom against his erection. It was good that it took so little to arouse him. He'd be like granite before she finished with him tonight. Her hand insinuated between their bodies to mould the substantial ridge straining against his trousers. With a content sigh, she scraped her nails over him, before she traced the shape of the head with her thumb.

"Dangerous territory, Jett," he warned.

She smiled. "I like this kind of danger." Still, she removed her hand and stepped slightly from him, staying in front of him to mask his evident arousal.

"Please," she said to Zora and Bram. "You must go. I do not want anything to happen to you. In another day, this will all be over and you will be safe here."

Bram glanced at Thad while he cradled the child to his shoulder. He seemed completely at ease with fatherhood, though less than five minutes into it.

"Thanks for inviting us into danger," he

said tone full of both amusement and ire. His emotions ran so strong, they flooded through Jett. Joy to have his wife and son. Love. Relief to be reunited with his friend. Anger at the danger, yet excitement, too.

She understood. She'd been overwhelmed with strains of the same emotions since she'd united with Thad.

"He didn't know. We thought we were safe here," she continued quickly.

Bram handed the baby to Zora and rose. "What's the danger?" He looked back to Thad. "How can I help you?"

"You can't. You saw what he did to Zora." Thad clasped his comrade's arm in friendship. "Take your family home. I will visit soon. I have missed you, friend."

Bram gave a single nod. "And I you." He made a face. "And I never thought I would."

Jett crouched beside Zora while the men spoke. "You should nurse him soon," she said, nodding towards the babe. "Your milk will come quickly, and he will be hungry."

"I don't understand how this is possible." Zora smoothed her child's downy hair. "After what I went through with Bram, though, anything seems possible. I don't question much anymore, I just go with it."

"You mean with the curse?"

"Yes, and breaking the curse. Thad had me naked beneath him, fully believing I was sacrificing myself by having sex with him, all for the benefit of releasing Bram from the curse."

Jett raised an eyebrow, jealous anger making her words precisely even. All of the ire she'd suppressed came flooding back. "Exactly what was he doing?"

"Besides pressing his cock to my vagina? Bram goes a little crazy whenever he remembers Thad touching me."

Jett glanced up at where the men still talked, unaware of the female conversation. "That hardly seems like it was necessary."

"According to Thad, it was completely necessary. I had to prove my love for Bram. Show how far I'd go to save him."

Thad had a lot of explaining to do.

"But he didn't actually. . ." she trailed off and Zora shook her head.

"No, I don't know how...but, in the end it was all Bram." She patted Jett's knee. "He may have pushed the limits, but I don't believe it was ever his intention to actually have sex with me. It was all a test."

"Ready to go?" Bram asked. He held out his hand to his wife.

Jett looked up to see both men standing over them. From the look on Thad's face, she knew he'd heard part of the conversation. If was he was smart, he'd also know he was about three seconds from a smiting. She could see him shuffling explanations in his head while Bram and Zora prepared to leave.

As if she'd believe any of them. How would he feel in Bram's situation? Did he have any concept of the torment he'd caused?

Anya entered, interrupting her thoughts to announce dinner.

"Please see that the meal is delivered to the Wingate's home," Thad told her.

"That's not necessary," Zora protested.

"It is. We invited you to dinner and now you must leave. And you have a new baby to care for. It's the least I can do for you," Thad assured her.

"Anya," Jett said, drawing the handmaiden's attention.

"Yes, goddess?"

"After you've seen to the meal, please come to my chamber. I desire your assistance."

The woman smiled, fully understanding Jett's meaning from the explanation the goddess had sent to her telepathically. Thankfully, handmaidens were well versed in what the goddess required.

Thad was in for a surprise. Hopefully, he'd learn something from it. She couldn't allow him to abuse his abilities.

"Shall we go upstairs?" Jett asked as soon as the couple had departed.

Thad nodded warily. Perhaps, she'd been a little too cheerful.

"We need to discuss your curse-breaking methods," she added.

"What Zora said is true. I never intended to fuck her. I told you before, you're the only one I've wanted."

"What you want and what you do can be two completely different matters," she argued. What she was about to do, would prove that without a shadow of a doubt.

As they entered the room, Thad began to unfasten the green gown that she'd donned again when she'd returned from her confrontation with Nara. His hands slipped inside to cup her high, firm breasts.

A knock on the door came almost immediately and he groaned. "Servants..."

"This one is following my order, remember?" she said as she disengaged from him, but not before he gave her nipples a pinch that sent arousal flooding her cleft and regret flooding through the rest of her. She did not like disciplining those pledged to her. She preferred the role she'd taken with Thad the past few days. Unfortunately, submitting to a mortal was problematic for a goddess.

She crossed to the door to let Anya inside.

"What do you need her for?" Thad asked, obviously grumpy from the interruption. Jett smiled serenely. She didn't answer. Instead, she opened the door.

The handmaiden had changed into a flowing blue robe that tied at the waist. She loosened the tie as she entered.

"What's this about?" Thad demanded.

"Exactly how far are you willing to go to prove you want me?" She indicated to Anya who let her robe drop. It fell to the floor along with Thad's jaw.

"She's here so you can fuck her," Jett told him. She drew her fingers along Anya's breast and the handmaiden's eyes closed slightly. She breathed unevenly as Jett raised her vibration slightly and began to thumb a pert pink nipple.

She led Anya to the sitting room couch and urged her to sit, reclining slightly against the armrest. Jett disrobed and knelt next to the equally naked woman. Leaning forward, she took a peak into her mouth while she moulded the corresponding supple flesh with her other hand. A thrill marched through her at the feel of Anya's soft flesh pressing up into her own chest. It was so different from the feel of Thad's solid chest. The handmaiden's soft abdomen cushioned where his hard stomach did not.

Thad sputtered a few feet away. "What is this about, Jett?" he demanded.

She eyed him over the breast she licked, the scent of vanilla filling her senses. Anya moaned, her head dropping back.

"What do you think it's about?" Jett asked. She moved so that she sat behind Anya, cradling the girl between her legs. The handmaiden's thighs parted to give Thad an enticing view. It was impossible to miss her arousal, particularly when Jett skimmed her fingertips through the girl's raven nether curls and parted the creamy flesh there. She made small circles over the maid's clit while Anya cried out her pleasure. "She's wants you to touch her, Thad."

His hands thrust into his pockets as he obviously held himself back. He backed against the wall. "She doesn't want me. She never really has."

"This shouldn't be so hard, Thad. You've fucked her before."

"That was before you."

Jett shrugged even though his words burned through her. She wanted to cry for the emotion he roused in her.

Goddesses do not cry, she reminded herself.

"The acolytes and handmaidens exist to fulfil the god's and goddess' needs. I required this of her, and she's ready to fulfil my desire. She wants to fulfil my desire. And she wants you." Anya's thoughts opened to her. "She always has, on some level."

The handmaiden was a highly sexual creature. Excitement reeled through her at the prospect of participating in this activity. It was good. Jett would never force her servant to fuck anyone if she did not desire it.

Thad licked his bottom lip, swallowing hard as he watched her fingers play over Anya's cleft. His cock pulsed against the fabric straining to contain it.

"Just tell her what you want of her. You have

my permission. For this. I won't smite you," she continued, hoping her words were true. "I'm giving her to you. What do you want?"

His head tilted as he regarded her. He obviously didn't quite believe her assurance.

"What are you up to?"

She smiled. "What do you want?"

"I want you to kneel before me and take me into your mouth."

"No. This is between you an Anya. What do you want from her?"

He stared at the handmaiden, his eyes slightly glazed. A flash of disappointment shook Jett, but didn't sidetrack her resolve. He was a mortal male after all. What did she expect? That he wouldn't be aroused by a naked woman writhing with pleasure? She'd chosen her course of action. She had to go through with the punishment.

Why did she feel more punished?

"Jett, don't..." he pleaded.

At Jett's silent command, Anya was off the couch before Thad finished speaking. Kneeling naked at his feet, she worked the button at the mouth of his jeans, slowly lowering the zipper. His cock burst out of his slightly lowered pants. Anya quickly caught him in her small hand. Her fingers didn't meet as she pulled them up from root to head of his staff.

Jett's thighs quivered and dropped farther apart as she remembered how well he filled and stretched her. How she wished she could send Anya away and let him possess her again. Pain built in her middle, as her over-aroused body demanded him.

She couldn't. Hoping to relieve some of the tension screaming within her, she skimmed her fingers over her belly to splay them over her weeping cleft. Her breath wobbled from her. She needed to fuck him. She wasn't cut out to dole out this sort of punishment. She could barely withstand seeing the other woman touch him.

Through half-lidded eyes, she watched Anya take him deep in her mouth, her cheeks hollowing as she milked him with her lips. She bobbed, working forward and back on his member. A strangled groan wrenched from Thad. His eyes closed at the pleasure he experienced, his hand cupping the back of Anya's head. His other palm flattened on the wall. Jett lashed it there with an energy band much like he had captured her earlier. With her mind, she gently moved his other hand to a similar position. A band circled it and his middle, holding him securely to the wall.

Thad's eyes flew open. "What are you doing?" he demanded.

She slipped a finger inside her folds, arching, a sigh parting her lips. "What does it look like?" she asked.

"Let me go so I can touch you."

She shook her head though she wanted to do as he wished. "Enjoy Anya."

The maid ran her hands over his legs and torso. She temporarily abandoned his cock to push away his pants then pulled his shirt from him, aided by Jett's magic. Her nails dragged over his small nipples, raking down to the thin trail of hair that led to his manhood. He grunted when she sucked him into her mouth again, his hips thrusting forward.

His lips parted slightly, his hips working his shaft in and out of Anya's mouth. Jett waited until he was fully engrossed before she continued his punishment.

"Come for her," she whispered to Thad. "Prove

how devoted you are to me by coming. Do you want to fuck her?" she asked. "Do you want to bury yourself deep inside her?"

Thad's head rocked back and forth against the wall as he was torn between his pleasure and her words. "Only you," he rasped. "Release me and I'll prove it."

"But that's not what I asked you to prove. You must prove your devotion to me to break the bands holding you." Now, he knew what Zora must have felt.

Holding his gaze, she spread her arousal along her folds, then brought her fingers to her lips, licking them off. Desire burned in Thad's eyes. Desire that had nothing to do with the handmaiden sucking him. His fingers flexed. He wanted her.

Good. She watched him as the door opened and the other nude servant she'd beckoned entered the room. Gregor didn't pause as he crossed directly to Jett.

"No," Thad bellowed. And now he understood Bram's pain. It was untenable what Thad had done to Bram to break the curse. It was her duty as his goddess to show him exactly why.

Gregor knelt between her thighs spreading them further apart. His fingers dug into her legs as he held her captive. He pulled her forward so that she rested at the very edge of the cushions, her legs draped over his arms as he clasped her ass.

"No! Get away from her!" Thad bellowed.

Ignoring his command, the acolyte pressed his mouth to her mound, lapping her arousal. His lips wrapped her clit, nipping at it, dragging her close to climax. The sweetest agony rocked through Jett, her hips lifting from the couch as he stabbed his tongue into her.

"Jett, no," Thad begged. Through a haze of pleasure, she watched his face contort. He barely seemed to notice Anya still licking his member as his hips moved unconsciously against her. Anya gripped his thighs as she pressed in. The energy of her aching desire threaded around Jett, lifting the goddess to new heights of pleasure.

"She wants you to take her," Jett moaned as Gregor worked her closer to orgasm. Her inner muscles pawed at his tongue and fingers, wanting more. Anxiously, she slid her hands over her torso, lifting her breasts in her palms. Her nipples were like small marbles rolled beneath her fingers.

"Do you desire me enough to fuck her?" she gasped around the tremors raking her cleft.

"Make him leave," he demanded.

Gregor rose over her, replacing her hands on her breasts with his. He nuzzled her neck, while his body wedged between her legs. The weight of his substantial cock pressed over her pussy.

"He seems quite agitated, goddess."

"Shut up," she whispered, taking his mouth. She thrust her tongue against his as she writhed beneath his hands, wishing he could be Thad. Wishing it was her Warlock who held her pinned to the couch. Despite the carnal pleasure Gregor roused in her, she never wanted to do this again.

In her mind's eye she saw Anya rise and try to kiss Thad, but he turned his face away, staring at Jett. He had a stronger hold over himself than she'd imagined. His chest heaved with the battle he fought.

Before he was not a man humbled by his punishment and brought to his knees by the knowledge of the wrong he'd done. Anger turned his features to stone as his determined stare pinned her full of fury and possession.

"Anya come to us," Jett commanded. "You may join us if he will not show you proper attention."

The handmaiden rushed to Jett's side. While Gregor, kissed a fiery path between Jett's breasts she pulled Anya towards her mouth.

"You've done well," she said quietly. "You'll have fun with Gregor later."

The girl gave her an impish grin. Jett trailed her fingers over the maid's stomach to work them into the woman's drenched folds. Anya thrust against her hand.

"Yes, goddess," she moaned, then pressed her lips to Jett's. Jett sucked her sweet tongue into her mouth, arching into the four hands that stroked over her, caressing, pinching, delving, moulding. *This* was the life on which Nara regularly expounded. Empty pleasure filled her only to gouge away a section of her soul. She could take all the two offered, yet not be whole without the one who truly filled her.

Jett pressed on to remember her main purpose as sensations washed over her pushing her towards a heart-fracturing climax. *Oh. Yes...Thad...His punishment.*

She released the energy bands that held him to the wall. He stumbled for a moment before darting towards them. Immediately, he crashed into the invisible wall she'd erected. She almost felt guilty as he was shoved backward by the energy. Almost. Anger at what he'd done to Zora and Bram still licked at her. Carefully, she sorted jealousy from punishment. Jealousy could only shred them both.

Gregor dipped his tongue into her navel and nipped her belly. Anya's small passage convulsed around her fingers as she cried climax into Jett's mouth. Jett continued thrusting into the damp heat, willing the orgasm to continue. Anya bowed under the magical enhancement.

"Oh goddess, oh goddess!" she cried as Jett pulled her mouth away. Gregor moved up Jett's body pressing his cock into her mouth. She sucked eagerly, glad he was a bit smaller than Thad as he thrust enthusiastically into her mouth. He captured Anya's breast in his mouth, transforming them into a writhing three-headed beast.

Thad clawed at the wall. Jett feigned at ignoring him as she milked Gregor's wide cock, using a little more magic to enhance the man's pleasure and make it possible for him to become hard again as soon as he came. And he would come.

Her tongue pressed the vein on the underside of his arousal as she worked up and down him, alternately moulding him with her tongue and raking him lightly with her teeth. His fingers speared into her hair, fisting as he drove deep to her throat.

"Jett, no!" Thad begged, his hands pummelling the invisible wall. "I'm sorry. I was wrong."

At the moment, she believed he'd say whatever was necessary to get her to stop. Anya screamed as she sank into another orgasm, her nails scrapping Jett's belly as she flew out of control. Jett added extra pressure to Gregor's cock to send him to flight with Anya. Immediately, he cried out, exploding down her throat in gelatinous pulsing spurts.

She swallowed convulsively, trying to take it all. He pulled from her lips, softened for a moment before he swelled once again.

"No," Thad moaned.

He pressed to the wall watching Jett give and receive pleasure, dreading the moment Gregor would leave her mouth and shove into her cunt. Thad swore. His. She was his. The servant would take what belonged to him, piercing his soul for all eternity.

Despair filled him as desperation clawed down his spine. Jett was his and he couldn't breach the wall she'd erected. He had to get to her. He had to make her stop. This is what he'd done to Bram. He was sorry, oh gods, he was sorry. He hadn't realised what it was like to have the woman he loved ready to take another man into her supple, welcoming body.

Just three feet from him, Gregor pulled from Jett's mouth and moved between her thighs, completely hard, though he'd just come. His arousal prodded at her opening, seeking to entrance.

"No!" Thad thundered, panic slamming him as he threw his body against the wall. The acolyte and handmaiden disappeared as he shoved through, coming down on Jett like a man possessed. He didn't give her time to react as he dragged up her hips and ploughed into her drenched channel, pistoning hard without giving her time to adjust.

"Mine!" he bellowed out of control.

He'd lost any finesse, any façade of gentleness, as he raged over her, storming her fortresses, a man gone mad. His stronghold had been threatened and now he reassured himself it remained his.

Her inner muscles clawed at him as he drove forward, and she shattered in his arms. He bent over her, sheltering her body, claiming her mouth as glass exploded around them and climax after climax wracked her body, bowing her beneath him. She trembled out of control while she sobbed his name.

"Mine!" he cried, a mantra of possession as he

kept moving, too far gone to slow now. His release tore across his body, seeming to rip his groin in two with its violence as he came.

He continued to pump forward, his life draining into Jett as he slowed. He buried his face in her throat as they both calmed.

"Don't *ever* do that again," he grated as his soft member pulled from her slack body. She hugged him close. Softly, she stroked his damp hair and made light trails down his back with her fingertips.

"I never wanted it to be anyone but you," she replied.

He raised up on his elbows and his emotions still far from controlled.

"Promise me Jett. Don't let another to touch you. Man *or* woman."

"Unless you're there to control their minds? Or it suits your purpose?" she asked her brow raising. He wanted to throttle her or fuck her until she couldn't think. She had no right to punish him. She had even less right to let another touch her. She belonged to him. Didn't she get that?

The anger seething through him wouldn't easily recede. Scowling he climbed to his feet, shoving back a groan at her flushed, sweat-covered body sprawled on the couch. Faint bruises showed on her hips where he'd held her too tightly. He closed his eyes to shut out the vision. He had to get away and clear his head before he surrendered to his emotions and pounded into her again.

On resistant legs, he turned away. He might as well shunt his aggression towards Airyon. The way he felt right now, he'd incinerate the god.

Behind him, he heard Jett sit as he yanked on his pants, but he refused to look at her.

"Where are you going?" she called after him.

"My office. I have work to do," he bit out.

"Thad..."

"Get some sleep. I'll be back soon." He opened the door, turning for a moment when an afterthought shot through him. "And stay the hell away from the servants."

Chapter Thirteen

YOU CAN'T SAVE THEM ALL.
AND WHEN I CLAIM YOU,
YOU WON'T BE ABLE TO SAVE HIM,
EITHER.

Jett stared at the scroll that had been in her hand when she'd woken just before midnight. Her skin crawled to know Airyon had been so close to her and she hadn't sensed him. Obviously, he meant to play with her. He could have easily whisked her away without anyone knowing until it was too late.

Her brow furrowed as she scowled at the missive. What in Torment did Airyon mean? She was certain he knew she'd returned Zora to her body. Apparently, he'd decided he'd kill Thad whether she surrendered to his demands or not.

Airyon could decide that all he wanted. She'd protect Thad with her life, if need be, and Wrath would get nothing.

She spread out her awareness, searching for Thad's vibration. Though he'd said he would, he hadn't returned to the room last night. She'd spent the night alone in the huge bed that dominated the sleeping area. She quickly found his presence where it had been since he'd left her. The far corner of the house. Frankly, she was surprised he hadn't retreated to his cave. She got the feeling though that he didn't want to leave her alone.

His energy still stewed, though he'd settled into a more sedate rhythm now.

Plagued by her own worries, she'd kept a constant vigil throughout the night. She had less than fifteen hours until the time Airyon had designated for her to come to him. In that time, he might do anything to sway her.

He wouldn't succeed, but she needed to remain ready for battle. As her awareness had sharpened, alert for anything, the energy she'd noticed when they'd first arrived, disturbed her. It wasn't ominous and certainly didn't emanate from Airyon or any of his minions. Still, it unsettled her.

She glanced out the window at the snow flurries. The energy was something other than the unseasonable weather here. The earth was unbalanced. Its distressed cries flooded her as it experienced whatever magic Airyon cast over it. She had to stop him. From the vibrations coming to her, she wasn't sure her people or the earth could take even fifteen hours more of his abuse. She could only hope the other planets under her control were not subject to his attacks. She thought not since his intent was to seek her, but she couldn't be sure.

Short of returning to the godly plane, there was little she could do to discover his actions. That was the most unsafe place for her to be. Airyon was strongest there, while she was strongest here within the Zodiac Quadrant—her holdings were her places of power. She was a goddess in the Zodiac Quadrant. On the divine plane she was ordinary and one of the lower echelons of deities.

While there were tiers of gods lesser than her, she didn't possess any power close to that of the inner circle of the higher gods known as the Council. Airyon ranked so close to her he could use his cunning to outwit her and she'd be his prisoner.

Going to Nara to retrieve Zora's soul had been dangerous. Had he realised what she'd done, he could have grabbed her then. It had been the last thing from her mind. Now it had to remain the first thing. Under Airyon's control, she'd be unable to protect her people...the handmaidens and acolytes...or even her warlocks. Especially her warlocks, and especially Thad. She didn't doubt from Airyon's message that Thad was a target.

He fingers clenched. She couldn't afford to wait for Airyon to visit again. She'd need to call him out. If he didn't appear, she'd need to go to him. It was a deadly option, but one she'd have to face.

Girded for battle in the white robes signifying her station, she padded barefoot down the hall and searched for Thad. The garment was a message. Enough was enough. She would confront Airyon and end this.

She didn't doubt Thad would attempt to stop her. All his protective emotions for her would fly into action when he learned her intentions. He'd try to stop her. As much as she'd like to comply, she couldn't. She was the Goddess and this was her duty.

The peculiar energy that had nagged at her amplified as she approached the eastern side of the house. What on earth had happened there? It was as if her power radiated to that area, directly from the heavenly plane.

Her brow wrinkled. What magic had Thad wrought?

A cacophony of sound barraged her as she

neared his hiding place. She entered the room to find Thad sitting in a swivelling chair, a circle of moving pictures surrounding him. There had to be twenty of varying sizes.

When he saw her, he quickly masked his horrified look and lifted his hand. He pushed a button on the small black device nestled in his palm. Immediate silence rang loudly around them. The pictures disappeared, leaving behind blank shiny boxes.

"What were you doing?" she asked, making a sweeping gesture at the curved wall before him. It reminded her of some sort of primitive viewing room. The gods had similar but more advanced technology.

"Nothing," he replied.

She pressed her lips together at his lie. Her foot tapped on the thick white carpet. "I thought we were far beyond untruths."

"I meant, it's nothing for you to worry about." Which meant she probably should. His eyes narrowed on her goddess garb. Slowly, he placed the control device on the surface of his desk and stood. Studying her, he circled his work area to stand before her.

It struck her how different their relationship was now. Mere days ago, he wouldn't have stood inches from her and stared directly into her gaze. She wanted this forever.

"Why are you wearing that?" he demanded.

"The time has grown short. I must confront Airyon before he destroys the earth."

"How do you—"

"Know?" she interrupted. "The earth's pain calls to me. My people suffer while I hide. I cannot hide any longer."

"Jett, no. They'll suffer more if Airyon—" He

broke off.

"Kills me?"

"If he hurts you," he finished. She sensed there was far more behind 'hurt' that he didn't say. She knew the consequences of defeat at Wrath's hands.

Thad slid his arms loosely around her waist. "I don't want anything to happen to you."

"I have to stop him."

"I know, baby, I know." Dropping to his knees, he caught her hand and bowed his head over it. She bit her lip as he pressed his mouth to her palm. "Jett, I need you to do something for me." He paused, his forehead resting on the inside of her wrist. "I need you to stay until I get back."

"Back? Where are you going?"

"I have tasks I must see to in my quadrant. I must retrieve some of my work from my apartment in New York. Just wait for me. An hour. Please." He stood and kissed her gently, lingering on her lips as he urged them apart to taste her mouth. A melting sensation trickled through Jett as he pressed her to his chest. "Promise me. Please. We'll come up with a plan."

Jett sighed into his mouth. She could wait an hour.

He pulled back. Silently, he gazed into her eyes, stroking his thumbs along her cheeks. "I'll see to my tasks and return quickly. By my guess, the Festival ends tonight, doesn't it?"

"Yes."

He pulled her to him, pressing her hips to his. "How long will it be before you're mortal?"

Jett smiled. He was avoiding the treachery that still lay before them, an obstacle they might not survive. She wasn't surprised by his evasion. The frail human mind couldn't withstand the sustained pressure.

She nipped the underside of his jaw. She'd like to dodge what was to come, as well, but knew she couldn't. "Soon. At the longest, a few weeks."

His eyes darkened, possessively. "You'll finally be completely mine, and I won't have to share you with the rest of the worlds. You'll be safe."

"Soon," she whispered.

* * * *

Thad's absence, the threat of Airyon, the deity-mortal problem and their solution warred inside Jett, all of it chafing like mismatched shoes. Nothing was sinking into its proper place, even the prospect of forever with Thad. Perhaps it was because she doubted that their forever would ever happen, but something wasn't right.

Restlessly, she'd roamed the house, mulling their situation in her head and planning her attack on Airyon. There was little she could do but take him unaware. Her footsteps seemed to whisper surrender as she wandered from room to room. That was an untenable solution. She'd sooner destroy her holdings herself. At least she could make her people's death merciful. Wrath would not.

Her fingers trailed the wall as she pondered. A tingle shivered up her arm and she paused. Without looking around she knew she'd wandered to the eastern side of the house. Here, a now familiar power radiated into her senses.

This was her fifth pass and the fifth time she'd been electrified by the energy.

Of course! How could I be so stupid?

Thad's cave stood on the eastern portion of his land. He regenerated there. In the beginning, he'd hidden there. There was power there. How could she have forgotten? Ignoring the cold, she dashed outside. Immediately footwear appeared around her feet. She barely noticed as she strode towards his cave.

She wasn't certain where the entrance lay. The one time she'd been there before, she'd locked onto Thad's vibration. It drew her to him.

She sighed. Had she been on earth so long that she'd humanised? Hardly. Goddesses did not need doorways. Closing her eyes, she transported inside. The magic didn't matter. Airyon knew exactly where she was and probably exactly what she was doing. It wasn't difficult to visualise the glee filling him at her agitation. It was merely a matter of time before he returned for her.

She wouldn't go without a fight. One could only poke an animal for so long before it bit. She wouldn't be mindless in her attack, but by the gods, she would bite Airyon and destroy him.

Power flared through her as she materialised inside the cave, the unexpected surge driving her to her knees. A natural energy geyser. It stroked into her as powerfully as Thad's cock. Yes, oh yes the power. It infiltrated her cells and galvanised her abilities weakened by the drag of the earth's atmosphere. Glorying in it, she arched, letting it fill her.

Her unprepared womb tightened in reaction. The delicate muscles rippled while her cream flowed around the power driven into her through her core. Stronger and stronger it grew until her cries filled the cavern. Her skin glowed with golden rays, illuminating the dark.

Raising her hands, she splayed her fingers. Wave after wave of release shattered through her, exploding from her fingertips. It raced into the walls of the cave, shooting out to spread the earth with her healing power.

She collapsed, her cheek pressed to the cold stone floor. The healing hadn't been enough to counteract the evil Airyon wrought on her people, but it would heal much of the damage.

Her hand flattened to the earth. How had she been so stupid? How had she not known? It was no coincidence Thad had made this his hiding place, the place where he rejuvenated and honed his craft.

While she rested and readied herself to heal again, invisible tendrils of power wafted up her arm and curled about her. Mentally probing the floor she found the energy that radiated into the house and had disturbed her since her arrival. Four ley lines intersected here and formed a knot of sorts. Anyone pledged to her could draw from its power. It would protect them—even from the God of Wrath.

She could draw from it. This was her essence in one of its purest forms. Earth energy. Direct from the mother of earth. Herself.

* * * *

Thad perched atop the torch of the Statue of Liberty, and surveyed the incoming storm. The location was the perfect vantage point. The only better place would be the top of the Empire State Building—but the observation deck there would be teeming with people this time of day. Even with the oncoming storm, people wanted to see the terrible majesty of nature.

A category five hurricane headed for New York City, and the city was in a state of pandemonium. Hordes of tourists and residents rushed to evacuate the city before the force hit dead on by the end of the day. Too many would be trapped when the tempest pummelled the city.

His long hair whipped around him, lashing his skin in the gale force winds that threatened to topple him from his perch. He struggled to remain upright, magically anchoring himself so he didn't fall into the white capped waves engulfing the base of the statue. Hands held before him, he tried to redirect the storm. His muscles screamed from the effort, but he couldn't rest.

If he could manage to send the storm on a southern trajectory, landfall would come where cities were better prepared. It would downgrade to nothing more than a tropical storm before hitting.

He'd controlled the weather more times than he could count—usually wielding it not repelling. He could stop this storm with a little effort.

Doggedly, he pushed against the swirling winds with all his energy. His teeth gritted against the effort. He'd never encountered a storm so stubborn. But, then, he'd never encountered a storm powered by Airyon. Never giving up, he shoved a wall of counter-energy against the front. The waves grew silent while the hurricane slowed. Lethargically, it turned, brooding as it headed south.

Satisfied with his success, Thad let the wall drop. The storm snapped back like a stretched rubber band. It's fury stronger than before.

That had never happened before!

Someone was deliberately guiding the storm. Someone stronger than he. A hurricane striking New York would devastate the city and reshape the landscape to unrecognisable formations.

He had to stop it. The reshaping would kill

millions. Thad refused to give up. If he didn't succeed, he'd have to alert Jett. She'd threaten to smite him for keeping this from her and he'd endure her anger for days. Or longer. If Airyon levelled New York and killed millions, her anger would know no end. Nor would her grief.

Digging deep within himself, he searched for the same power he'd shared with Jett to resurrect the guard. It would take the same force here.

I am a god, he thought. *You will obey me. The elements bow to me.*

Pulsing energy flew from his palms, the streams nearly visible as they rushed towards the storm and pierced the walls of pressurised air. Clouds scattered momentarily to let through bright blue sky. A moment later, they slammed back together with a resounding slap of thunder.

You will stop!

A second set of energy streams poured from his hands, commanding nature. He would stop the destruction!

He didn't notice the huge bird diving towards him until it was upon him. Lifting one hand, he directed a blue beam of power at the vulture. *A vulture? In New York City?*

The bird continued towards him, unaffected by the bolt he'd shot. His brow furrowed. How could it? Even the storm bowed to the authority emanating from him.

Airyon. Wrath had transformed.

The grey and black bird suited the rogue god, but didn't give Thad pause. He slashed at it with razor sharp swords of air. Airyon didn't slow, though blood poured from his wounds.

The vulture changed its angle, its talons clawing the air as they aimed for Thad. He aimed another sword of air between the bird's feet, up beneath its breastbone. Screeching it reared away before attacking from another angle.

Thad was unable to stop it as razor sharp talons tore across his neck, shoulder and chest. Blood gushed down his body. He frantically tried to heal himself while the bird wheeled around to make another assault. The scavenger was Airyon. If he could kill or disable him now, Jett would be safe.

Angrily, he abandoned the air manipulation he'd used to work the hurricane and turned to a stronger element. His most powerful. A barrage of fireballs raced towards the vulture. The powerful blast sent the bird off-course, but didn't deter it for long, though its feathers continued to smoulder. Screaming its displeasure, it darted towards Thad.

He dodged, nearly falling from his perch, despite the magical anchor. This wasn't going as well as he'd hoped but at least it seemed that in this form Airyon was unable to smite him.

Quickly, he sent a wall of flame at the vulture. It dodged beneath it and barrelled into Thad. Claws ripped across his abdomen. Suddenly, Airyon transformed. He hung in midair a few feet away, his face full of rage. Wrath. Raising his hand, he hurled a lightening bolt—*a smiting bolt*—at Thad.

Instinctively, Thad shot up his hands to ward off the attack. Airyon's energy ricocheted without harming him as it knocked him off balance. His arms flailed and he toppled backward. A smack resounded through the air as he crashed onto the narrow ridge at the base of the torch.

Immediately, Airyon loomed over him.

"What did she ever see in you, mortal?" He laughed with evil triumph and raised his arm. Another bolt glowed in his fist.

Thad dodged.

Airyon's bolt hit the spot where he'd lain, disintegrating the narrow shelf. The floor fell away beneath him, careening to the cement platform beneath the statue. He plummeted with the raining pieces of torch.

Death was certain. He'd avoided smiting only to be broken by the fall and washed away by the raging ocean.

His soul howled as he flailed to slow his fall and gain any handhold. He'd failed mankind. He'd failed Jett.

He'd be separated from his goddess forever.

The God of Wrath soared after him, his intent clear. Killing Thad. Wrath was not content with this death. He wanted it completely at his hands.

In the mere seconds he had, Thad sent another barrage of fire at Airyon, gratified that the man grimaced in pain as the attack hit its mark.

Closing his eyes, Thad visualised himself home.

He was dying and he couldn't heal himself. He prayed he could at least say goodbye to Jett before he died. One last kiss of farewell to last an eternity.

A moment later, he slammed into the ground, and his pain disappeared along with his consciousness.

* * * *

"My goddess, we must ask why you haven't helped us?"

Jett studied the three warlocks across from her, careful to keep her face from revealing her thoughts. She searched for a reply to the Southeastern Warlock's question. Storms of massive proportions were wreaking havoc on the delicate balance of the earth? "I didn't know" hardly seemed like an appropriate response. She'd sensed unrest. The natural disasters should have spoken to her.

She couldn't admit she'd been distracted and lose what little faith remained in her people. Airyon was destroying her holdings and devastating her people. In the last day, he'd flown out of control. He was a frenzied god desperate to have her under his control by any way he could obtain the power.

Thad knew.

The way he'd hurried her from the truck stop. The way he'd stared in horror at the viewing screens and shut them off to keep her from seeing them. His lie. He'd lied to her. His irresponsibility to her people stunned her. How could he let so many people die? The very reason she'd run from Airyon was to protect her people. By hiding the truth from her, Thad was killing them just as surely as Wrath killed them.

And where was her Warlock now? He'd claimed to have business to oversee. Was he trying to correct the imbalance by himself? Damn him. Damn him! He thought to protect her from her duty.

With certainty, she knew he planned to take her place before Airyon. It was a sacrifice he'd happily accept.

Then he'd come after her.

Anger surged through her. How dare Thad! He went too far. He wanted her to stay with him, but this was too much. Despite their future plans, she was still his goddess. He was her pledge. He knew it was her responsibility to monitor world events, particularly natural phenomena. He knew she wouldn't let storms and weather abnormalities run rampant like this.

He knew she would not accept the threat to his life or this wildly foolish sacrifice.

When he returned, she'd strip him of power. His disregard for the fragile lives in his care and in the care of the other warlocks proved that he wasn't worthy of the position she'd given him.

Her heart ripped when she realised, she couldn't join her life with his either. She couldn't become a quiet mate who deferred to him in all matters and let him hunt and forage for her, so to speak. She'd had control of her life and watched over the lives of those throughout the Zodiac Quadrant since her creation—far less than the million years that Thad had attributed to her, but still long enough that it was deeply ingrained. It was as much a part of her as her flesh. She couldn't separate herself from it, even for Thad.

She'd see to the problems Airyon had precipitated around the world, and then deal with Thad's deceit. Rebalancing the earth would be simple in comparison to what she had to do to him. If the three warlocks didn't still kneel before her, she might have burst into ungoddesslike tears at the pain that tore at her chest. A silent cry strangled in her throat.

How could she hurt him?

Divine justice required she see him punished, but the thought sent despair trembling over her. She had no choice. By all laws, Thad deserved to be smote and sent to Torment for his extreme disobedience. It was to her discretion. What he'd done was beyond tolerance.

She would not condemn him to Torment. He'd have her eternal separation instead. It was the only other option in the narrow band of the law.

Her hands shook slightly as she regarded her

pledges. She crossed her arms over her chest to keep her reaction secret and regarded them each with displeasure. It was misdirected. She didn't feel any ire for the three men who brought the news—just complete irritation at the man who was supposed to be committed to her.

He'd betrayed her trust at the first opportunity.

Thad, why did you do this to us? Her fingers tapped on her upper arms. Carefully, she kept her anger from her tone. "Warlock Pennington is even now attempting to overcome the disturbances in his territories. You should do the same in your own."

"Yes, goddess," they replied as one, right hands fisted over their hearts, heads bowed.

"I am resolving this issue on a different level, unseen by mortal eyes. These problems are not earth-based but will soon cease."

She didn't mention the Festival. It wasn't necessary that they knew of the regeneration or that Thad protected her from the God of Wrath. They need only know that she had things under control.

Or to think she did.

Each of the men had already given her a report on the activities in their territories. It was catastrophic. Animals rampaging, natural disasters of all sorts, people in panic.

Despite her anger, she suddenly needed Thad with an intensity that surprised her. She needed his arms around her, lending her strength. It was laughable, a goddess needing strength from a mortal, especially a mortal who'd betrayed her. When had she come to depend on him?

A century or so ago...

She'd always held him in different regard than

the other warlocks in her allegiance. She'd rarely thought of them outside of the tasks they were assigned. Not so with Thad. He'd plagued her thoughts and dreams for longer than she could remember.

How could she put him away from her? She would have to suffer through whatever pain resulted from their separation and hope that she healed in time. Perhaps the Higher Power would wipe memories of Thad from her mind.

She thrust away the thought. She didn't want to forget, no matter how painful. Though things had not turned out, and she would not become mortal and live with him as his wife, her time with him had been special. She never wanted to forget despite how it ended.

She wouldn't forget. A millennium from now, images of him would still haunt her. She longed to forget this new information and go through with their plans. She too would be punished if she turned a blind eye to this transgression. More so, how could she trust him after his blatant disregard for her people?

A loud hiss echoed through the room, the sound of space being ripped asunder as a traveller transported into their presence. Thad had returned.

She turned her angry gaze to the shadow forming before her.

Thad.

He materialised sluggishly, alerting her to his dangerously low energy. Despite her anger, concern took over. Concern quickly transformed to alarm.

As Thad transported, he hovered a moment in a shimmering transitional plane, not quite there, not quite where he'd been. If he could not breach this plane he'd be forever trapped between states. Possibly in horrific pain.

"Jett..." he whispered.

Gods no!

Panic filled her. Latching onto his waning vibration, she lent her energy to draw him. Suddenly, he appeared fully in her presence. He floated in mid-air, his limbs hanging limply towards the ground. His pasty skin blued as he neared death.

A breath later, he slammed onto the white carpet with a dull thud, his arms and legs twisted into unnatural positions. Blood oozed from his body so profusely she couldn't tell where he was hurt, where the blood came from.

She dropped to her knees beside him, her hands stroking his aura as she tried to assess his damage. Intense pain wrapped her, an empathic shadow of what he suffered.

Airyon's mark radiated from him. Airyon had done this.

As she experienced Wrath's attack raking along her skin through the cellular memory Thad projected, terror tore through Jett. Thad had weathered the attack and escaped with his life.

For how long?

Intellectually, she'd known Airyon might target Thad. She'd hoped he wouldn't—that Thad might escape his notice and stay peripheral to her battle to retain power. He'd ended up dead centre instead. She hadn't protected him.

She glanced up at the horrified warlocks. "Leave us, and go with care. We are under attack."

Without watching them depart, she turned her full attention back to her lover, unwilling to answer questions or worries. Time didn't allow. His vibration faded even as shock settled over her. She wouldn't let him die. Not like this, not because of her. Her previous anger was shoved aside. It would wait until he was healed.

"Why did you do this?" she whispered. "Millions could have died."

"Ten times...more than that...if he gets you," Thad answered with much effort.

Oh gods. He hadn't been as self-serving as she'd thought. He'd visualised the greater good. He was wise, while she played the fool.

Thad hadn't betrayed her trust in him.

Her anger dissipated leaving only desperation.

Closing her eyes, she held her hands over his torso, focusing on the wounds of his upper body. So much pain. So much damage.

A fine mist rose from him, visible only to her godly eyes.

"No!" she sobbed, clutching at it. "No! I forbid you to leave."

Hastily, she murmured an incantation, panic filling her as he slipped through her fingers.

Chapter Fourteen

Thad's body was too damaged to contain his spirit. He couldn't remain on the earthly plane without a vessel. Jett did the only thing she could.

She pulled his spirit within herself.

A burning, too-full-for-her-skin sensation came first. Thad struggled, intuitively sensing something was wrong.

"Be still," she commanded as she moved her hands over the torso of his corpse, healing the torn flesh. She straightened an arm, knitting the bones with her touch. With enough time, she could heal his body so it could contain him again. These damages were easier to repair than those of a smiting.

Emotion drove her, strengthening her will.

"What have you done?" he asked.

"You've died. Nara would never have returned you to me so I've kept you here, the only way I know how. I've temporarily brought you inside me."

She repaired another portion of his chest and moved lower. The damage was extensive, talon marks peeling back his flesh and muscle. It was a miracle that he'd survived to return to her.

She'd kill Airyon. Her own wrath escalated to unscaled heights. She'd take immense pleasure in giving him to Nara's whims.

"A word, sister."

Jett glanced up to find Nara standing a few feet from her as if she'd conjured her with a thought. From the irate expression on her sister's face, she knew she'd had nothing to do with summoning the Goddess of the Veil. Nara was here on business.

"Nara? Why are you here?"

Her sister raised an eyebrow and sniffed delicately. She glared at Jett, her eyes narrowing as she looked at the twined souls within her.

"Why do you think? This is the third time in less than a week you've denied me a soul destined for the veil. I've come to retrieve what is mine."

"You can not have him."

"You can't deny me what is mine. It's divine law, and I've let you break it one too many times. You must release him to me." Nara reached out her hand. A forceful tug pulled across Jett's abdomen as her sister attempted to pull Thad from her body.

Jett mentally grabbed him, holding him within her and weaving a few more threads of herself through his soul. "You cannot have him!"

Nara snarled, jerking harder. "Release him."

"No." Jett tightened her grip on Thad. Looking away from her sister, she focused on repairing his body. The sooner he was healed, the sooner he would be safe inside his body. Nara couldn't remove a living, breathing soul. Much as it infuriated her, it was outside her scope of power.

Inside her, a strange pressing sensation pushed on her bones. Thad braced himself to prevent his removal. Good. If he worked with her, he would be more difficult to steal.

Nara pouted, beckoning to him with her hand. "Come on, love. Come play with me. We'll have lots of fun. I promise."

In Torment! Jett couldn't stop the screech that tore from her, nor could she halt the fireball she instinctively hurled at her sister. It engulfed Nara, who laughed from within the flames before she extinguished them with a sweep of her dainty fingers. Not so much as a scorch mark marred her skimpy pale blue robes.

"Impressive," Thad murmured inside Jett. *"A little jealous?"*

"Shut up."

"I'm just saying—"

"Do you want *to die?"*

From the corner of her eye, she saw Nara pull a golden rope of energy from the air. No! Jett had seen it used before. Nara bound recalcitrant souls with the cord, dragging them back to the veil with her. Although not much dragging was involved. Once she got her rope around them, the souls usually did whatever she wanted. They had no choice.

Jett frantically repaired the last section of Thad's body.

He nipped the inside of her neck, taking advantage of his position within her. *"Want to die? Not particularly. Not now that I've found such delightfully, divine accommodations."*

"Do not get too comfortable. You are not staying." But she couldn't move him back to his vessel until she got rid of Nara. This was a fine mess. Her sister wouldn't leave without him and Thad wouldn't be safe until back into his own body. Jett couldn't move him under Nara's watchful eye. With his soul inside her, she couldn't transport either.

"I'm not going with her," he bit out in determination. Did he really think she'd let her sister win?

"Of course, you are not."

"Stop delaying," Nara demanded.

"He is my pledge. He belongs to me."

"Do I now?" He stroked her womb, sending a flood of arousal through her and reminding her that she belonged to him.

"Not now!" She grated. She'd heard about how carefree a soul could become when outside its body, but really? Had he no sense? *"You will distract me from saving your ass."*

"Stop worrying so much. She's not taking me with her."

His cavalier attitude set her teeth on edge. Obviously he didn't realise the danger Nara posed to his future on earth.

Her sister's eyes narrowed and a knowing smirk lifted one side of her mouth. "Pledge? He's the one isn't he? He's the one you finally gave up your dreadful virginity to."

"You make it sound like a disease."

"Only if it sticks around for five millennium." Her hand planted on her hip as it cocked to the side and she held out her other palm to placate Jett. "Look, I'm sorry that he's the one, but he has to come to the veil now."

"Ooh...come to the dark side, Thad," he said in a spooky tone.

"Stop joking about this!" Couldn't he be serious? This was a matter of his life or death.

Thad stroked the inside of her breast, sending a tingle through her nipple. *"Hey, I've looked Death in the eye today and I'm still alive. Death's kind of pretty, too."*

"Do you want me to save you or not?" Jett

snapped. With him inside her she couldn't slap his hands away. And this was not the place to think about sex. With Thad stroking her, it was hard to focus.

"Ah baby, you know I think you're prettiest," he placated.

Nara fingered her rope, a thinly disguised threat. Jett knew the Goddess of the Veil would yank Thad forcefully from her if necessary.

"Technically, you are dead, not alive," she corrected. *"I am supposed to let you go with her."*

He latched onto her ribs again. *I'm not going.*

"Could we not make a deal?" she tried. Like she and Airyon, she and her sister had equal power. Equal but different. When it came to souls, Nara had the upper hand. Jett couldn't strong-arm her into conceding.

"We already have a deal and you haven't made good on it."

Jett sighed. "You know I will."

Nara tossed back her hair in a completely haughty manner. "No deals."

"Did she learn that move from you? It's sexy."

Jett scowled at his comment. *"Keep it up and you are going with her."*

Fingers teased along her insides, leaving tantalising ripples in their wake. *"I will never part with you."*

Nara lifted the golden rope into the air. "Time's up, sister." Her eyes looked sad. "I'm sorry. This is my business."

"Nara, please..." Jett begged. Terror sang through her. She and Thad would have no choice in separation when Nara bound his soul and dragged him to the veil.

It was little comfort that her sister had reached

her allowed limit of pets for the season. She couldn't put Thad in her service, unless she freed another and petitioned permission from the council. She hated to do that, but for Thad she might. If she enslaved him, he'd essentially be a sex toy to the Goddess of the Veil until statutes dictated she free him—about every hundred years—when she'd start a new crop.

Worse, she'd part Thad and Jett for eternity. Once he was behind the veil, Jett couldn't have access to him. No one breached the veil without assistance and there was no one who would help her, 'for her own good'. Her people would think she'd lost her sanity if they knew her love for her mortal warlock overlord.

Desperately, Jett closed her eyes and tried to transport away before Nara could capture Thad. With the extra energy flowing through this place, perhaps she could manage. Her body refused to budge. Thad's soul inside weighed too heavy within her. She was anchored here until she could return him to his nearly restored body.

Nara wasn't chancing it. Her weapon dropped around Jett. It cinched tight before its divine essence sank through her skin to bind around Thad. White hot heat roiled through her while Thad struggled against the lasso.

"I'm not going with her! I'm not leaving!"

"Let him go!" Jett demanded. Her words shook at the struggle within her. Her body began to lose form, shifting like soft clay squeezed in a toddler's hands.

Nara laughed. "Sorry, sister. He belongs to me."

"Like hell!" Thad's struggles increased, even as Jett felt him pull from her body. No! She couldn't lose him so easily to Nara. She wouldn't let Airyon

win. Mentally, she clutched at his vibrational threads, but it was like grasping sand.

She was losing him!

Suddenly, Nara's golden rope fell away. Its ends dropped to the ground in limp, shredded pieces.

"That's impossible," she murmured.

"Why, She-Styx? Your power isn't infallible."

Nara swung her attention to the speaker. "*Airyon.* Go away scum. I'm working."

Airyon skimmed his eyes over Jett as her form returned, then shifted to the shredded lasso. He turned back to Nara, seeming oblivious to her glare. "Working? Is that what you call this?"

"Would you know work if you saw it?" Nara snapped.

"Would you?"

Nara screeched. If it were in her power, Jett suspected the other goddess would kill the God of Wrath. Her sister's fingers curled. Her full attention narrowed on Airyon as her blue eyes splintered with ice. Airyon would regret his taunting when Jett turned him over to the goddess.

Her gaze shooting back and forth between the bickering deities, Jett debated returning Thad to his body. He was safer from Airyon while his soul was inside her. He was safer from Nara while inside his own body. Jett could protect him from Airyon, but not Nara.

She had to reunite soul and body.

She doubted Nara would notice. Airyon might, however.

Taking advantage of her sister's distraction, Jett leaned close to Thad's body. Quickly, she repaired the last of the damage Airyon had done all the while keeping an eye on the other two. She'd never seen Nara so enraged as Airyon traded barbs with her. And Airyon...he'd opened himself up for her to easily target. If Thad hadn't weighed her body, Jett would have killed Airyon herself. Nara couldn't because of limits on her particular power, but *she* could.

Jett pressed her open mouth to Thad's. Her arms slid around his waist.

"Go home Warlock Overlord. Let go and fall backward. Your body will pull you inside."

Following her command, Thad slipped from her body and into his own as easily as if they'd been making the move for centuries. Nara and Airyon never noticed. Thad's restored arms banded around her tightly. His mouth moved powerfully beneath hers, rejoicing in his life as sparks flew around them—from Airyon and Nara's 'conversation.'

Jett lifted her head, glorying at the ragged breath against her lips and the jagged rise and fall of his chest. Warmth refilled his muscles. It flooded into her, assuring her his strong heart beat again.

"Take us from here," she whispered. "Go to your cave."

"Yes, goddess." His sturdy arms tightened infinitesimally, his mouth taking hers again. Power sluiced around them, pulling at them as they flashed to his hideaway.

The energy geyser flared as they landed over the ley lines, limbs entwined. Its essence shot through them. Bound them. Jett gasped as the arousal she'd experienced laced through her. Her muscles trembled with the force.

Thad's surprised gaze locked with hers, a ruddy flush slashing across his cheekbones, as he experienced the same.

"I need you. Now," he growled. His fingers

already worked to divest her of her clothing.

"Yes," she agreed. She needed him just as badly. It was a celebration of their lives, of his joy at reunion with his body and continued union with her. Her joy at thwarting death, continuing her time with Thad. Somehow they'd work out forever. Somehow. . .

They came together quickly, both climaxing at once. Afterward, Thad stroked his hands over her. "I'd thought I'd lost you."

Jett shifted, enjoying the feel of him still embedded deep inside her body. He rotated his hips bringing a moan to her lips. He captured it with a heated kiss as his hands skimmed her hips again. Slowly, he dragged his palms along her body until he cupped her face.

"I want to have a child with you."

Jett's eyes widened. She hadn't expected that.

"Thad..." she began.

"I know we can't until you become mortal. I just wanted you to know. A child with you...Jett."

Her belly trembled as his words sank through her. Oh how she wanted to have a child with this man she'd loved for so long. Tears welled in her eyes and blurred her vision and his beloved face.

"We can't—I can't—if I become mortal—look what happened when you fought Airyon. He killed you. Who would protect you? I couldn't bear that. And, who would protect my people and keep him from destroying them?"

Hurt anger filled his eyes before it disappeared behind a stoic mask. He withdrew with a nod and began to pull on his clothes. "Where does this leave us, Jett?"

She looked away, as she too pulled on her clothes. Despondently, she shuffled over to the log-hewn bed and sank onto the edge. She rested her elbow on her knees and stared at her loosely twined fingers. "The festival will be over in hours. I must go back."

Her answer ignited something inside him, something he'd vowed to hide with that mask. "No."

Jett's head snapped up, an unbidden thrill accompanying his declaration. "No?"

"We have not come this far for you to up and leave as if what's between us has no matter."

"Of course it matters. My leaving won't change that."

He punched his arms into the sleeves of his shirt. "I will not lose you to that asshole. You belong to me."

"I am a goddess. I belong to no one."

His raised brow challenged her, telling her he knew otherwise. "You're not leaving."

"And who will stop me?"

"You think I can't?"

She knew damned well he could. She didn't really want to go. Where there was no divine will, mortals could find an opening. She sighed. She didn't want to argue with him, not now when their time was short. She would leave eventually. There was no choice. "Very well. I'll stay. For now."

"For*ever*," he countered.

"There isn't a way."

"We'll find a way. You belong with me." He pulled her off the bed and back to him, his mouth blotting out all argument. Her body pressed to his.

Jett knew she'd pushed him to his limit, and she let him win for now. Thad wouldn't use words to argue with her. He'd use the method at which he excelled. She groaned as he pushed his hand up inside her robe and palmed her bare breast.

Gently, he plumped the nipple. Already she ached for his touch again, the reassurance of his body over hers. When he covered her, she could forget her responsibilities, forget everything that would keep them apart.

There was only here.

Only right now.

With Thad.

Slowly, he laid her back on the bed and spread her legs. His fingers dragged upward, spreading her folds and holding her open for a quick swipe of his tongue before he climbed her body.

"You make me crazy," he muttered. With great dedication, he investigated the underside of a breast. He licked the crease where the mound met her chest. His mouth trailed up the under-slope to her erect nipple. She squirmed as he nipped at the aureole. Her fingers knotted in his silky hair.

"Take me Thad," she begged. Her hips lifted and she rubbed her aching cleft against his belly. Her legs wrapped his thighs, her heels digging into his ass to urge him to her. "Fuck me. Now. Anyway you want. Just…please…yes!" her cry echoed in the cavernous space as he ploughed into her and gave her everything she pleaded for.

* * * *

They'd made love over the ley lines again, but sometime in the afternoon, they'd returned to the rustic bed Thad kept in the cave. He'd assured her it had been cleansed since the Bram-Zora incident. She didn't know how long they'd been there, but Airyon and Nara hadn't followed. They would eventually, but right now, they hadn't figured out that the cave was masking Jett's presence.

She stretched between the starched, natural

cotton sheets then settled deeper into the feather pillow. A sense of drowsiness surrounded her like dozens of wispy clouds.

Perhaps it was in part the knowledge that she and Thad were completely safe here. Her power was strong over this ley line grid, while Airyon and Nara's powers were diminished. Neither could hurt her or her warlock in this place. They were even weaker than Thad.

She pulled Thad's white button-down shirt closer around her. Somewhere in another chamber, he worked on diverting an unscheduled natural disaster. He'd insisted that she remain here and 'keep the bed warm'. She'd have argued, but the disaster aversion was usually easy work for him.

Assuring her that he could take care of the problem, without seeking out Airyon or leaving the cave, he'd given her the spare shirt he kept here and dressed in the spare pants. His others were shredded and covered in gore. With a lingering kiss, he bid her to rest.

Still it troubled her. An unscheduled disaster equalled Airyon. Obviously, he'd finished arguing with her sister, he sought to draw her into battle. Guilt weighed on her. She should help Thad. She would have already, but he seemed to have something to prove. He could protect her. He could take care of things. He was worthy of her...

Gods! How much worthiness did a person actually need? No mortal, and few gods, could be as worthy as Thad. He was one of the great ones, the stuff of legends. In a thousand years, her people would tell tales about him.

She lifted the lapel of the shirt, smiling at the memories his scent brought forth. He was great in more ways than one. Perhaps she should track him down so she could rush his task to completion, then trace that chiselled curve that ran from his hip to beneath the waistband of his pants.

Her cleft vibrated with desire again and she threw back the sheet. She could lay here wallowing in desire or she could go find him, divert disaster and investigate that sexy ridge with her tongue. Tough choice.

"This is how I'd like to see you all the time," a sarcastic voice murmured, dragging her from her mental perusal of Thad's body.

Jett bolted from the bed, glad the long tails of Thad's shirt covered her. "Airyon. What are you doing here?" she demanded. "You have no power here."

He looked around, his expression unsurprised. "I suppose not, my betrothed, but you'll have to leave here sometime."

"Do not call me that."

"Why not? It is your station."

"In your mind only."

His smile reminded Jett of a cat, and she was the trapped bird who'd dared to try and fly away. Casually, he reached into the air and retrieved a scroll. *The Daily Deity Report*. He tossed it onto the bed at her side.

"Take a look," he instructed.

Her jaw locked in at his off-hand attitude. Begrudgingly, she stole a glance at the scroll. The words stole her breath from her lungs.

Airyon, God of Wrath, and Reddjedet, Goddess of the Zodiac Quadrant, Join at end of Festival

"It's a lie!" she protested.

He shrugged. "No one knows that."

Her heart sank as she continued to read. The Festival was soon over and the article stated that the Higher Power had called her home. All her choices were gone. It was a command no one could ignore without dire repercussions.

"So, as I said," he continued, his eyes growing feral, "you have to leave sometime, and when you do, I will be waiting. You will be fine, but when your mortal lover tries to follow you, he will die."

Jett howled in fury and hurled a bolt at him without a fraction of a thought. He'd never hurt Thad!

Airyon neatly dodged the smiting she'd slammed towards him. "Temper, temper," he chided. "I am looking forward to killing him, you know."

He dodged another bolt, while he examined his nails in false boredom. She knew her attacks were too close for his comfort. Damn her rage for making her inaccurate! He should be dead by now! Her next attack singed across the top of his shoulder.

"Of course, the choice is yours," he offered, slightly out of breath.

"What choice?" she demanded.

The Higher Power had called her home. She had to go. She had to leave Thad alone.

"Come willingly with me, join with me, and I will leave him be. Your life in exchange for his life. A good deal, don't you think?" His stare challenged her as he boldly walked towards her, taking his life into his hands. Her aim was far better the closer he got. He grabbed the edges of her shirt, spreading it wide as he yanked her towards him. She gasped as the cool silk of his shirt came in contact with her bared breasts. He insinuated his thigh between her legs and pressed against her exposed mound.

His fingers dug into her buttocks, grinding her to him while the other hand fisted in her hair.

"Mine," he grated. He pumped his arousal against her while his mouth covered hers, punishing her lips apart to allow his tongue to spear inside. He seemed impervious to her pummelling or her clawing, even gaining strength in it. Evading her knee, he released her with a smile.

"A taste of what is to come," he promised. "Do not try to outwit me. My followers will kill him if you betray me." His thumb flicked over her breast and she shuddered, swallowing bile. "I will look forward to later, Reddjedet."

With a laugh, he disappeared before she could respond.

Jett yanked her shirt closed. Tears pricked her eyes at the empty and repugnant future that lay before her. She had no choice. It was go with Airyon or give Thad a death sentence. When given that choice, there was really no choice at all. She couldn't assign Thad such a fate. Her love for Thad would allow only one action. Sacrifice her love and give him up. Somehow, she'd have to say goodbye and leave him without him stopping her.

He'd see it as betrayal, as her choosing Airyon over him. She was the wife of his heart, the one he wished to be joined to for all time. She'd promised she would never lie with another. Tears rolled down her cheeks, dropping onto her chest, wet flags of sorrow. She'd have to break her promise and live with the eternal guilt. It was the only way to save the man she loved. Thad would never understand this truth, the reason for her action. He'd fight with everything in him if she revealed all her feelings, all she sacrificed, for him.

Perhaps it would be better that way. If he never knew how much she loved him, what she'd given up for him, what she'd taken on for him.

A jagged sob wrenched from her and nearly robbed her ability to stand. How would she bear an eternity of Airyon?

"Jett? What is it?" Thad asked urgently as he burst into the room. He stopped short at the scorch marks on the cave wall and her distraught appearance. Concern filled his gaze as he took in her distress.

Squaring her shoulders and swiping futilely at her wet cheeks, she tried to hide her tremble. She failed miserably. Another gasping sob rattled up her chest.

"What the hell happened?" he demanded, rushing to her and enfolding her tightly in his embrace. She sank into the welcome comfort. His arms squeezed almost painfully around her. She wondered if he thought to make her a part of him, inseparable, so that he might protect her.

If only he knew how soon they *would* separate. Thank the gods he didn't.

"Airyon..." she started. Her voice broke as she said the name of her tormentor. How would she endure an eternity at Wrath's mercy? How would she endure her betrayal of her people? Worse, how would she endure an eternity without even the sight of Thad's face? When she left here today, she'd never see him again. She couldn't. For both their sakes.

She wondered if here where her power flowed so strongly, if she should try to wipe his mind again. This time she'd do everything necessary to make sure she was successful. He'd never forgive her if she failed and he realised what she'd tried to do. Again. Indecision warred within her, a civil war of options with the ultimate enemy the same for all sides—herself.

If she failed, it might be better. Thad would harbour anger against her for the rest of his life. In his anger he might be able to move on. If she wiped his memory, he'd have a residual longing he wouldn't understand. She closed her eyes. With that longing he might never be able to move on and live his life normally.

It would be better to leave him with the hurt of her apparent betrayal. She'd leave him with his memories and strip herself and the power she'd given him from his life. He'd no longer be a warlock overlord, no longer be pledged to her. He'd be like every other mortal—the gods would be invisible to him.

She'd be invisible to him.

When Airyon wasn't aware, she'd look on Thad, watch him throughout his life, she'd watch him love another woman and perhaps seed children. She'd be there, yet he'd never see her or her pain.

Damn Airyon! Damn her weakness! Though she was equal in power to the God of Wrath, he held leverage over her that she couldn't ignore. Thad's life. The lives of her people. She couldn't let him continue to ravage the planets. Even without her love for Thad, her people required safety. And she could have their safety. Airyon would sign that bargain in blood before she gave him anything. Thad's life. Her people's lives. He'd never be able to break the promise without eternal consequences.

In that and only that did she take sad pleasure. Airyon thought to use her power to strengthen himself, but he had no idea what he would get. He'd get power from the joining, but it would be impotent power. There would be nothing he could do. He'd never be able to ravage her people and use his wrath.

They'd be safe.

Thad would be safe.

She'd be alone. Save for the initial, repugnant joining, she'd never be with Airyon. She'd certainly never take pleasure in him. It would be impossible to use his body to slake her needs.

She might vomit.

Chapter Fifteen

"Just hold me. Please," Jett begged Thad.

He enfolded her in his arms and cradled her against him. "What the hell did he do?" He didn't wait for an answer, her shudders and tears apparently enough to answer his question. "Goddess, I'll kill him!" he swore.

Jett shook her head, panic sending a chill through her. Gods! If Thad went against Airyon, it would negate all she'd done, and would do, to save him. She couldn't let Thad get himself killed.

"It is not important," she lied. "Forget about him. I do not want you to get hurt."

"I won't let him hurt what is mine."

"He did not hurt me," she answered unable to deny she belonged to him. At least for now. And he'd always have her heart, even if she was physically with Airyon.

She couldn't meet his eyes and instead focused on buttoning the shirt she wore. Her fingers fumbled numbly with the holes and small plastic disks. Tears blurred her vision as utter sorrow took firm root inside her. It was over. Everything she wanted, and secretly hoped for the past two hundred years, was over.

Gently, Thad pulled the fabric from her useless

fingers and pushed aside the shirt's lapel to reveal a bruise left behind by Airyon. "I don't believe he didn't hurt you."

Jett wrenched the shirt back over her, grasping desperate anger to hide her pain. "What is it with you?" she snapped, trying to sidetrack him. "Protecting me all the time? I am the goddess, *your* deity. I gave you power. I don't need you to protect me all the time. And I certainly don't need protection from Airyon."

Thad crossed his arms over his chest, his eyes narrowed, his challenge clear. His throbbing temple dared her to deny his power. His clenched jaw screamed his refusal to digress.

"I'm the only one who can protect you from him," he replied, his tone calm opposition to hers.

She squared her shoulders, crossing her own arms across the unbuttoned shirt and the ample flesh it revealed. At the moment, reclaiming her position was more important than a little nakedness. Somehow, someway, she had to make him understand. He was not more powerful than she was. He had no divinity or power over the universes. She alone commanded the future of earth and her other planets.

This was her burden, not his.

"Why is it so important to you to do this?" she attacked. "Why do you refuse to leave it to me?"

He laughed bitterly, a flash of uncertainty tainting his blue eyes. His fist clenched against his biceps. "It's what men do. We defend what is ours."

"I—"

He moved like lightning, coming at her before she could react. His finger pressed over her lips. "Don't you dare deny that you belong to me."

She scoffed, not denying the truth of his statement. His words melted her. Challenged her. A denial would give him power, because he'd know she'd lied. Instead, she answered with a question. "How can a deity belong to a mortal?"

Thad smiled, and she knew he'd spied her weakness. His hand caressed down her neck, easing aside her crossed arms. He drew apart the edges of the shirt. Tenderly, he dropped a lingering kiss over the bruise. He tended it with his mouth, laved it with his tongue, as if his very attention could erase the damage and heal her.

When he drew back, his razor-sharp gaze pierced straight to her heart. The steel in his voice belied any tenderness. He was a warrior, battling for his very life. He refused to surrender. "We're a man and a woman. Nothing else matters. Everything else is background. And you *do* belong to me. I will not lose you. If I have to revert to caveman tactics to prove it to you, I will. I've already got the cave," he concluded, a poor attempt to lighten the situation with a jest.

Her resultant laugh echoed rusty and slightly hysterical against the stone walls of his mini-fortress. She spun away from him. He'd fight her every step of the way on this—she knew that now, had known that before this disagreement had ever started.

Her plan clicked in her mind. She'd have to leave when he didn't expect it. Then she'd disguise her path to keep him from following her. What good would it do if she left and Thad trailed after her? No mortal had ever entered the divine realm, but that didn't mean Thad wouldn't try. He'd already breached countless other barriers. Following her to Eden wouldn't be insurmountable for him.

She didn't doubt for a moment that he'd try to

come after her and succeed in entering her realm if she didn't do something to prevent him. The fact no one had done it before didn't mean that Thad couldn't. His power exceeded that of any mortal she'd encountered, including all the warlock overlords who'd pledged to her throughout the centuries.

She'd made a mistake, but one she couldn't feel remorse over, though now it would cause her difficulty and pain. She should never have enlisted Thad as an overlord. He possessed power outside of what she'd granted him. He'd had them long before she'd engaged him in her service. She couldn't help but think he'd been well practiced in these magical skills, as well. She'd merely amplified them and given him a few new ones.

He wouldn't be easily eluded when she fled.

Masking her roiling emotions, Jett sank into his embrace. They didn't have long before she must leave him. Airyon wouldn't be patient. If she delayed, he'd try to lure Thad outside of her place of power. She didn't want anyone to interrupt her last moments with the only man she'd ever love.

She lifted her mouth to Thad's.

"I love you," she whispered against his lips.

"Oh Goddess," he murmured, sealing the words between them with a kiss that couldn't be called anything but claiming. And that was exactly it, he was claiming her. She fought the tears that burned in her eyes. She couldn't cry now. There were centuries of time for that later. She opened to him now, splaying her fingers on his broad chest and finding the nipples there. She caressed them until he groaned, his arms becoming bands around her.

He lifted her as if she weighed nothing and carried her towards the bed. She snuggled into

him, nipping at his neck, enjoying how he made
her feel small and protected and pushing from her
mind that she was neither. She was larger than
life, the protector. But she let that go, revelling in
Thad.

And he wasn't feeling nearly as tender. He
seemed to have a point to prove as he carried her
to the bed. He skimmed the shirt from her body as
he walked, then worked the closure of his pants.
In a moment, they were both naked. Jett gasped
when he dropped her onto the bed, but her gasp
turned to moans when he followed. He dropped
his head to her chest, taking a plump nipple
between his lips. Ruthlessly, he suckled while he
smoothed his hands up her arms until they were
stretched above her head, her chest raised to him
as an offering. She sensed the bands of power
looping around her wrists as he lashed her to the
headboard.

He stared down at her, his dark eyes glowing
with challenge.

"Mine," he growled. "You're not leaving me.
Tell me you'll never leave."

Her lips pressed together, and she realised
she'd have to lie. Against her mental decision, her
head rocked back and forth, denying his demand.

He turned thunderous. A growl of outrage split
the room. "You belong to me!"

"Thad..."

"No!" he exploded. "No more. If you won't
admit with words that you're mine, then I'll let
your body speak."

"No," she pleaded. Her wretched body would
betray her. It would give him every answer he
demanded. Answers that would be true and yet
lies. She couldn't stay with him.

She fought to get free of the energy bonds,

confused that they should have the ability to hold her. Was her time on earth dulling her powers? Remembering her battles with Nara and Airyon, she knew they were not.

How was Thad able to subdue her?

Awareness prickled down her limbs as he spread her thighs and lay on his belly between them. His powerful hands held her legs apart while he explored her swollen folds with his mouth, sucking, probing, tormenting. Her heels dug into the mattress and her hips lifted as his tongue flicked the expanding bud revealed by her arousal.

"Mine," he grated as his mouth claimed her. "My sheath, my Eden. No other will ever claim this pussy. You're mine. Tell me. Tell me you'll never leave me."

"Thad," she panted, her hands flexing above her head as she strained against the bindings. She needed to sink her hands into the long tresses falling around her hips and pull him closer with a demand for the release that lingered a breath away. "Please."

"Tell me," he demanded. His tongue slid along her while her vaginal walls began to tremble. "Tell me."

"Thad!"

"Tell me!"

Jett whimpered and squeezed her eyes shut as tears seeped down her cheeks. She pressed her face into her arm. She couldn't lie to him. Not now, not for a sexual release that would seem tawdry later when faced with her betrayal. She wouldn't lie to him for sex.

"You belong to me," he asserted.

"Yes," she answered. That was true. A sob swelled in her chest as he left her, but a tingling on her hip caught her attention. Her eyes popped open in surprise. Thad still knelt between her knees, his gaze intent on the place where his palm rested on her pelvis. Pleasure seemed to emanate from him, creating a warm vibrating net around her, capturing her, holding her to him in a web of belonging she knew she might never break. Slowly, he slid away his hand and she saw the mark. Two interlocking rings. Eternity. It shimmered like gold in the dimly lit cave.

"You belong to me," he rasped, dragging his finger along the small symbol. "This will remain as long as you are mine, to the end of our days."

His cock prodded the entrance to her sheath before she could confirm or deny his claim. Determination filled his countenance. He would not take no, or any denial, for an answer. He was claiming her, staking his right. The web around her intensified, wringing reaction from her as he surged forward to fill her deep recesses.

"Yes! Gods, yes!" she cried, straining to meet him as his wide erection stretched her with his possession. She thought he'd move wildly, their union hot and fast, but instead he set a slow, simmering pace that had her head thrashing on the thin pillow as he drove her to desperation for release.

He was waiting. Waiting for her confirmation that she'd stay with him, that she wouldn't put herself in danger, that she'd never give herself to another—even out of duty.

Despite his efforts, pleasure erupted from her middle. She refused to rein it in or hold it back. It exploded along her limbs as it sent her on a ride that tore a scream from her lips and clenched the same from Thad as his release overwhelmed him. She twisted spasmodically as her muscles clamped around his manhood, milking everything from him.

He clutched the sheets on either side of her head as their orgasm overtook them. The cloth hissed as it tore under his unchecked strength. Her climax radiated beyond them in an eruption of brilliant light, shaking the bed, the table beside them falling over. A loud rumble punctuated the moment as a crack tore along the ceiling.

Thad's arms tightened around her until she could barely breathe. Suddenly, the pressure released, and he collapsed above her.

The power bands disappeared.

She didn't want to move, but now, now was the time.

Thad murmured a protest as she slid from his embrace. Spent, he flopped onto his back, an arm thrown over his face. Tenderness welled inside Jett. She wanted to cuddle into him. She wanted to whisper naughty things to him that would start the reaction in her once again. To soar with him one more time...

With sadness, she acknowledged, she must act now or never. She must act now while he least expected it, or he would try to stop her. If this display was any indication, he'd succeed in stopping her, too. It confused her that he'd have such power—she'd have to question the Council regarding it. Later, after she'd dealt with Airyon.

Trailing her hands along Thad's arms, she straddled him and covered his mouth with hers. His earlier protest became a groan as she teased his tongue with hers and grasped her fingers around his wrists. She held them over his head in a gentle love clasp.

On and on, she kissed him while holding him that way. Taken in by her guise of bondage-love play, he didn't realise strand over strand of magical power wrapped his limbs, binding him to the bed. She wrapped them loosely. He'd never know what she'd done, until he tried to move. And couldn't.

Her body wept for the ridge that rose beneath her mound. Her cleft begged to take him one more time. With tears in her eyes, she refused. She couldn't delay. Airyon might return any moment. Her palms trailed over his powerful chest as her lips left his. Carefully, she climbed from him.

"Goodbye my love," she whispered. Her legs wobbled as she stood beside the bed. Gods, what he'd done to her... She could barely stand.

Thad's eyes flew open as realisation settled over him. He tried to get up, reach for her, but the bands knocked him backward.

"Jett! Release me!" he demanded. His muscles bulged as he fought.

Her heart broke as he struggled, and she steeled herself against her crumbling resolve. Moving to the end of the bed, she faced him and held out her hand. Gently, she traced her love over his body, arousing his pleasure centres to somewhat mask the pain of what she must do. He might sense the pleasure, but he'd know the mental anguish of her removal.

"No!" Thad gasped, immediately grasping what she planned. "No, don't do this!"

Lifting her other hand, she methodically began to sap her power from his body. After she finished, he'd have none but his own innate abilities that had been gifted him at birth.

Thad strained against the bands holding him. The energy shifted and anticipated his every move. "Jett, don't do this."

She shook her head. "I have to go home, to Airyon, to end this. You are no longer in my service."

"Damn it! Let me go," he demanded, his frustration winning out over his coaxing. "Jett, don't do this. Let me fight him with you."

She shook her head and pulled the last of her power from him. Her eyes and her hands closed, sealing the recaptured energy within herself once again. When she opened her eyes, finality crushed through her, hollowing out her heart.

"Goodbye," she whispered.

"No!" He pulled so hard against his restraints blood trickled down his arms. Automatically, she healed the wounds and added cushion, still inescapable, beneath the bonds. Thad's struggles shook the sturdy bed while his pleas became incoherent, breaking her heart with what she'd done to this superior man.

Fighting her emotions, she forced her expression to blank and met his panicked eyes. This was a man realising his most prized possession was about to pass from his grasp. His desire would forever be outside his hold.

And she had to hurt him beyond what was bearable to make him stay behind.

Lifting her chin and donning her stance of power, she stared into his eyes. Dread filled her, her stomach wrenching with the repulsion of her task. She had one final step to drive the core of her message and determination home. Everything in her protested, but she had no choice. He had to know their time was over. He couldn't come after her.

She opened her fingers and swiped her hand over her hipbone. With the slight touch, the mark he'd put there disappeared leaving smooth unblemished skin. Her control nearly snapped at the anguished look that covered his face, and the cry which followed. Despite the cushioning she'd conjured within his bindings, new blood spouted from his newly healed wrists. The bed frame creaked as the headboard began to splinter.

He'd do bodily harm if she wasn't swift to depart. The struggle would wear him out, but if he continued as he was, she feared he'd break a bone or tear muscles.

Another swipe of her hand had her clothed in a shimmering white sheath. The time had come for her to return to her seat of power. Playtime was over.

Resolutely, Jett enacted the final portion of her escape. She ignored the pleas for her to stay, for her to let him protect her. His emotion-filled appeals ripped out her heart. He was mortal and she was not. They couldn't be together. She had a duty.

By doing her duty, she'd allow him to recover. He'd live.

She'd love him forever.

"Airyon," she whispered. She reached out her hand. He appeared at her side, wrapping her in his embrace and glaring triumphantly at Thad. His head bent and Jett sank into his kiss. She flashed them from the room, with Thad's outraged bellow of pain echoing in her ears.

Chapter Sixteen

Thad collapsed against the bed, regrouping his strength before he undertook the toughest battle he'd ever fought. Clashing with Airyon had almost killed him, but in comparison, it was nothing.

Jett was in for the fight of her life. If she thought she'd won, she was dead wrong. She'd caught him unaware, and that would never happen again.

Pain and betrayal tore through him at the memory of Jett's hand in Airyon's. It shredded his gut and destroyed everything he thought he'd known about her. Had she used him? Played with him? Had their time meant nothing?

He'd sure as hell find out. Reddjedet owed him answers. And a whole lot more.

* * * *

It seemed centuries since Jett had been here, not days. Mist-laden air spiralled around the vast expanses of iconic columns. She'd seen pictures of her home once in earth's books—a mortal gifted with a glimpse of the heavens so that he could share it with the world. Ever after that vision had been copied until it became the accepted depiction of the god's realm. Now her people saw it as a mythical place, while they had no idea how close to truth their drawings were.

The white everywhere reminded her of Thad's homes.

The edges of the structures blurred. Not from the mist, she acknowledged, but from her. Even here, she'd never escape the memories of love written on her heart. How was it that her soul already ached for its mismatched mate, her body called again for the perfectly matched fit of his possession? Had she not been a virgin and unaccustomed to a man but a week ago?

The short time did not matter. Thad had become the other part of herself. The male part of her whole, ensouling her being to a level of vitality that mocked the half-existence she'd been living.

She couldn't go on without him. She had to find a solution—take care of Airyon and go back to Thad if he'd accept her. She did not have to consent to a future without him. If in the end, she must give up her divinity and live life as a mortal in order to have happiness, happiness which was the Higher Power's wish for her life, she'd do that.

But first she'd have to stop Airyon from preying on mortals, preying on lesser deities. He'd chosen the wrong goddess to enrage. She'd crush him into the marble.

As if summoned her thoughts, Wrath appeared in the antechamber of her dwelling place. The sight of him combined with the realisation that Thad completed her was a slap to the face and a kick to look for a suitable solution. There was no need to accept the future he prescribed. She would not sacrifice herself for the well being of her people. It was a cowardly thing to do, not brave, and it was beneath the deity they deserved. She had not become their revered goddess by backing down from a fight and meekly conceding in the face of battle.

Her determination focused, and she knew what she had to do. It would be a risk. She might not have Thad after the way she'd betrayed him with her illusion of Airyon, but she certainly didn't have to accept a future with the real God of Wrath.

"I see you've come to your senses and left him, my betrothed," Airyon sneered.

Yes, she'd certainly come to her senses. She fought the cynical smile that tugged at the edges of her lips. She'd enjoy scorching his obnoxious hide. She'd enjoy smiting Airyon until only ashes remained.

"Do not speak to me."

"That will be difficult as I intend to join with you by day's end."

A shiver raked down her spine. She knew what the joining entailed. If she lost her battle with him, he'd rape her. She'd never willingly submit to him, victor or not.

She could *not* lose.

"I'd rather spend eternity in silence than ever hear your vomitous voice again."

"Ouch!" he laughed. "Well, sweet, get used to it. I intend to speak to you every day for the rest of eternity as I direct and siphon your power for my own uses. And as I take your hot little body the all ways you let him and more."

Jett looked away. Bile rose in her throat, its acrid taste choking her.

If it came to it, she might be forced to join with him. She'd never do so willingly. She'd never willingly part with her power, either. If she had to fight him the rest of her days, she would. Airyon might fool himself into thinking he'd have free access to her power, but he'd be a despondent god when he learned how little access he'd have. And he'd never be able to touch Thad—she'd see to that promise in Airyon's blood.

"My goddess..."

Jett turned towards the voice. Anya? Of course. Anya was her handmaiden, conscripted to aid her goddess however or wherever necessary.

"How quaint. Your mentor has sent you his handmaiden, just like in the days of his grandfather," Airyon grated, misinterpreting the reason for Anya's presence. "You'd think he'd have learned to carry his own messages after what happened to him."

"You will not speak of that betrayal in my presence," Jett snapped.

"Oh pardon me...I forgot. Bannor was your mentor. Before he was sent to Torment."

"My goddess," the handmaiden interrupted again to draw her attention. Pain etched Anya's face, reminding Jett of the rumour that Bannor had had close ties to one of his handmaidens. Apparently, it was less rumour than truth. Perhaps Anya had used Thad every bit as much as he'd used her. He'd seen her as a replacement for Jett, while Anya had used him to assuage the pain of losing Bannor.

"I have been sent to prepare you for audience with the Council," she glanced at Airyon, "to discuss pressing issues."

"The Festival has not concluded."

"You're to be ready for immediate inquiry at its conclusion. The time draws near."

Jett nodded. They would want to discuss Wrath's activities, but since he was not called as well, she also stood accused. No doubt her activities over the last days were called into question. Despite how anyone might view what she'd done, she could not be contrite for her time with Thad. He was her true mate, despite anything that might occur in the eons to come. If she lost her battle with Airyon, she might be forced to join with him, but she'd never truly belong to him, she'd never submit. She'd sooner go to Torment.

Preparation for this meeting could not have come at a more inopportune time. She needed these few hours to plan her battle with Wrath. She glanced at him and saw the triumphant knowledge in his eyes. He understood exactly what this appointment would cost her. In his opinion, he'd already won.

"Run along, my betrothed," he said in a voice so sweet it could wither mortal flesh. "We wouldn't want to keep your masters waiting because you are not ready." He closed the space between them in a blink of time. "But remember who will soon be your master."

"Not as long as I still exist."

"Oh, sweet, don't you know how it invigorates me when you fight?" He rubbed against her side, revealing his arousal.

Jett didn't attempt to hide her disgust. She moved away, putting several feet between them while she addressed Anya. "I'll be to the preparation chamber shortly."

"Do not delay," the handmaiden urged. She reached out and put her hand on Jett's shoulder, a forbidden gesture. After what had passed between them and what Anya had been to her mentor, it was acceptable. She looked directly into Jett's eyes. "Do not fret, goddess. Many know of your plight. Many would seek to aid you, given the leave." She paused, indecision crossing her eyes. "Including Warlock Pennington," she finally went on.

"He will not aid me."

"He is determined to have you."

Jett shook her head. To have. Not to love. He wanted her and she'd betrayed him. He wouldn't want her any longer. Not as a mate and partner. And he'd never admitted to loving her. She could have probed his emotions to find out for sure, but she'd respected his privacy, wanting him to tell her on his own terms when he was ready. Now he never would, even if that feeling had existed. Jett didn't foresee him easily forgiving her.

"He cannot assist me. He is mortal. Even if I knew a way to rid myself of the vermin plaguing me," she ignored Airyon's growl, "we could not be together."

"And you would let that stop you from finding happiness? There are ways. I have served the gods long enough to know—"

Anya's suddenly words cut off suddenly and she crumpled to the ground, her scream piercing the mist-laden serenity. The scent of scorched flesh permeated the air. A smouldering circle of black marred the chest of otherwise pristine white garment. The charring spread as Anya convulsed at Jett's feet, agonised shrieks ripping from her as Airyon's attack burned her from the inside out.

"You always have talked too much," Airyon sneered.

Jett dropped to her knees. Fruitlessly, she tried to heal the wound from Wrath's bolt. She encountered destruction with every probe of her power. The fire moved too quickly, had destroyed too much to save Anya from death. Every attempt to restore met defeat. Unlike others he'd instantly killed, he'd purposely attacked Anya with the intention to not only kill but to torture.

The handmaiden's fingers weakly clenched Jett's arm. Her pain sapping into her goddess.

"You can defeat him," she whispered, her words barely audible. Her hand slid away as her body disintegrated and her essence glided from Jett's dwelling, pulled towards the veil by Nara's invisible rope.

Airyon smirked and reached out his hand. "See, you cannot stop me. Come now. It is time for us to align."

Jett glanced at the outline of black ashes on the marble at her knees and power built in her hands. Without thought, she drew back and hurled a ball of fire. Let that be his answer. He dodged, but she did not let that stop her.

She would destroy him.

Unfolding to her feet, she shot twin bolts of energy for his heart.

He disappeared, only to reappear near the doorway. "Come now, sweet. Don't fight so hard against the inevitable."

Airyon was cunning, a strategist by his nature as God of Wrath. She created and maintained the balance of life. Battle was not in her makeup. Given the chance, he'd obliterate everything important to her, including Thad. Especially Thad. The way he'd killed Anya was a message. Thad's death wouldn't be instantaneous. Airyon would make him suffer.

She knew better than to trust Wrath would blithely forget about Thad if they joined. He'd hold Thad's well-being over her head for her love's entire lifetime. Thad would never truly be safe, no matter what agreement her tormentor signed. In blood or not.

She had to stop him. Somehow.

"It is not yet sunset," she growled.

He rolled his eyes and sighed with extreme irritation.

"Why delay?" he asked, slowly and pointedly articulating each word to hold his entire opinion. Any of her actions to put off the inevitable would be pointless.

"I must meet with the Council." Her gaze challenged him. She would not meekly fold to his demands—he should have determined that by now. Despite his leverage over her, her power equalled his. "As you have heard, I have been summoned."

"Those fools!" Airyon exclaimed. "You're a fool too. Why do you meekly do as you are told?"

"It is my purpose."

"Your purpose is to join with me. Our alliance will make us the most powerful gods in any quadrant. Our power will surpass that of your puny Council. We will bow to no one."

Horror shot through her as she saw the true scope of his plan for her powers. He didn't want her holdings. He wanted to rule the heavens.

"Do not say that!" she demanded.

"Why not? No one will stop me. No one will believe you if you try to alert them. Really, who would try to usurp the Higher Power?" He pressed a hand over his heart and looked taken aback. "'A lover's quarrel. That's all it is. I don't know what has come over her.'"

"Traitor!"

His laugh rattled through her as he dissolved from view, the rasping sound echoing in her chambers long after he'd departed. Oh gods! What was she to do?

This went far beyond her and Thad. Airyon was right. After her long duration on earth, no one would believe her if she told of Airyon's plans. They'd think she'd been affected by mortal thinking, that she'd succumb to their weaknesses or perhaps a disease.

She'd seen what had happened to the gods of the past, the ones that had spent so much time on earth. They'd lost credibility, eventually lost power. Athena, Aphrodite, Apollo. . . Zeus and Hera. They existed on another plane now, living out eternity while their duties were sustained by others, their powers so depleted that they endured only in legend.

No one would see Airyon's strategy until it was too late.

Her arms wrapped around her middle. And gods help her! She felt too weak without Thad. What had happened to her?

A gentle breeze removed Anya's remains from Jett's dwelling, almost unnoticed as she paced and planned. She could not ignore the scroll that materialised where the handmaiden had lain, the seal on it unmistakable.

With a silent word of thanks she grasped it.

"Take me to the one who summons me." If anyone understood separation from their love and the power of betrayal, he did.

* * * *

Thad jumped from the bed the moment Jett's energy restraints released him. From habit, he reached his hand and summoned his clothes, remembering too late that he didn't have that power any longer. Jett had taken his powers.

His shirt snapped into his hand and his eyes went wide. She'd taken her energy from him. He'd felt it as it scraped from every cell, ripping away, seeking to unwind from the places where it had twined with his own essence. Apparently, she hadn't been able to remove everything.

With ease, he shot off a fire ball, blasted a bolt of energy, transported to the mansion, moved the puffy white clouds overhead... As he experimented with his powers, it appeared he'd lost damned little if anything. Jett hadn't succeeded in taking any of his power, unless his own innate talents had grown so powerful that they'd surpassed what she'd given him.

None of it made sense. How could his mortal abilities be better than the goddess-given gifts?

And he'd felt her removal by each agonising increment. How could she remove herself and leave his powers? Had she not told him he was no longer in her service?

Fine, just fine. He didn't want to be in her service anyway. He wanted to be her mate.

He tore through his chambers, shoving his clothes on while he went. The fabric made sounds of protest with the force of his action as he nearly ripped the seams.

While he'd been bound, his anger had grown and grown until he wanted to pummel something—not Jett, never her, though in honesty a fair portion on his anger was directed at her.

She'd left him. *For Airyon.* That was on whom Thad's anger centred. He was the one Thad wanted to take out. When Jett put her hand into Airyon's, Thad couldn't contain his howl of outrage.

How dare she?

Whether she removed the mark he'd given her or not, she belonged with him. *To him!* They were bound. Thad would allow no man to touch her. She was his and no one, god or otherwise, would take her from him. He would reclaim her even if he had to go to the ends of the earth to find her.

He came to a dead stop at the thought.

He'd go to the ends of the earth and, perhaps,

beyond. To the heavens if necessary. And he knew where to start. Jett's audience chamber. It was neither on earth or in the heavens but in between, and it was the best place to start looking for her on his mission to find his goddess.

Jett wouldn't like that he'd come after her, but she could get over it. The goddess was his.

Closing his eyes, he visualised the room and prepared for battle. Mentally, he erected a shield of power around him and transported. He had no way of knowing if he'd encounter Airyon or the god's minions. If he did, he'd be ready.

The room was dark when he appeared, the torches extinguished when Reddjedet was not present. That magical procedure turned out to be a good thing, since several of the torches had been upturned and now lay on flammable objects. Many were crushed into reedy powder on the floor.

With a swoop of his hand, Thad levitated the undamaged torches back into their iron holders. Another circular swipe created a light blue ball of light above his outstretched hand.

As the glowing blue orb illuminated the entire area, his anger surged. The torches were not the only victims to Airyon's wrath. He'd destroyed the room. Jett's throne lay in splinters, the fabric shredded. The entire dais was scorched and collapsed. The jewel-toned murals, tributes to Jett, were ripped, as well. Some were pulled from the walls, some appeared as if giant animals had clawed through them. One side of the gold, double doors in the back of the chamber hung drunkenly to the side, revealing a darkened passageway.

Everywhere Thad looked, destruction met his gaze.

Anger gave way to fear for his goddess. This was the person with whom Jett had left? Airyon would destroy her. He'd crush her delicate form as easily as the pulverised torches.

A howl built inside Thad. He couldn't tolerate the thought of her hurt.

He wouldn't allow it. He wouldn't allow anyone to hurt his precious goddess. Much as he'd claimed to be her god, much as she might claim to have released him from duty, he was still pledged to her. He still worshiped her and always would, although the meaning and depth of his worship had changed.

He had to find her.

Surveying the destruction around him, he sensed his first step towards finding Jett would be down the newly revealed passage behind the gold doors. As he crossed to it, his footsteps echoed on the bare marble, emphasising the emptiness of the space and echoing the hollowness of his soul. Without Jett, he had nothing. His being was empty without her essence inside and beside him.

She'd torn herself from the very root of him when she'd left, stripping herself from him. She thought she'd taken everything but she'd left residue. He felt her. He sensed her turmoil now, and her need for him.

Why did she separate herself from him? Why didn't she allow his assistance? *Airyon.* There was no other answer. Jett was protecting him from Wrath. Thad swore. He didn't want or need protection. He needed her.

He ignored the truth that he'd nearly died last time he'd faced the god. The previous battle was different. He hadn't expected Wrath. He hadn't had this desperation inside him.

Last time you had all your powers, a voice whispered in his thoughts.

With a grimace, he focused on the gate.

'Where no mortal shall tread' was emblazoned on the arch above the doorway. He paused and pondered the possibilities. What would happen if he crossed? Guards? Death? Smiting? Would it draw out Jett?

A warning was a warning, but how many warnings had he ignored over the last two hundred years? At least one for every year in Jett's service. Deliberately, he stepped over the invisible border between the mortal and divine realms and quickly brought his other foot to rest beside the first. He'd seen too many action movies to believe he was home free, but as he waited a moment, nothing happened. No spiked beams swung at him, no collapsed floors, no huge boulder. Nothing. Was it possible the gods thought the warning alone would keep mortal men from trespassing? Surely not. After all, humans would be human. Very little stopped them from crossing the line, particularly if there were no clear consequences. It was the way of man.

To his surprise, instead of a chasm opening beneath his feet, the torches in the passage flickered to life, their pale green flames casting an eerie glow over the plain hall. The nondescript quality of the passage surprised him. There were no hangings, etchings or inlays, just bare marble walls. Nothing signified he'd crossed into the divine realm.

He extinguished the energy ball over his hand. If there was illumination here, he preferred to save his energy for the battle that was sure to come. He realised at once, his orb had cast most of the light in the tunnel. With it now extinguished, the tunnel grew dim and a bright light became apparent in the distance. Cautiously, he took another step and headed towards the glow.

*Go into the light...*his thoughts taunted.

Perhaps he should turn around.

A crack of thunder forestalled his decision and heralded the arrival of another—a god? A guardian? An acolyte? Thad wasn't sure. He stood his ground, his fingers flexed and ready in case he had to fight.

A man draped in white cloth stood before him with beefy arms crossed over his semi-bared chest. His forbidding granite-hard face and heavy-browed gaze pierced Thad.

"Thaddeus Pennington," he said, his voice a rolling boom in the tunnel. "You will come with me."

Before Thad could flinch away, the being grasped his arm and they transported into darkness.

Chapter Seventeen

Jett knelt in the dank, dimly lit chamber, her head bowed. Her gown clung to her in the miserable heat while the humidity pasted tendrils of her long red-blonde hair to her face.

"Master Bannor," she murmured in greeting to her mentor.

"Rise, my child, there is no need to kneel before me. I am banished. Disgraced and removed from power."

"Betrayed," Jett ground out.

He shrugged, his show of nonchalance in no way hiding his deep feelings on the matter. "Nevertheless, in truth, it is I who is now required to bow before you."

"Never," she answered. Rising, she met his gaze. "How can I serve you?"

"You must destroy the one who betrayed me. You must stop him from preying on other gods. You know of whom I speak. It is a mission of which you are already aware."

"Airyon," she confirmed. "I was not sure it was him."

"No one knows. Only he." He tipped his head. "And I."

Bannor indicated a pair of shabby chairs

behind them and went to seat himself. He waited pointedly while she decided to sit. She'd never been allowed to sit in his presence before. Even now, condemned to Torment, a golden light haloed him while he leaned back in his chair, his long fingers steepled before him.

He glanced away only when a third person, a handmaiden, joined them. He took the maid's hand, a sad smile lighting his eyes as his thumb caressed the back of her wrist.

Jett understood the sadness. When Anya had died, she'd had the choice of eternity in Paradise behind Nara's veil or here in Torment. She'd chosen Torment in order to be with her love. While her being here obviously soothed Bannor, he visibly regretted the future she'd chosen.

"Anya tells me there is a human with whom you have...grown quite fond."

"Yes," Jett admitted, tamping down the accompanying pain. Torment amplified pain. All sadness, all pains, all negative emotions were magnified here. Not only were occupants separated from the divinity, but they watched painful events take place, powerless to stop them. Jett had no doubt that Bannor had witnessed Anya's demise. He'd likely witnessed her choice of destinations, Paradise or Torment, while he screamed with frustration.

"I have witnessed your time with Thad," Bannor admitted, confirming that he knew far more than a mere whisper of knowledge from his lover. "I have tried to counsel you but of course, I cannot be heard from here."

Jett nodded, hot tendrils splaying up her face. What exactly had he witnessed? She didn't want to know.

"There is no need to be embarrassed," he told

her, glancing up at Anya as he obviously thought of their relationship prior to his banishment. It was a relationship forbidden in the heavens and forbidden to resume here. As shades of their physical selves, they could be together but never engage in physical love. Another torment. "The Higher Power created the love you expressed with Thad. It is not wrong to share your affection and desire."

"He is mortal," she whispered.

"And so you left him."

"I seek to protect him from Airyon."

Her lord sighed. She could almost hear him thinking, *Foolish, foolish child.* She didn't feel foolish. She felt empty. But his sigh said it all. He found her unwise. She wasn't. She was protecting Thad. If leaving him was the only way to save him, she'd do what she had to do.

Bannor leaned towards her, holding her hand between his clammy fingers. "You've made a mistake. He is not mortal, child."

"What?" she exclaimed. Her hand flew to her mouth and she immediately bowed her head. "Pardon my reaction and my disbelief. How is it that you say that Warlock Pennington is not human?"

"I sense many changes in you." He tilted his head and amusement lit his eyes.

"Yes," she answered. He'd witnessed her relationship with Thad. Of course, he knew there were changes in her. She bit her lip to hold back her disrespect. It was Torment bringing it out. She'd never have felt irritation and impudence towards her mentor before.

"You have given him your virginity."

Jett waited. Everything in her screamed for him to get to the point. He seemed to be dropping puzzle pieces on an invisible table, waiting for her to put two and two together. Unfortunately, whatever he clearly saw remained a mystery to her.

"And?" she asked in a carefully measure tone.

"That is the heart of it," he explained. "You have joined with him. By that, you gave him a gift that can never be taken from him."

"The virginity of a goddess?"

"No. You gave him immortality when you gave him your love and trust. He would not otherwise have been able to take your virginity and seal the pact you unknowingly wrote. He is destined to rule by your side. His powers are growing and will soon be equal to yours. You are part of each other. Have you not sensed a piece of yourself is missing since you have been separated from Thad? Airyon cannot force you to join with him. You are already joined with another. The only way he can take your power is to destroy Thad."

"Thad is immortal?"

"Didn't you know that when you gave yourself to him, you gave him immortality?" he asked. "He is in more danger after gaining immortality than before. While he is gaining strength, he is untrained in his powers and what he can do. By your action to evade Airyon, you created a path for you and Thad that did not exist before. You are halves of the same whole now. Ordained to be joined. It is still up to you, though. You can choose to work together or not. You can choose to be together forever...whole. Or you can choose to be separate and become fractured pieces of what once was. Never happy." He regarded her with an expression as close to sympathy as a deposed god in Torment could get. "And always feeling as you do now."

"He will not want me back. Not after how I left him." Emotion trembled in her chest. She had to get herself under control before she took on Airyon.

"Do you really believe that? Did you not hear his cry when you left him? I did. I do not believe he is so willing to let you go. You must go to him. Now, before Airyon realises the change in Thad."

Oh gods! Airyon thrived on preying on vulnerable gods. If Thad was equal to her, he had the power to fight Airyon but little knowledge in how to wield it. Wrath would sense that, too. He'd be overjoyed to siphon away Thad's energy.

She had to get to Thad before her nemesis did.

She turned her gaze back to Bannor watching him embrace Anya and hold her tightly—the extent of what they were allowed to have here. They had more than she and Thad had now or would have if Airyon managed to destroy one of them.

"Can we really be together?" she whispered.

"The future has not yet been written. The two of you can defeat Airyon. You are two and he is one." He glanced at her belly. "And you have much to live for. Your union and your heir."

A wild flutter in her abdomen answered his statement. She placed her hand over it, feeling a vibration of life she'd missed in her turmoil. "An heir?"

"A girl." He smiled. "Created when you joined with your mate over your place of power."

A child? She had to tell Thad!

Oh gods! She had to get to him before Airyon.

She knelt hastily. "Thank you, Master Bannor. I will defeat your betrayer."

"One more thing," he said quietly.

"Yes?" she asked in surprise. Did he know of Airyon's weakness?

Bannor turned to his lover. "Await me in the outer passage. Stay close to the protection of my door. You will be safe there."

Anya nodded then hugged Jett. "Blessings until we meet again, my goddess."

Bannor waited until Anya had departed, watching her in adoration as she went. He moved close to Jett as soon as the heavy door closed.

"How may I serve you?" she asked.

"Hades and Persephone have finally convinced Demeter they are happy together. They have gone away for a brief time alone." He moved close, his lips pressed to her ear. "Now, while the gates of Torment are weak by his absence, help me from here. Hide me in your territories and reanimate Anya."

Jett had never denied her mentor any request, and though he'd been betrayed, what he beseeched was paramount to treason. If she did as he asked and Airyon defeated her, she would be condemned to eternity in Torment. As her other half, Thad would be condemned, too.

Sorrow filled her. Bannor solicited her help not for his sake, but for his lover's. He sought only to save her. And perhaps, to be able to spend some time in her life. Jett's heart wrenched. This was the one thing she couldn't do for him.

Slowly, she shook her head. "I am sorry, Master Bannor. I cannot."

Bannor stepped back and sighed. He looked sadly at the door where Anya waited beyond sight. "I understand. I should not have asked you."

"But I know why." Wouldn't she do the same for Thad? Hadn't she already? "I wish that I could grant you this."

He nodded. "There is more than yourself to consider." His smile didn't reach his eyes, and he placed a hand on her head. "Have faith, child. You will win this battle. You have my blessings and strength, weak though they are."

"Thank you, Master Bannor." Though he'd been stripped of most power and disappointment at her refusal cloaked him, his support bolstered her for what lay ahead. She would defeat Airyon in his honour.

She held her arms out to her sides, slim wings reaching for the sky, as she prepared to transport to Thad. "Until we meet again."

* * * *

"Thad!"

Jett's call turned to a gasp. Around her, the cave lay destroyed, books ripped apart and linens shredded. The bed where she and Thad had lain was burned. The other furniture in the cavern was in pieces.

Airyon hadn't restricted his attack to the places she'd touched. The shelves lining the perimeter of the chambers were cut in half. Clay apothecary jars were smashed, their contents spattered and oozing onto the ground. Even the cave's walls had giant claw-like gouges raking down them. Nothing remained untouched. Without the amplification of her power to protect it, Airyon had come here and demolished Thad's refuge.

Anger scorched through her as she stared at the bed where she'd shared her love with Thad. It was nothing more than a pile of coarse ashes. The floor over the connection of the ley lines was splintered, another show of anger. He couldn't destroy it. The power grid was impervious to his rage. Still he left the marks of destruction.

"Thad!" she screamed.

Her spirit shot through the warren of rooms made by the adjoining caverns.

No Thad.

Quickly she propelled the same way through the mansion.

No Thad.

New York.

No Thad.

Frantically, she scanned the planet for his energy. Horror and destruction met her, but no Thad. He'd disappeared as completely as if he'd been wiped from existence.

He wasn't dead. At least, not on earth. While his spirit would have been within Nara's possession, Jett would have found his residual energy lingering near his body. He'd simply vanished.

Airyon had taken his body.

A sob of despair welled inside her and drove her to her knees, there over the ley line connection. Even as the energy geyser touched her, her spirit wailed for her loss. For her stupidity. Thad didn't know she'd been unable to remove his powers. He wouldn't have followed her. He'd been helpless against Wrath.

She was as much at fault for his death as her nemesis.

Pain lashed through her as she curled in a ball above the geyser, her palm pressed to the floor and her tears pooling on the stone floor. Great sobs tore from her chest and scrapped past her closed throat. Pain ripped through her middle.

She'd lost Thad. Without him, she'd lose her child. His essence was imperative for growing the babe.

Without ever touching her, Airyon had destroyed her.

For a long time she couldn't move. She could

barely breathe. Slowly, cold determination built in her as her cheek pressed to the cold rock. What happened to her now didn't matter.

She'd destroy Airyon for this.

She'd see Bannor received his wish. She might not have her love, but she'd see that he had a chance to have his. Whether she died or not, she'd be in Torment without Thad. She might as well do some good for someone while she could. If she helped Bannor and Anya, it couldn't be undone even if she died. No one would know where in her territories she'd hidden them.

Mentally, she girded herself for the battle to come. Airyon demanded she join with him by sunset. He would be dead by then.

* * * *

"Master Bannor." Jett's voice rang through the dank chamber. Bannor looked up from his embrace of a tearful Anya.

"Reddjedet. I did not think to see you again so soon."

"I've come to grant you your request." Without wasting time, she strode to the couple.

"What has happened? What changed your mind?" Concern filled Bannor's face. He realised the magnitude of her actions and the repercussions that would follow if she were caught. He above all others would know that her actions would condemn her, unless she was proven heroic by Bannor's absolution. "What has happened?" he repeated.

"There is not time for that," she answered. "Hades will know what I am about—I will have to work quickly."

"Are you sure?"

This was right. If she was condemned for doing the right thing, there was something wrong in the heavens. There was already something wrong. Airyon was allowed free reign when he should be in the worst part of Torment.

She pulled Anya to her feet and turned to Bannor. "Since I will not need to create a new corporeal body for you, I will send Anya first. She will take longer. Anya, because Airyon destroyed your flesh, I will have to create a new body."

The handmaiden nodded. She embraced Bannor tightly, her face pressed to his chest. She whispered his name as he pressed his lips to her hair.

"Thank you, child," he told Jett, placing his hand on her shoulder. "I am in your debt."

She shook her head. "There is no debt, and you may curse me before this is over. To mask your location, I will not be able to send you together. And in her new body, Anya will not remember her past. I will be unable to reveal her location, either, without risking her discovery."

"Bannor!" Anya cried.

"It's our only chance," he whispered, emotion brimming in his eyes. "I will find you. When I do, you'll remember. Trust me. I *will* find you."

The hollowness inside Jett echoed with the devotion between the two lovers. If only, she hadn't sacrificed the love she had for Thad. By leaving him alone, she'd signed his death warrant instead. And now, she'd sign her own.

Dead or alive—without Thad, it would be Torment either way. Steeling herself against the consequences, she summoned the power to reanimate Anya and save her friend. Immediately, the walls of Torment responded with an ear-piercing alarm. Beyond the walls of Bannor's chamber, the clamour of pounding feet and howls rose. There were no secrets here. She'd have but minutes to complete her task and escape.

She wouldn't need more than that.

Fully empowered, she clasped Anya's shoulder. "We must hurry!"

For agonising minutes, Jett split her being between Torment and earth as she spun a new being for Anya. The moment the vessel was complete, she thrust Anya into it, closing the passage between the handmaiden and Bannor so that the path to the new being could not be traced.

Anya was safe.

Jett turned to Bannor, knowing there wasn't a second to spare. The handmaiden might be safe, but without her heart's mate, she'd spend her life searching for something or someone she'd never find. If Jett failed, she'd have consigned the woman to a fate worse than the Torment she'd escaped.

"Tell me where she is," Bannor begged as soon as they were alone.

Jett shook her head. "I cannot. This is your quest. Find her. Prove yourself, and with your actions, disprove the lies that condemned you here." She paused. "For *all* our sakes.

"Anya is under a veil of protection," she continued. "If ever she is in danger, you will immediately be taken to her so that you may protect her. She will not know you, and when she is safe, you will return to where you were before transporting. Until you find her of your own accord, I can give you this gift alone to find her." She splayed her fingers on his temples. "Know her by this vibration."

A bellow filled the chamber as Hades' minions

flooded through the door. Jett's eyes went wide. Acting reflexively, she clasped Bannor and transported from the room amid curses and screams.

* * * *

Jett had never experienced unwelcome in Eden, but now, as she sought the respite of her home, she sensed she didn't belong. It didn't matter that what she'd done was with the best intentions—righting a wrong that had been done.

She'd broken the code of honour. She'd rescued not one but two from Torment, and even rescuing one would forever condemn her unless Bannor redeemed himself.

She could not feel remorse for her deed, however. She'd been correct to right the wrong. It should have been done long ago. For now, she had to avoid detection and avoid death. Though she'd charged Bannor with redeeming himself, she'd eke an answer from Airyon by whatever means necessary.

She'd get her answers or die trying. She had nothing to lose.

Thad was dead.

A sharp tremor wound through her. Jett swiped away a tear. She'd know soon if Hades had detected her presence in Bannor's cell. The God of the Underworld would know that another god had assisted Bannor, but her master had mentored many. Each one would be suspect in his escape. Once the culprit was pinpointed—if the culprit was pinpointed—there would be nowhere to hide.

Condemnation would come. Her powers and her territories would be stripped from her. Then her freedom would be removed. She'd spend the remainder of eternity in Torment.

Still in her one transgression, she found comfort. Bannor and Anya would find each other. Eventually. They'd know happiness. Happiness denied her, even if—when—she defeated Airyon and revealed his betrayal of her master.

Her fingers spread over the place where her baby rested, her final connection to Thad that would soon wane. "I *will* defeat Airyon and I *will* wring his confession from him before I deliver him to Nara. Bannor will be redeemed."

Could she barter with Nara for the return of Thad? Surely, her sister wanted something else. Perhaps she'd be in a conciliatory mood once she had the object of her desire within her grasp.

Jett smiled, the object of *her* desire would brighten her outlook, too. A glimmer of hope shone on the horizon. All was not lost. She shook off the after-affects of Torment's morose spell. Determination lightened her steps as she marched to the starburst of bright tiles decorating the floor in the centre of her home.

She spread her arms, becoming one with her divine strength. It flowed into her and through her as she communed with the heavens to regenerate the energy she'd depleted during her time on earth and Torment. The electrified bands of power snapped around her.

"Just about done?"

Jett peered through a wavering cloud of energy to see the Goddess of the Veil leaning against the wall a few feet from her. Couldn't her sister ever announce herself?

"Nara," she acknowledged through her teeth.

"I don't want to interrupt you getting all pretty and all."

Fuming at the interruption, Jett completed

her regeneration. The beams of energy closed, disappearing from sight. "What do you want?"

"I trust you're preparing to finally bring Airy to me."

"Finally! It is not as if—" Jett broke off her fingers clenching. It wouldn't do any good to alienate her sister. "Is that why you are here?"

Nara rolled her eyes. "You summoned me. Gods! You couldn't have been thinking any louder. It's a wonder the entirety of Eden doesn't know what you've done."

Jett glared at her. "My thoughts are not loud."

"Really?" Nara replied sarcastically. "Could have fooled me."

"You were deliberately invading my mind."

Nara shrugged. "Sometimes, I like to use this stupid, useless gift of mine. You may know about it—"

"It is not useless. It helps you protect the veil—*when* you use it properly. Why were you in my head?"

"You want to breach the veil—that's why. So if you could tone down your thoughts. . . they're like a shooting star stabbing through my third eye."

"I want Thad back."

"I can't help you there."

"To Torment with that! Why not?"

Nara made a show of looking around the chamber. "Mmmmm...perhaps because...I don't have him."

"Do not play with me, Nara!"

Her sister laughed. "Believe he's dead if you please, but he's not within my realm." She leaned forward, mirth lighting her violet eyes. "Gods don't spend eternity in my realm. The Valley of Rest awaits them, a time of regeneration followed by new life. Wake up and smell the ambrosia! You know that as well as I do."

"You spend too much time on earth. Even I do not speak as my people do," Jett chided, the weight of Nara's revelation bombarding her consciousness. It was nearly too much to contemplate. Or hope.

"Lighten up, goddess! Your worlds don't need a stick in the mud. They need the woman you're becoming."

"How did you become so wise?"

Nara snorted her disagreement with the assessment. "Guarding the veil is boring. I study the Scrolls of Eternity to pass time."

And play with your slaves, Jett added silently.

Her sister laughed easily reading the thought. "All work and no play, makes Nara a grouchy girl. So when do you think you'll be delivering Airy?"

"Today."

"Excellent."

"Nara?" Jett called, stopping her sister as she prepared to leave. "If Thad's not with you, do you know where he is? Is he regenerating?"

"He's not dead, sister." She winked, raising her arms to transport. "Go kick Airyon's ass and live happily ever after. Oh, and you'd better let my niece come visit me."

With the last word, she disappeared, leaving Jett staring after her.

Did everyone know about the baby?

Shaking her head, Jett prepared to transport to Airyon's holdings. That would take him by surprise. He'd never expect her to come to the sunless planet where he dwelled when he wasn't spreading his wrath throughout the countless universes.

"Goddess Redjedett!"

She jumped, turning. The Council's messenger stood in the doorway to her dwelling. His arms crossed over his chest as he regarded her. His eyes narrowed as he swept his gaze over her. "You are called before the Council. Immediately!"

Before she could transport an iron manacle appeared around her ankle. Jett flinched as it bit into her skin, anchoring her to Eden.

In a flash, the messenger disappeared. There was no need to wait. There was no escape once the band circled her ankle. Besides, she had no where to escape to.

She'd been discovered.

The Festival of Regeneration was over.

Perfect timing.

* * * *

"Wait here."

Thad looked at the hulking guardian beside him. "Where are we?"

And why did they have to wait? Was he dead? Was this the place of judgment? Wait! There was a waiting room for judgment? Did he get a number? He didn't feel dead. And he'd know. He'd been dead before—well mostly dead anyway.

The man gave a slight bow, reminding him of a disgruntled genie of the lamp, then disappeared without answering.

"So apparently, *we* won't be waiting," Thad muttered. It would only be him. Now alone and curious, he peered about him. Nara was nowhere to be seen. That surprised him. Didn't she preside over the dead? What had Jett told him? Nara guarded the veil—the path to paradise.

Nara had nothing to do with Torment. If Torment was where he'd landed for eternity, it would explain why she wasn't here. Somehow, this place didn't strike him as particularly tormented.

A guise perhaps.

The goon seemed to have left him on some sort of Greekesque porch. Tall columns fronted the area while behind him lay a solid marble wall with a giant doorway.

He wasn't going through it. Last time he'd ventured through a mysterious portal, he'd been hijacked here. If this truly was a holding place before entering Torment, he wasn't waiting around to be judged.

He'd found a way in. He'd find a way out. Then he'd find Jett.

Maybe he was closer than he thought, though. The mists and architecture hinted that perhaps this was Jett's Eden. It certainly appeared the way picture books represented heaven. If that was the case, then it followed that he'd find Jett here.

Damning the consequences—if he were to enter Torment anyhow, how much worse could it be? Thad started down the steps that led from the 'porch' and into the mist. Hazy, white and pastel robed figures moved about between the wide-spaced buildings. It reminded him of an ethereal city—and perhaps this was. A quiet, somewhat musical murmur wafted across the air as gentle as an early summer breeze. It calmed the turmoil in his spirit and reassured him he would find Jett. At the same time, the energy within him surged, agitated and growing within this divine plane.

He'd never felt so powerful. Odd, especially since Jett had tried to strip it from him. Was he somehow leaching from this place and its inhabitants? Were the other beings gods or were they acolytes and handmaidens? Whoever they were they took little notice of him as he strode among them. Fine with him. He had to find Jett before she did something stupid like join with Airyon.

His blood ran cold at the thought that she might have already. If that was the case, he'd find a way to undo it. Jett belonged to him, and there was nothing Airyon could do to change that.

He deliberately pushed aside the thought that Airyon could kill him. He wasn't going there. The power surging through him spoke of Wrath's defeat. He wouldn't kill Thad again.

As he lost sight of the place where the hulk had deposited him, it occurred to Thad that he had no idea how to find Jett. He couldn't very well go from being to being asking for her. He couldn't go knocking from door to door. Gods! There weren't even any doors in this place.

If he asked for her, he might as well alert the media that a trespasser had entered the inner sanctum.

"Thad."

He looked up in surprise. So much for moving about unnoticed. A stern man stood before him, a golden light haloing his white-draped body. Despite his outward demeanour the man's eyes danced with amusement.

Is that good or bad?

"You must learn to listen. My acolyte instructed you to await me."

Okay, bad. He'd need to work around this somehow. He was not going to Torment, and he was not abandoning Jett. Thad drew himself up, determined to challenge this god if need be.

The being placed his hand on Thad's shoulder, showing a power so great Thad knew he'd never defeat him. This power vibrated far greater than Jett's, even before she'd muted her energy levels.

"Who are you?" he asked.

"I am Miccal, head of the Council that rules over the twelve quadrants—including the Zodiac Quadrant. And for now, I will excuse your lack of protocol and respect. There is much in which you must be instructed."

Gods! He didn't have time for that. Even now Airyon could be forcing Jett to join with him.

"He is not," Miccal answered. "Yet."

"You can read my thoughts." It didn't surprise Thad. After the last two hundred years, nothing surprised him—at least, nothing like this. Jett managed to surprise him all the time.

The 'yet' sank in suddenly and sent another bolt of urgency through him. "Where is she?"

"Soon enough. Come with me, Thaddeus Pennington, and I will help you find that which you seek."

* * * *

Jett knelt before ten of the twelve council members who oversaw the quadrants. Master Bannor had not been replaced and the twelfth member was mysteriously missing. Silently, she awaited their condemnation. In their eyes, no matter her motives she deserved punishment.

She'd stolen property—that's what Bannor was considered, Hades property—and she'd hidden that property away. She'd helped a criminal escape. It didn't matter that he wasn't guilty.

"You may rise, goddess," the Council instructed, their voices joining as one.

Keeping her head lowered, she did as they asked. Around her their essences flowed, skimming her body and probing her secrets. Their ghostly hands touched her everywhere, pulling her robe from her so that she had nothing to hide.

"We know as you know that he was not guilty."

Her head shot up and she quickly scanned the white robed council members. Their hoods were pulled up, shadowing their faces. They surveyed her unmoved as their minds and energies continued to stroke her.

"What do you mean?" she blurted. She panted as her legs were shoved apart and a pillar of energy parted her folds. It skated along her rapidly moistening cleft, sending pulses of power into her clit.

Never had she been treated thus. Of course, she'd never been called before the Council either. Bands of air captured her arms, pulling them behind her back while the investigation continued.

"Long has the God of Wrath sought power and vengeance on other gods. Because of his nature, he is not subject to this council. He is a rogue with no master. When he betrayed your master, we allowed the belief that Bannor had terrorised the people of his quadrants, partaking of the men and women as he pleased."

"Yes," she whispered, as her breasts were moulded. She dropped to her knees, her head falling back. She could barely concentrate on the words.

"We allowed your master to go to Torment. He knew Airyon's secret. Eventually, Airyon would have visited him, and Bannor would have destroyed him. He is the strongest of us. Banished from the Council he could easily have gotten rid of his enemy. We cannot. The Council may not kill."

Her cunt convulsed as a surge of energy shot into it, stretching the tender walls. All the while ten pairs of hands held her. No place went untouched. Rubbing, stroking, probing the Council found her secrets. Joy and confidence filled her, replacing all the fear and worry.

"What are you doing?" she gasped, arching into invisible fingers, her eyes closed. It seemed the Council touched her everywhere.

"Strengthening you."

"How—" Her question turned to a cry as energy moved in her again accompanied by another energy taking her ass and spiralling up into her middle. Her breasts were squeezed, the touch moving outward to pull her nipples. She moaned, filled with too many sensations at once. Her arousal dripped from her spread pussy to the floor between her knees.

"Bannor cannot kill Airyon now. That task falls to you. Defeat him and you will be pardoned for the crime you have committed. Fail and you will be punished."

A sharp smack across her buttocks drove a gasp from her. She bent forward on shoulders and knees, her arms still bound behind her and ass high in the air as the energy fucked her. Hands supported her, thrusting her helpless body back onto the forces ploughing into her. Orgasm coiled within her, driven tighter by another strike across her rear.

"Fail and you will go to Torment in Bannor's place."

"I will not fail," she vowed, her voice high on the brink of release. "I will not fail."

She screamed as starbursts exploded behind her lids, her body convulsing as the Council's energy surged through her. Her arms and legs stretched outward as she hovered slightly above the ground. Gently, the hands lowered her and she lay panting against the cool marble. The manacle, which had anchored her, fell away.

"I will not fail."

* * * *

Miccal led Thad back towards the structure where he'd been instructed to wait. As he followed feeling like a chastised schoolboy—and just as rebellious and resentful of it—a woman dressed in a white sarong exited the building.

Jett! A serene light shone in her eyes that he hadn't seen before. She appeared powerful, with a secret knowledge in her satisfied smile. How could she look so happy when he wanted to howl at the moon for protest of her departure?

She wasn't tormented by it at all the way he was.

He couldn't accept that. He didn't want her unhappy, but he refused to be without her. She belonged to him. And damn it! She'd said so. He wouldn't let the two of them suffer because she was out of her mind with some insane goddess-woman-hormone-imbalancing PMS.

She could smite him all she wanted to. He'd walked in the home of the gods. He'd endure her wrath. He wasn't letting go.

"Airyon!" she yelled, her authoritative voice ringing clear in the misty air. Thad surged forward without heed to what Miccal would say or what protocol he should remember to use.

Before he could call her name, Airyon appeared on the porch behind her. He wrapped his arms around her waist. Jett startled, her eyes growing wide. She pulled at Airyon's grasp while he said something into her ear.

Thad dashed towards them. Airyon would not

steal Jett when Thad had only just found her again. More importantly, he would not allow Wrath to hurt her. She was his goddess and he'd die before he'd allow any harm to come to her.

* * * *

Jett struggled against Airyon's grasp, pain tearing through her middle as he speared tentacles of power inside her to hold her still. This was not what she'd intended when she'd called him out. He'd deliberately appeared behind her, taking her by surprise.

Had she failed the Council already? No. He might drag her away, but she would still win.

"You're mine now," he growled in her ear.

"I will never belong to you."

"Oh, yes, I know. You think you've given yourself to him," Airyon laughed. His warm breath dampened her ear. "But I will kill him. Then I'll take you for my own, as was always intended to be."

Ice flowed through her, splintering into her middle. "Do you really want a mate who will hate you for all eternity?"

"Wrath *is* my business. A little hate doesn't bother me." The band around her middle tightened, and he bit the skin between her neck and shoulder. "It excites me, sweets."

He wrenched her from her home and into darkness of his transport tunnel. The sound of a bellowed protest following them filled her ears. Whoever sought to aid her had come too late.

She was afraid. What would happen if she couldn't defeat him?

Chapter Eighteen

"No!" Thad's protest ripped from him along with what seemed half his soul. One moment, Jett and Airyon had been there, the next all that remained was a shimmering aura where Jett had been.

As it spiralled away, Thad dashed after it before the trail dissipated and she was left alone with Airyon while he tried to discern where Wrath had taken his mate. The thought of her alone at his hands was almost more than he could bear.

His life was a waking nightmare. Just as he reached the shimmering mist, it disappeared leaving him grasping at nothing as Jett's essence wrapped around him and vanished. He ground out a curse that would have had the gods blushing if they'd heard it. This was untenable! Perhaps he was in Torment; finding and losing Jett was his punishment.

A hand settled on his shoulder, its searing vibration telling him the appendage belonged to Miccal.

"Calm yourself, my child—"

My child?

"—Your mate is not lost."

* * * *

Pleasure suffused along Jett's limbs as she returned to consciousness. *Thad.* It had to be. Only he stroked her this way, only he made her feel on fire with his caresses.

Her legs spread open and hung over the side of the bed, while he parted her folds. His tongue delved along them, flicking and probing while she twisted with the tendrils of rapture radiating from her centre.

It felt so good...

Still, unease nipped at the edges of her euphoria. Something wasn't right. Her position was...uncomfortable. And...this wasn't the firm mattress beneath her. It cushioned her body as well as rock.

She couldn't move her arms and legs.

As she struggled to open her eyes, a murmur around her caused her brow to crease.

What in the worlds?

"Good, you're awake."

The sardonic voice yanked her from the fuzzy place between the worlds of sleep and wakefulness. Jett's eyes went wide as the gravity of her situation returned to her. Airyon had stolen her from her home. She'd bitten him during the transport and he'd knocked her unconscious while attempting to dislodge her teeth.

She had no clue where he'd brought her. It wasn't one her holdings—her weakened state revealed that. Anxiously, she tried to sit up but couldn't. Her arms were pulled down towards the floor and chained. Her legs, bent over the end of the table on which she lay, were manacled as well.

She couldn't see Airyon, her view blocked by her skirt bunched at her waist. But she could feel him. Oh gods! She could feel him. He knelt between her parted knees while his fingers stroked inside her and he continued to taste her.

"I know why your mortal craved you," he rasped before he spread two fingers inside her and plunged in his tongue.

Her pelvic muscles convulsed in response, tightening, sending more cream to feed his appetite. Breathing became tortured, each breath catching on the guilty bliss he produced.

"Just give in," he whispered as she clawed her nails into the stone table, sending gravel pinging to the bare floor. "I'll give you pleasure like you've never known."

"No," she moaned. It was tempting, oh so tempting when he sent such pleasure spearing through her womb. She could forget everything and give herself into the sensations. It was an illusion. She could enjoy now, but afterward... afterward she'd have let Airyon capture her soul. She'd have failed her people and betrayed Thad, the man to whom she truly belonged.

"I'll make you beg," Airyon promised.

Her head thrashed from side to side. She couldn't forget herself. This was wrong. How could she feel such pleasure from her fiercest enemy— the man who sought to control and destroy all she loved? Yet, as she fought against his touch, persistent tendrils of pleasure raked through her core.

"Oh gods!" she cried as her body convulsed, ecstasy flying to her toes and fingertips.

"Oh yes," he laughed, holding up a glistening hand. "My people! See how the goddess prepares for our union."

My people? A frantic glance around her revealed hundreds of beings witnessing her humiliation at Airyon's hands. He'd chained her to an altar in the centre of some sort of small coliseum. They 'had the floor' while the others in various levels of undress watched avidly from the tiers of seats. Excitement sparked through the crowd. This unholy union would trigger a civilization-wide orgy.

Airyon would fuck her while his world watched.

Heat rushed up her chest to her face. So this would be how it was. He'd put her on display. He'd steal possession of her channel with a multitude of witnesses—in the relative safety of his holdings. It made sense. He needed to join with her before his people to prove his possession of her—whether or not he used rape to make his claim. This was also the one place he could suppress her energy. Here he could take her, though she'd be unwilling, and no one would stop him. She was at his complete mercy.

She gritted her teeth against the sensations he evoked. Had he used some sort of magic on her? None of his subjects would believe her unwilling, the way her body betrayed her to him. The stroke of his fingers coaxed forth another round of shudders.

As if answering her troubled musing, Airyon rubbed an elixir on her folds. While she tried to twist her hips away, he sent stakes of energy though her once again, pinning her abdomen and thighs where he'd arranged them.

"Are you so desperate for power that you would rape to achieve it?" she asked, her words altering in pitch as the emollient sank into her skin. Both hot and cold together, it drove her insane with want. Her folds swelled as they reacted to whatever he'd applied. She writhed against her restraints while he continued to stroke her, coating her inner walls as well until she was a mass of quivering sensation.

"I will not rape you. You will beg me to take you. You will be mine to mould and command, just as your holdings will be mine."

As she fought to hold off the mindless need pounding into her, she feared he spoke the truth. She couldn't fight this. If only she could get her hands free. Her heart pounded with helpless dread. Desire weakened her limbs. Much more of the magic he wrought over her and she'd plead for his cock—any cock—to be buried within her.

No she wouldn't! She was stronger than her weak flesh. She needn't give in to the carnal temptation he presented.

Airyon stood and addressed his people. "Witness as I prepare the sacred portal. Soon, we will share in the power of the Zodiac Quadrant."

A cheer went up.

Not, if she had a say in it!

"Behold, the sacred member."

Her eyes went wide as he opened his pants to reveal a penis to rival Thad's in thickness, if not length. Despite the need screaming inside her, begging for a man, any man, she fruitlessly fought against the chains. The metal clanked with her efforts but gave no sign of breaking.

She was stronger than her need. She was! She wouldn't mindlessly submit to Wrath just to have a cock inside her to ease the ravenous hunger.

With a smug smile, he stroked his palms up the inside of her thighs and up over her pubic bone and beneath the fabric of her dress to her belly. His lips parted his eyes growing heavy with need. While he stared into her eyes, he dropped a hand to his arousal and stroked his fingers along it.

He was deep into the joining ceremony. Even

in the face of her exposed flesh, she didn't believe he could want her so much. She was a path on his quest for universal domination. He wanted to rule over the gods.

His arousal and distraction because of it seemed to say otherwise. He wanted her far beyond his need for power. Was it her resemblance to Nara? Though they were not identical in looks, his residual feelings might home in on the similarities in their features and vibrations.

He let out a shuddering breath as he continued to touch himself with one hand and stroke her with the other. Prickles launched an assault on her resistance. Gods! How could she endure this?

Now was the time to attack, while he was weakened by his desire, but without her hands, she couldn't direct her diminished powers. She cursed her own impotence. Her shoulders burned as she yanked against her restraints.

"I'm not yours to take!" she cried. "Let me go!"

He smiled languorously. "I don't think so."

Her bindings creaked, scraping against the stone where they were embedded. They didn't release. She tugged harder, hope strengthening her. "I reject this union. Even if you take me, it means nothing."

Airyon skated his fingertips along her thighs again and pushed her knees further apart to insinuate his body between them. She groaned as he rubbed his aroused cock along her mound, his wide tip catching at her hungry opening.

"Oh, I think it will mean something," he whispered as he bent over her and sucked the tip of her breast into his mouth. The light fabric between his tongue and her skin rasped against her nipple, provoking it into a rigid peak. Her chest arched into him. In her trussed position, the muscles of her back pulled painfully in counterpoint to the pleasure he doled out above her. He slid a hand beneath her to keep her bowed.

"Stop," she begged.

"This is my power on you," he rasped in her ear. He thrust his hips against her, his member prodding her, but still not entering. "Imagine my power within you."

A surge of need set off tremors in her belly. She'd refuse but her cursed body would betray her. It was a matter of moments before he would slip beyond his restraint and sink inside her. And much as it shamed her, she knew she'd have little protest beyond her negligible verbal complaint. Her body would welcome his entrance.

Gods! She needed Thad. Closing her eyes, she pictured him, willing his energy to come to her aid.

Airyon could do his worst, arouse her traitorous body, but he'd never really have her. It was Thad she desired. Thad who'd taught her body to anticipate the act Airyon described. Thad who was the other half of her soul.

"Thad, please. I need you," she whispered.

"Unhand her!"

"Thad!" she cried in joy. Her mate stood a few feet away, his face thunderous, his white-blond hair flying about his head as tendrils of power spiralled around him. Thank the gods! And he appeared very much alive!

"Gods curse you, mortal!" Airyon bellowed, turning from her and glaring at Thad while closing his pants. He stumbled against the wall of air that slammed into him. Thad growled as the god caught himself on Jett's open thighs. *How dare he touch my woman!*

Thad struggled to control his anger as electricity built in his fingers. Airyon was too close to Jett. He had to free her before he attacked in earnest.

Remember you are one with the goddess. Miccal's words from moments before rang in his mind. He'd free Jett and they'd battle Airyon together.

Jett struggled to see him around Airyon's wide shoulders. Her face was flushed and her hair in disarray from her captor's exploits. Her agitated breaths pulled against the manacles that held her to the altar, the thick metal bands gouging her delicate skin.

Rage burned through Thad, coupled with heart-sinking shame. The sight presented him when he arrived in Airyon's fortress was no better than the one he'd presented Bram that day so long ago in the cave. Just as he'd prepared to take Zora, Airyon prepared to take Jett. Thad had never intended to take Zora, however. With stark clarity, he knew the fear and possessive outrage that had been Bram's that day. Even if Thad realised Airyon's motives now were far different from his own that day, Bram had had no way of knowing Thad's intentions.

But Thad had something Bram hadn't possessed.

With the complete force of the anger boiling inside him, he sent dual spirals of pressurised air at the Airyon. Surprised by this second attack, the god toppled sideways and landed on his ass a few feet from Jett. He immediately jumped to his feet and drew a sword of fire from the air.

Thad glared at him. He would not lose this fight. Not this time. "You will stay away from her."

"Make me."

The flaming blade swung through the air, the tip sweeping close to Thad's face. He dodged backward.

It surprised him that Airyon would choose to use such a medieval-modelled weapon when he had other greater sources from which to draw. Thad drew his hands together in fists before him, then pushed them forcefully to his sides. A wall of energy crashed into Airyon and shoved him aside. With another sharp motion, Thad sent the chains on Jett's wrists and ankles clattering away.

She scrambled from the altar, her dress sliding back into place, but not before he saw the mark on her hip. His mark of possession. The wench hadn't erased it at all, only made him believe she had. Satisfaction erupted within him. It fed his determination to take her from this place—not that his determination needed feeding. She was his whether she chose to acknowledge it or not.

"I think I mentioned you'd need my help." He was done letting her try to protect him. It was time she understood her position at his side, not in front of him, ordering him, protecting him, or accepting his worship. She'd receive an entirely different form of worship from him now. And *his* protection.

"Always," she acknowledged. Her hand touched her stomach as she eyed Airyon and edged closer to Thad. "We are one."

Regaining his balance, Airyon bellowed at the crowd, which had thinned considerably since Thad had arrived. A pair of men, similar to their master's stature, separated from the throng. Their bearing spoke of death for the interloper. So did the red flames of anger that licked up Airyon's body as he glared at Thad. "I've been looking forward to killing you."

"Then you'll be disappointed. I've come to retrieve what is mine."

"She is mine!" Airyon protested. His sword sliced into the floor. The building shook and a chasm opened between them. Jett stood on the wrong side.

"Jump!" Thad called. "I'll catch you."

Immediately, thorny brambles, with snapping blooms the size of his fist, sprouted from the gaping expanse. The chasm grew wider as spears of jagged rock poked up amid the thicket.

Jett backed away from Airyon as he advanced on her, his intent clear. His hands went back to the fastening of his pants. The two men grabbed Jett's arms, dragging her back to the altar and holding her down. One of them yanked her dress up to her belly while Airyon advanced.

Screaming, she kicked at him.

Thad was in Torment. He'd thought finding and losing Jett had been hell? Controlled by the sadistic god on the other side of the chasm, the brambles parted just enough for him to see the horrifying tableau on the other side.

"Transport," he begged.

She shook her head, her hands twisting as she tried to get them in a position to smite any of the three men around her. "I can't."

Only then did he see the serpentine band that wound up her calf, lashed around Jett to prevent her escape. The end trailed across the floor to Airyon. The length shimmered, mutating with each of the god's movements, a living extension of its master. The prismatic surface reflected his dark nature, with fiery, ever-changing colour. Thad knew immediately that the tether wasn't formed of any breakable substance.

Bound by it, she couldn't come to the relative

safety of his side of the fissure. He'd go to her and fight the three men at close quarters.

And figure out how to release her from Airyon's hold.

His thoughts centred on her, Thad transported to the other side where he appeared crouched over Jett. Frightened, Airyon's minions jumped away, releasing her, while Wrath crossed his arms over his chest and glared.

"You're really annoying, mortal."

Angrily, Thad raised his hand just as he'd seen Jett do many times and pelted a smiting bolt towards his opponent. It halted almost as soon as it left his hand. *What the hell?*

Thad's eyes widened at the slim hand reaching around his body. Jett's fingers fisted and yanked away the arrested attack.

What the hell? He thought again. *She protected Wrath?*

Airyon laughed in delight. "Smite me, mortal, and you kill her. Oh the drama! What to do, what to do?"

Chapter Nineteen

What to do, indeed.

The coil on Jett's leg tightened as Airyon laughed.

"This isn't happening," Thad muttered, as he climbed from the altar, all the while staring at the tentacle. He wouldn't know its properties, but she did. She'd experience everything Wrath experienced, she'd feel everything he felt. It was a cowardly ploy, but potent. Airyon's trick would effectively restrain any attack Thad might think to make. For that matter, anything she did would be suicidal. Since her death would mean Torment not the Valley of Rest thanks to her aid to Bannor, she wasn't willing to risk it.

"Is this what you did to Bannor?" she asked. She could impart the information Thad would need to help her mentor.

"Bannor?" Airyon echoed in surprise. He seemed genuinely surprised at her assumption. "No, I did not do this to him. His power was too great."

"But yet you betrayed him."

He raised an eyebrow and tilted his head slightly, answering neither yes nor no.

"Who's Bannor?" Thad asked.

"It was Anya, wasn't it?" Jett continued. "You

did this to Anya. You thought you could get him to do whatever you wanted when you had Anya where you wanted her, didn't you."

"It is an effectual means to an end," Airyon concurred.

She wanted to howl. Wrath was slick as they came, never giving enough information to condemn himself. A mocking glimmer in his eye told her he knew exactly where her line of questions was leading, and he wasn't planning to let her lead him merrily down that thorny path.

His mouth tilted up on one side and the coercive tentacle on her leg slithered upward to stroke her inner thigh. Her breath caught in her throat as a rash of gooseflesh raced across her skin. While she watched, his eyes clouded slightly and his lips parted.

Jett fought her smile. Fool. In his haste to fetter her, he'd failed to shield himself from her sensations. He could no more hurt her than she could hurt him. And now that the spell was in place, it was too late to change it without removing the tentacle all together.

Airyon's eyes narrowed as he realised his error at the same time as she. Her mind raced at the implications. Her body still hummed with the arousal he'd coerced into her with his misuse of power. She could use this mistake against him and free herself. But how?

From the corner of her eye, she spied one of the minions closing in on Thad and her. The man's hand glowed fire red as he prepared to launch his attack. Gods! Airyon had bestowed powers on some of his followers, as she had on her warlock overlords, which meant they were just as deadly.

She yanked Thad down against her as the fireball sailed past, bouncing off the protective ward she'd placed around them. Angrily, she twisted beneath her mate and raised her arm to retaliate with a direct and fatal blow, but Airyon had already turned on his follower.

"Idiot!" Airyon thundered at the man. With a sweep of his hand, he knocked his follower to the ground. "You nearly hit the goddess."

Thad's eyes narrowed, his face inches from hers as he sprawled over her, while the dissipating ward held them close together. "He's trying to defeat you, yet he doesn't want you harmed in any way? I thought he was ready to defeat you by any means necessary. Am I missing something?"

"He doesn't want the pain to debilitate him. If I'm burnt, he—"

"Pain to debilitate him? Does this lash work in reverse?" Thad interrupted.

"Yes. He feels what I feel," she answered quickly.

"Can you put another wall between us?"

"Of course." With a sweep of her hand, she erected a wall of energy between them and their opponents. "Why? I can't hold him off with this forever."

Thad smiled, a wholly devious smile, before he pushed aside the fabric covering one of her breasts and lowered his mouth to her beaded peak. "I'll bet pain isn't the only way to debilitate him. Raise your vibrational level as high as you can."

"It won't affect him. He's as powerful as I am."

"Trust me." His tongue traced the outline of her nipple, setting off a tsunami of ripples in her belly. The desire she could barely hold at bay exploded inside her. Languidly, she arched beneath him, both ignoring Airyon whose hands were pressed to the energy wall, and relishing the moan he could not suppress as Thad pleasured her body.

"I think he likes it," Thad whispered.

"I think he'd like to kill you," Jett laughed against his ear. "Airyon's definitely into women and women only. This will be too much like being made love to by a man for him to enjoy."

Thad turned her face to his, his mouth plucking at her lips. "Should I stop?"

Jett sighed. "Absolutely not."

"Good." His mouth covered hers, his tongue sweeping inside. Relentlessly, he made love to her mouth. He possessed it as she knew he'd soon possess the rest of her. Suddenly, he pulled away and kissed his way to her naked breast. As Thad sucked the point deep inside his hungry mouth, she watched Airyon clutch at his chest, his expression ruddy as the sensation overtook him. Good. Let him suffer from his dirty trick. He had been very, very bad, and now he had to pay.

Determined, Jett sank into the pleasure of Thad's ministrations, her focus almost solely on finding her explosive release. The merest fraction of her attention split to maintain the wall—but the rest of her was his.

Warmth built between her thighs as her arousal deepened, the cream in her cleft flowing freely. She wanted Thad buried there. Now. Restlessly, she lifted her hips into him. Her hands scored down his back to clutch his buttocks and drag him closer.

"Don't make me wait," she begged.

"I want you on the edge," he rasped between his teeth. "I want you screaming over the edge."

"I'm there. Please, Thad. Now."

Releasing him, she fumbled with his pants while he shoved up her dress.

"No!" Airyon exclaimed as their intent became clear. He pounded on the wall. The tether tightened on her leg—if he sought to stop her, he'd chosen wrong. The tentacle couldn't control her actions. It certainly couldn't control her thoughts.

With perverse satisfaction, she imagined the tightening to be Thad's hand. He crawled over her, his body close, but she sensed he held back slightly to keep from crushing her to the stone. How could he not know that it was what she most wanted? First, she had another lesson for Airyon. What she wanted most would have to wait.

Agilely, she slithered from beneath Thad.

"Sit," she ordered, patting the altar.

He regarded her speculatively, his eyes darkening when she licked her lips and momentarily dropped her gaze to his erection. She met his eyes as he sat up. She placed her hands on his knees and steadied herself as she knelt between them.

"No!" Airyon bellowed, the thuds against the wall intensifying as he panicked. The sound of an energy attack sizzled around them. Dangerous. Though the smite could have ricocheted back at him, Airyon was desperate. Jett smiled at the knowledge. He'd do anything to keep from feeling what she was about to do. But would he release her?

Jett levelled her resolute gaze at him. "Let me go."

His face hardened.

Still watching him, Jett leaned forward and flattened her tongue to Thad's arousal. Thad's fingers speared through her hair while she licked down the length of the shaft, slowly, feeling every veiny ridge of the meaty flesh.

Gods he was beautiful. And it *was* a wondrous thing, the cock. She focused on the firm flesh beneath her lips. She licked him greedily already anticipating the feel of this long, thick *magnificent* creation probing her vagina and burrowing deep inside.

His musky scent enflamed her senses, drawing her into its siren song.

She pressed forward, her breasts gently scraping the altar as she went. Her lips stretched around the wide head of his cock as she took him as far as she could into her mouth. Thad sucked in his breath, and thrust against her lips, driving to her throat.

From the corner of her eye she saw Airyon gag, then she closed her eyes. While Airyon would experience what she did, this was between her and Thad. She didn't want to see or hear Wrath. All that mattered was her connection with Thad.

He wasn't dead. He was here and they were touching as she'd mourned never touching again.

"Yes, baby," he groaned as she worked up and down his shaft. She caressed him with her tongue and tasted every sweet-salty bit of him. "Oh, yes, Jett."

His pleasure set off chain reactions along her nerve-endings, her body responding to his ragged voice. Arousal dripped to her thigh while her body throbbed. She wanted to taste him, to have him spurting into her throat. Even more she needed him deep inside. So deep.

Her fingers drifted to her aching cleft and dragged through the drenched folds. Oh, it was so good...

From a distance she heard Airyon telling her to stop, the words garbled as he tried to protest around the sensations in his mouth. Jett refused to feel guilt. He could release the tether at any time. It was his own stubbornness that continued the sentient connection.

As if sensing the same, the tether loosened, but not enough for her to get free. She redoubled her efforts, and subtly shifted her leg, testing the strength of the tentacle.

Thad groaned and she knew he was reaching the end of his control. Just when she thought she might go free of Airyon's grip, Thad grabbed her shoulders and pulled her up. He claimed her mouth in ferocious determination. With expertise that surprised her, considering she didn't think Thad had ever made love on an altar, he turned her and laid her on the smooth, cold stone. His gaze flickered with pent-up desire as he bent over her.

She flattened her hands on his chest and held him away. "There is something you have to know."

"I'll never be able to meet Airyon's eyes again?" he asked and she knew he wasn't completely comfortable with the fact Wrath could feel their every move. Even now, he stifled grunts as Thad's penis prodded her opening.

She tensed. She couldn't let him in her, though she wanted nothing more in all the worlds. He couldn't fuck her without knowing the consequences.

"Besides that."

"Okay...?"

"Even though we are in Airyon's territory, this is a sacred altar. If you take me on it, we will be joined for eternity."

His eyes grew tender as he regarded her. She could live in those depths if only she believed he wanted her there forever. As a mortal, Thad had no concept of forever. He couldn't know how long they'd truly be bound.

He nipped her shoulder and his hand flattened

on the place where he'd marked her. "I don't need an altar to claim you as mine. That was decided a long time ago."

Her body flamed. It protested her delay and demanded she let him take her immediately. Already she could feel the lips of her pussy pulsing with need of him. Thick cream coated her. The slide as she moved sent waves of exquisite pleasure hurtling up outward from her centre, rippling wider and wider until she thought she'd collapse from it. It was so good. Nothing could feel as good as he would when he pressed inside her to claim the empty space that belonged only to him.

His fingers stroked over her cleft testing her readiness. She could have told him how desperately ready she was, but he'd already found the proof. He didn't need her confirmation. His dark growl raked over her. Slowly, he dipped two fingers inside and she shuddered, so aroused already that her orgasm immediately raked over her.

"Thad!" she cried in unison with Airyon's cry of, "Nara!"

The tentacle fell away and she yanked her leg clear of it.

"I'm free," she breathed, jumping from the altar, while Thad collected himself.

"Are you going to vacuum now?" he muttered under his breath, clearly unimpressed by her vigorous departure as he too prepared to immediately fight Airyon. They didn't have time to linger in the bliss following her shattering climax. If they didn't defeat Airyon now while he was weakened, they might never have a chance to be together. Jett refused to let that happen. She'd lost Thad once. She wouldn't lose him again, especially not to a ruthless despot like Wrath.

"I'm dropping the wall," she warned Thad,

already gathering the power within her. "You take out the minions and I'll attack Wrath."

Airyon glared at her as the wall dropped and she hurled a spiral of energy at him. Though the orgasm had momentarily freed her from his grasp, it hadn't slowed his reactions. He deflected her volley and threw one of his own as easily as if they were playing a child's game. It screeched over her right shoulder narrowly missing Thad.

Their precarious position sank like a weight in her stomach. Though there were two of them, her power was diminished while Airyon's grew stronger. Desperation clawed at her resolve. She would not be defeated.

The life of her child depended on it, as did her future with Thad.

Anger sizzled along her veins while her power rebuilt in her hands, stronger this time. If Airyon thought she'd been reunited with her lover only to have him killed, he was dead wrong.

She moved around Thad so that her back pressed to his and they could fight from two directions without being taken by surprise from the rear. He deliberately shifted to face Airyon, ignoring her directive to attack the other two men.

Wrath hung back. He seemed happy to let his people attack. Jett was sure he meant to drain their power. He'd fatigue them before he swooped in for the kill.

It wouldn't work.

She sent a fork of energy at one man, doubling him over. Another attack sent him to his knees. She had no desire to kill him—he was an innocent bystander sworn to Wrath's service. Methodically, Jett fought never letting Airyon far from her sight, never losing track of Thad's condition in the battle. If necessary, she'd find a way to transport him from here. Somehow.

Her muscles burned for exertion, but she couldn't stop. Any hesitation and they'd be overpowered. Airyon would be on them and Thad would be dead. Her fate would be another sort of death when she lost her love.

She would not. A smite tore through two men while another threw a woman into the temple wall. She crumpled to the floor. Jett lost sight of her when another wave surged towards her. Her hands burned, her fingers aching from the continuous surges streaking from them.

Beside her, Thad's heavy breathing signalled his weariness. Neither could take much more. Then suddenly, *finally*, they were alone with Airyon. Most of his people had fled and the foolhardy who'd remained were dead. He glanced around, a king surveying his kingdom. Still he appeared unconcerned. He even smiled when he again turned his gaze on her.

She panted, calculating his first move. It terrified her that his first move would probably be to eliminate Thad.

"Wrath is mine," Thad growled when she attempted to step in front of him. He held her aside, refusing protection. "I'm taking him out. No one touches my goddess."

"Wrath is not yours," she argued. Airyon leered at her, his black-brown eyes blazing pools of avarice. He still thought he could win. Even after every loss he'd endured.

He stood alone.

His lips twisted into a smug grin. "If he wants me, I'd be happy to let him try. I'll enjoy killing your lover."

"You would have to kill me first."

"Now, that love, will never happen. I intend to kill him and defeat you here, then I will take you to my palace where I'll chain you to my bed and defeat all your other defences. You will be totally mine. Your body. Your power. Your soul."

"Never."

Beside her, Thad growled taking a step forward.

Airyon held out his hands, the power fuelled by his province flowing into him in pulsing black ribbons. Slowly, he moved them in front of him. "Enough of this. Come to me Jett. It is destined that we be together. You are mine."

The black bands zapped forward and unexplainable terror pierced though her, emptying her soul. Desolation echoed within her as Airyon's power wrapped around her in murky streams that spiralled up her body. She couldn't break them and Gods! whatever he'd done to her, she couldn't summon the strength to try very hard.

"No!" Thad bellowed. He jumped before her, breaking Airyon's grasp on Jett. "You cannot take her!"

Jett fell to her knees. Airyon's negative energy had sapped her own energy from her body. Her limbs were leaden as she tried to raise her head.

"Thad. No," she whispered, barely able to speak.

Airyon laughed. "I had hoped you'd be noble, Warlock."

Instantly, the bands he'd wrapped around Jett, the bands that Thad had now intercepted, turned electric. White-hot lightning shot through Thad. His body bowed with the power.

He thrashed, struggling against it even as Jett tried to gather her weakened power. A fire ball from Airyon sizzled up his arms, charring skin which instantly healed.

"No!" Jett screamed, managing to raise her hands. Thad's arms raised as well. To ward off another attack? To fight? She didn't know.

Her hands glowed with the scorching fire of her unleashed rage. Airyon would not destroy her future. Airyon would not possess her. He would not hurt Thad. He would not live.

Twin bolts of blinding blue surged from her palms looping around those spiking from Thad's outstretched hands. They tore through Airyon's body. A stunned look crossed his face as he crumpled to his knees and then to the floor. His lips parted. No sound escaped as his head lolled. He hit the marble floor with a hallow thud.

Jett struggled to her feet as a fine mist rose from his body.

"Stop him!" she lurched after Airyon's spirit as it was drawn towards Torment. Hastily she threw an energy sphere towards Wrath's essence before it was too late and he was within Hades grasp. If Hades caught Airyon, she'd never repay her debt to Nara. And she'd never get away with removing another soul from beyond the veil again.

The orb engulfed the mist, trapping Airyon within. With a twist of her fingers the ball returned to her outstretched palm. Angrily, she turned.

"For the gods' sakes, Thad!" Jett swore. "Jumping in front of me like that... He could have killed you!"

"He didn't."

"You fought well," she admitted. She heaved a disgusted sigh. He was right but it didn't diffuse her anger. They'd deal with this later. *Later*. They had a 'later'. Something told her Thad would be unmanageable as soon as she revealed his status as a god. Somehow, it didn't bother her—much.

He was here. And immortal.

"It's about time you noticed. Why the hell do you think you have to keep protecting me?"

"You nearly died the last time you fought him. You did die. It was only by tricking Nara that I saved you."

"Why do you insist on revisiting that, over and over? I survived."

She refrained from muttering "barely" as they regarded Airyon's corpse. Thad tilted his head.

"You aimed a little low, didn't you?" he commented, sweeping his hand towards the char mark from Jett's smiting bolt. A blackened hole remained where it had pierced Airyon's groin.

She looked away. "Not at all."

"Liar. You missed."

"I wouldn't anger me. See what I did to him."

Thad stepped backward, then surprised her and lunged for her, sweeping her into his arms. "I'll watch my step."

"I thought you were dead," she said suddenly.

"Oh baby...I'm not dying and leaving you on your own. Gods know what would happen."

Holding Airyon's energy securely in one hand, she looped an arm behind Thad's head and drew him down to her. "I have to make a delivery to Nara," she whispered against his lips. "I have a debt to repay."

"I'll go with you."

She shook her head. She didn't want Thad anywhere near Nara, god or no. "I am safe now. Wait for me in the Throne room? We have unfinished...business."

His eyes darkened. "Hurry."

"It will take no time at all."

Closing her eyes, she transported to the veil. Nara stood beside it, leaning on an invisible wall, her arms crossed over her chest. While she tried to appear calm, wild excitement zapped through her, and her foot tapped in unconscious impatience.

Jett held up the sphere. "A present for you."

Her sister exclaimed, rubbing her hands together. "Airyon!"

"I repay my debt." She held the sphere from reach when Nara reached for it. While her debt to the council was automatically cancelled, she'd take no chances with the Goddess of the Veil. Debts and promises were the leverage to change worlds.

Nara nodded and pulled a scroll from the air. After showing Jett that it was the missive containing their agreement, she incinerated it. "The debt is paid."

With careful haste, she took Airyon from Jett. A wicked smile played over her lips as she regarded the misty grey contents of the sphere. All at once, the encapsulated essence darkened and began to bubble with marked agitation.

Jett's brows furrowed as she watched the interplay between the two. Airyon roiling, Nara petting the ball. What was the history between the two? Unless she missed her guess, Airyon had screwed with Nara and Nara was ready to get even.

She wouldn't stop her sister. After all, Wrath had been set to kill millions of people.

Nara continued to stroke the sphere. "Come now Airy-sweetness," she crooned. "I released all my other pets today, because I knew you'd be coming. I have such plans for you. How do you feel about chains? Do you have a colour preference?"

Jett shook her head, feeling a slight twinge of sympathy for Airyon. He might have preferred an eternity in Torment to an eternity at Nara's hands.

She had a feeling he was about to get a punishment the likes of which she'd never fathomed. "If we are finished...?"

Nara waved her away. "I've got this under control. Go have fun with your new god."

Jett's eyes narrowed. "He is not my god."

Nara laughed. "Maybe not in the Higher Power sense, but trust me, he is." She turned away, tossing Airyon's essence idly into the air and catching it again as she disappeared into the mist, but Jett could still hear her. "Welcome to my domain Airysweetness. You have no rank here and will have only the power I allow you. You will address me as Mistress..."

Oh gods! No wonder he'd been horrified to be in Nara's grasp. Nara unleashed—or with a leash—was a force to behold.

Jett did not want to dwell on her sister's antics.

Thad waited in the Throne room when Jett returned. Tension looped through his body as he sat on one of the thrones, his fingers tapping impatiently on the armrest. Jett smiled in anticipation of relieving that tension. She'd fulfilled her task to both Nara and the council. Now she could start her eternity with Thad.

Trepidation filled her. It surprised her that after all this time with Thad and all his determination to have her that she was nervous. She wished she could read his mind as she could much lesser beings. Thad was closed to her in that sense. And right now, she needed reassurance that he'd still want her when he discovered that not only would she not become human, but he was no longer human.

He jumped to his feet at the sight of her.

"I'm not letting you send me away, leave me, wipe out my memory, or anything else you might think up. I'm staying whether you like it or not. You belong to me. And don't give me the you're-a-mortal-I'm-a-goddess crap. We can work around that if you'll try. Even if you have to curse me again."

Obviously, he'd been working on his argument. She considered exchanging a few barbs to humour him but declined. The determination in his declaration didn't solve all her concerns but it went a long way towards soothing her worries.

Oh just get on with it! she chided herself. The sooner he knew his new station and accepted it, the sooner they could get on with more important things. Her pussy swelled at what she had in mind. Thick cream coated the plump lips while her being begged her to hurry.

"Thad—"

"You're not climbing up on your throne and deserting me again! If you think you can keep me from touching you—"

"All right," she replied before Thad could start another tirade.

"—then you're wrong!"

"All right."

"And you can forget about leaving me. You're mine. You're not leaving me."

She smiled and crossed her arms over her hard tipped breasts. "Okay."

"You're—what?"

"I'm not leaving."

He tilted his head, his eyes narrowing. "Why was that easier than it should have been?"

Easy? She tried to rein in her emotions. Even though he hadn't taken the opportunity to eternally unite with her in Airyon's temple, she knew he wanted her forever. "We're bound."

Thad stared at Jett his heart sinking to his toes. "You're forced to be with me?"

He wanted her by her own free will, not because of some divine decree that dictated that she remain with him. He wanted her commitment, her fidelity and most of all, her love. He wouldn't accept anything less.

She shook her head.

"No, I am not forced. I could choose to exist separately from you. But I choose not to." She bit her lip, looking unsure. "I chose to be with you. If that is your desire. It must be what you wish as well."

He tamped down the chorus of rejoicing that erupted within him. Much as he wanted to blindly accept her words, he could not. Two hundred years had taught him to never take Jett's decisions at face value. There was always a reason.

"Why?" He had to know. He had to know what was in her head. She'd had plans and motives in her head every step of their relationship. None of them particularly suited his state of mind. She'd never planned to be with him simply because she couldn't bear not to be with him. It didn't seem fair since he ceased to breathe whenever she left him. "Why?" he repeated. "Why now?"

"I..." Hurt filled her eyes and shot through him with more power than Airyon's attack had ever held. "Don't you want me?"

"Baby, I want you. Make no mistake about that. I just want to know what you're thinking. I *need* to know."

"I love you."

The perfect motive. He crossed the room in an instant. Her body melted soft and perfect into his

arms, while her scent rushed through his middle.
He might reach new heights on her sweet smell
alone. His cock hardened painfully. He needed to
be in her so bad.

"Goddess, I love you, too." His hands tightened
around her tiny waist. "We'll find a way to be
together. I was serious. Curse me again if it will
keep me from aging and allow me to remain with
you."

"I will not curse you." Her eyes gleamed with
wonder.

His jaw locked. Damn it. She might as well
kill him now. Would she stand beside him while
he grew feeble and unable to satisfy her eternally
youthful needs? She wouldn't stray from him, but
the pain of her pity... He'd never withstand it.

Her graceful fingers stroked away the lines he
knew wrinkled his forehead as his scowl deepened.
"Thad. There is no need to curse you. When I
gave myself to you...that first time...you became
immortal. You became like me."

He sucked in a breath almost unable to breathe
for the relief flooding over him. *Forever.* He'd
have an eternity of Jett. That might be just about
close to enough. Maybe. He grinned, joy warming
him and driving out the fear that had plagued him
since she'd left to deliver Airyon to Nara.

"I told you I was your god."

"The Higher Power might not like to hear you
say that." She grinned despite her admonishment.
Her hands slid up his chest, tweaking the small
nipples hidden beneath his shirt. She played with
his shirt buttons for a moment. Pushing them from
the holes was more effort than she apparently
wanted to exert right now. She waved her hand
and the garment fell open.

Hungrily, she kissed his the top of his stomach,

splaying her hands on his chest.

"I'll risk being smote," he groaned as she licked towards his navel. "Besides, I'm quite sure the Higher Power knows exactly what I mean."

"How could he not? He invented love." Jett laughed, the sound tinkling like chimes in the chamber. Her teeth sank into his hip.

"I'm sure that had something to do with orchestrating you into my arms."

"I will stay there as long as you want."

"How about a couple of eternities?"

She froze. "It sounds divine to me." Suddenly, she straightened deserting her adventure down his body. She bit her lip, a pretty pink tingeing her cheeks. Her hand pressed to her abdomen. "I have something to tell you."

"What is it?" His palm covered hers. It couldn't be what he thought...

Her eyes danced as she met his worried gaze. "We have created a goddess."

"We've made a goddess? We've...you're pregnant?" He crushed her to him as she nodded. A moment later, he dropped to his knees and pressed his lips to her flat belly. A ripple went through her.

Reverently, he splayed his hands over the place where their child rested. "It's more than I'd ever hoped." He looked up at her, his eyes misted. "Jett, I love you."

Her fingers buried in his hair. "I love you."

Standing, Thad gathered her into his arms. He pressed his lips to her temple while his hand skimmed up her side to cup her breast. Idly, his thumb flicked over her resilient nipple. Around them cool tendrils of magic spiralled around them as a transport tunnel opened and engulfed them. Thad held her tight as they hurtled towards their destination.

They landed in the white master bedroom of his mansion in Michigan. Here her power surrounded him and here he'd fill her with his.

He set her on her feet. "There's something I didn't finish earlier..."

"Then by all means, do." Her fingers slipped inside his open shirt, her nails grazing his skin. He recalled them digging into his shoulders. He wanted it again as soon as possible.

"Do I have to wear a toga?" he asked, wrenching the garment down his arms. He pulled her down on the couch where she'd pleasured Anya.

She turned and straddled him, her knees digging into the soft cushions, while she lifted her skirt. "They have their benefits."

She tore open the closure of his trousers. He sprang forward into her hands, hot and throbbing. He couldn't think. He just needed her. Had to be in her. Already a glistening drop of arousal leaked from him. Jett swiped it away with her fingertip and brought it to her lips, flicking it away with her tongue. He felt her tiny whimper to his root.

"What benefits?" he managed. "It's a dress."

She sank onto his ready cock, her liquid fire enveloping him as he stretched her tight passage, each inch of rippling tissue and muscle squeezing, drawing. Welcoming. She was his.

"See," she moaned. "Benefits."

"I can see they do." He grunted as her inner muscles clenched. He shifted his hips, ploughing upward into her welcoming channel. This was home. This was the place for which he'd waited for two hundred years. Now she was his and he would never let go. His arms tightened around her as her thighs clamped his hips. Yes, she was his.

She leaned forward so her lips grazed his

temple. Her tongue darted out to trace the shell of his ear. "And now, you understand why goddesses don't wear panties."

Thank the goddess for that.

About the Author

When it comes to books and movies, Brynn Paulin has one rule: there must be a happy ending. After that one requirement, anything else goes. And it just might in any of her books.

Brynn lives in Michigan with her husband and two children, who love her despite her occasional threats to smite them. They humour her and let her think she's a goddess...as long as she provides homemade chocolate chip cookies on a regular basis. Brynn is president of her local chapter of Romance Writers of America and also hosts a weekly writing critique group. She's conducted workshops at several writers' conferences around the country as she enjoys mentoring and meeting new people.

According to Brynn, her writing success can be attributed to 70's music, her local road construction crews, a trusty notebook, and of course, her husband (and willing research subject), AKA Mr. Inspiration.

Brynn loves to hear from readers. You can find her contact information, website details and author profile page at http://www.total-e-bound.com.

Total-E-Bound Publishing

www.total-e-bound.com

Take a look at our exciting range of
literagasmic™ erotic romance titles
and discover pure quality at Total-E-Bound.

Paperback copies are available online at
www.total-e-bound.com, www.amazon.com,
www.amazon.co.uk and from selected bookstores
in the UK, USA, and Europe.